Dixie Belle is a charming love story that will romance you, inspire you, and leave your heart merry.

—ANITA HIGMAN
BEST-SELLING AUTHOR OF *A MARRIAGE IN MIDDLEBURY*

Cissy Hillwood is about to learn that the journey from disaster to dream-come-true isn't always easy. Her Alabama spunk and charm add a delightful and romantic touch to her big-city adventure. Manhattan has an interesting impact on Cissy; happily, the reverse is equally true!

—TRISH PERRY
AUTHOR OF *THE MIDWIFE'S LEGACY* AND *LOVE FINDS YOU ON CHRISTMAS MORNING*

A charming story about leaving home to find new adventures, new friends, and best of all, finding yourself. A cast of fun characters, along with a touching faith message. Debby Mayne delivers.

—TARA RANDEL
AUTHOR OF *RIVAL HEARTS*

Debby Mayne is one of those authors who really knows the Southern woman, and she proves it again with *Dixie Belle*. I love that delightful fish-out-of-water perspective, and I was so happy to see Mayne do what she does best—weave the threads masterfully to create a community of characters to support the telling of a full and rich story.

—SANDRA D. BRICKER
AUTHOR OF LIVE OUT LOUD FICTION FOR THE INSPIRATIONAL MARKET, INCLUDING *RISE & SHINE*, BOOK 2 OF A CONTEMPORARY FAIRY TALE SERIES

UPTOWN
Belles
book one

Dixie Belle

Debby Mayne

REALMS

Most CHARISMA HOUSE BOOK GROUP products are available at special quantity discounts for bulk purchase for sales promotions, premiums, fund-raising, and educational needs. For details, write Charisma House Book Group, 600 Rinehart Road, Lake Mary, Florida 32746, or telephone (407) 333-0600.

DIXIE BELLE by Debby Mayne
Published by Realms
Charisma Media/Charisma House Book Group
600 Rinehart Road
Lake Mary, Florida 32746
www.charismahouse.com

Cover design by Bill Johnson

Visit the author's website at www.debbymayne.com.

Library of Congress Cataloging-in-Publication Data:
An application to register this book for cataloging has been submitted to the Library of Congress.
International Standard Book Number: 978-1-62136-524-2

E-book ISBN: 978-1-62136-525-9

First edition

14 15 16 17 18 — 9 8 7 6 5 4 3 2 1
Printed in the United States of America

This book is dedicated to my husband, Wally, who has been my partner and best friend through the good, the bad, and everything in between for the past thirty-plus years.

Acknowledgments

THANKS TO MY agent, Tamela Hancock Murray, for your steadfast support; my editors, Adrienne Gaines, Leigh DeVore, and Lori Vandenbosch, for showing me how to make my story better; and the rest of the team at Charisma House for pulling everything together in such a professional way. I appreciate y'all way more than you can imagine!

Chapter 1

WAIT RIGHT HERE, Cissy," Mama said. "I need to step into the powder room for a sec." She took a few steps, stopped, and spun back around to face Cissy. "On second thought, why don't you go with me?"

"No, Mama. I'll wait right here."

"You don't need to be alone right now." Cissy noticed the lines of worry etched deep on Mama's face.

"I'll be just fine." She pointed to a bench along the wall by the courthouse door. "I'll wait for you there."

"If you're sure." Mama pulled her bag closer as she backed away. "I'll hurry."

As Cissy sat down and leaned back, she sighed. What a day, and it still wasn't noon yet.

Spring had always been Cissy Hillwood's favorite season, but not this year. After finding out her former boy-friend Spencer McCully was a woman abuser and having him tossed into the slammer, she felt like crawling into the dirt she'd been digging in when he back-handed her a month and a half ago. Folks in Hartselle, Alabama, didn't take kindly to someone exposing their golden boy's faults. Of course, it was all her fault in the hundreds of pairs of eyes clouded by the football hero's glory days. Good thing Mama spotted Spencer in the garden threatening her and called the police, or else there's no telling what would've happened. Spencer had a violent streak, but Cissy was no sissy. She managed to keep him at bay by wielding the shovel until the entire police force arrived—all four of them. Good thing too, or Cissy might've had to help them out. Spencer sure was strong when he was mad, and boy howdy was he spitting nails.

But still…jail? She had prayed for resolution, but this is not what she had in mind. The very thought of being responsible for having Spencer handcuffed and put behind bars made her shudder. Cissy's teenage crush on Spencer ended the second he got possessive and said now that she was his girl he wasn't about to let her hang out at the Dairy Curl with her friends, even though she'd been doing that very thing since seventh grade. He actually came right up to her in front of her gal pals, mouthing off and acting all possessive.

She started to make her case, until he backhanded her. That did it. "We're done," she said as she cast a glance over at her dumbstruck friends who didn't even lift a finger to help. "No one hits Cissy Hillwood and gets a second chance." Before he could say another word, she ran to her car, slammed the door, and sped off. She still hadn't heard from the girls she'd known practically all her life, making her question how much they really valued her friendship. Yeah, Spencer was once the high school football hero, so everyone cut him some slack…too much slack, which was why he thought he could do whatever he wanted.

Mama came out of the women's restroom, her gaze darting directly toward Cissy. Relief overtook her panicked expression. Cissy stood and walked over to her mother.

"Hungry?" Mama looked a tad nervous as she guided Cissy down the courthouse steps and toward the minivan in the metered parking lot. "I thought we'd stop off at Belva's Diner for a bite to eat."

Cissy's stomach was still roiling from facing Spencer

Dixie Belle

and seeing the distasteful looks on everyone's faces, except the judge's, but Mama had been such a help during this whole ordeal Cissy wasn't about to deny her this small pleasure. After all it was Wednesday, and today's special at Belva's was chicken fried steak with mashed potatoes, gravy, and a side of salty green beans dripping in pork fat.

"Sounds good. Why don't we walk?"

"It's four whole blocks away." Mama scrunched her face. "And I'm wearin' my church shoes that rub blisters on my heels." She tilted her head and gave Cissy a half-smile. "But I know how you like to walk when you're troubled, so why don't I just take the car and meet you there?"

Cissy nodded. A few minutes alone would do her some good, help clear her mind after the stress of the morning. Mama lifted her hand and waved her fingers before turning around and hobbling toward the car. Cissy had tried to talk Mama into getting some new Sunday shoes that didn't hurt, but Mama refused to, saying she'd never find another pair that went with all her church dresses.

As Cissy headed toward Belva's she sucked in the crisp spring air, hoping to lift some of the heaviness in her heart. After she broke up with Spencer, why couldn't he just deal with the fact that she wasn't the kind of girl who liked being told what to do...or smacked? There were plenty of girls who'd love to be with Spencer, town football hero and the best auto mechanic south of the Mason-Dixon line—or at least that's what people in town claimed.

It was nearly noon on the cloudless day, sending people outdoors to eat their lunches on some of the painted green benches beneath maple saplings that lined Main Street. Cissy forced herself to acknowledge a couple of women she'd known as long as she could remember. "Hey there, Mrs. Stanley...Mrs. Parker."

3

Mrs. Parker scowled. "You're just too big for your britches, young lady. Why you went and done that to one of the finest boys in Hartselle..." She shook her head and clicked her tongue. "You oughta be ashamed of yourself, Cissy Hillwood."

"I...uh..." Cissy's jaw went slack.

"If I were you I'd stay home and not show my face for a very long time," Mrs. Stanley said, tag-teaming her friend. "No one's gonna want nothin' to do with you for fear you'll have 'em locked up if you don't like the way they look at you."

"But..." From the looks on their faces, Cissy doubted anything she might say would change their minds. "Have a nice day." She quickened her step and kept her head down all the way to the small diner in the heart of Hartselle. As soon as she and Mama walked inside, a hush fell over the place, and Cissy knew things would never be the same for her in the town she'd grown up in and loved.

"Cissy, honey, don't look now, but everyone's starin' at you." The only table left was smack dab in the middle of the dining room, so they walked over, sat down, and took a long look around. "If looks could kill..." Mama said softly.

The waitress arrived and held her pad at an angle so she wouldn't have to look directly at them. She stated the daily special in a monotone, took their order, and waltzed off without so much as a "Thank you" or "It'll be right up."

"Wasn't that special?" Mama said before leaning forward. "Listen to me, Cissy. You can't sit around doing nothing. You need to get yourself out there and find another job."

"Who's gonna hire me after what I did to Spencer?"

"You know good and well you didn't do a thing to Spencer. He did it to himself."

Cissy rolled her eyes. "Try telling Mr. Womack that."

"I always liked him until he fired you for no reason."

"Oh, he had a reason, all right. I ruined the life of our town's golden boy, and it doesn't look like anyone will let me forget it." She glanced around at the other diners and caught a few more glares directed her way.

"That brings me to something I need to discuss with you." Mama unrolled her napkin and waved her fork in the air. "I talked to Forest and Bootsie about what happened, and they think it would be a good idea for you to go on up there and visit for a while."

Cissy grinned. "Seriously? I've always wanted to go up to New York, but you wouldn't let me. You said it would be too dangerous."

"Seriously," her mama said. "I don't believe for one minute anything I said kept you from going. You're a grown woman, so there's no way to stop you, even if I wanted to. Besides, considering what's been going on around here with you and that lunatic boyfriend you got yourself involved with, I don't see how New York can be any more dangerous than Hartselle."

"Oh, I so agree." Cissy couldn't help the fact that her voice screeched with excitement.

Mama gestured around her. "I'd hoped things would go back to normal, but I think you're right. No one around this place will give you a chance...at least not in the immediate future."

"So what's the plan?" Cissy envisioned herself shopping on Fifth Avenue and having dinner in the finest restaurants.

"Call your Uncle Forest and make plans." Mama pulled a slip of paper from her pocket and handed it to Cissy. "Here's his number."

Shaking her head in wonderment, Cissy punched in Uncle Forest's number. He answered before the first ring ended and brought up Mama's suggestion of a visit himself. "I never thought I'd live to see the day your mama would encourage you to leave Hartselle, let alone come up to New York City." He chuckled. "Bootsie and I have your room ready and waiting."

"Um...I need to call and make reservations. What day—?"

"As soon as possible. I can't keep the job open much longer."

"Job?" Cissy held out the phone and looked at it to make sure something wasn't stuck in the earpiece.

"Yeah, didn't your mama tell you? One of our sales reps for Zippers Plus up and quit, so when your mama asked if you could come up here to get away for a month or two, I told her about the job."

Strange. Mama hadn't even hinted at anything so permanent, but it sure sounded good to Cissy. It was high time for an adventure, and boy howdy would this be an adventure. "I can come whenever you want me."

"Then let's get off the phone, and you get started on making yourself an airline reservation. Here's my credit card number."

"You don't have to—"

"I know, but I'm your boss, and that's how I roll."

"Okay, I've got a pen and paper." She jotted down the information she'd need to book her flight.

"Do it now and call me back when you have your flight booked." *Click.*

Cissy couldn't help but smile as she pressed the off button on her phone. New York City! She'd be a city girl. Visions of herself walking down Madison Avenue, decked out in the cutest outfit ever, maybe even meeting a decent guy with a job on Wall Street… She frowned. Okay maybe not Wall Street but a good job somewhere near her uncle's company. They could meet after work for dinner and maybe even stop off at a Broadway play every now and then. Of course, she'd have to ask him about his faith. She didn't want to take a chance on falling for the wrong guy…or a replay of the Spencer incident.

"So?" Mama looked up from her plate. "That was a short call. What did he say?"

Cissy spread her arms wide. "I'm movin' to New York."

Mama's lips twitched, but Cissy couldn't tell if they were about to smile or frown because she caught herself and gave Cissy one of her I'm-the-mama looks. "Hold your horses, *Miss Impulsive*. You better think about this first. Are you *sure* you want to get a job in New York?"

Cissy started to bob her head but thought better of it since it annoyed Mama so much. "Yes. First of all, I'll be able to walk down the street without everyone whispering about what a loser I am for tossing Spencer into the slammer." She held up a hand and tapped her fingers as she counted the reasons to leave. "Second, I'll have a decent job working for someone I can trust. And third, I just happen to know you had this all worked out before I even called Uncle Forest." Cissy stared at her mother.

Mama nodded as she glanced away. "True. To be honest, I didn't like the idea of you getting a job up there at first, but Forest reminded me how long it'll take folks here to get over what happened."

"Wait, that's not all. I have more." She tapped her thumb. "Fifth, I might be able to get a date since no one there worships Spencer. I'm sure there are plenty of very handsome men in New York."

"Can't you go a little while without having a date? Seriously, Cissy, this is the kind of thing that gets women into trouble."

Cissy shrugged. "I enjoy hangin' out with guys. Well, at least the good ones."

Mama rolled her eyes as she let out a breath of exasperation. "I don't know what to do about you, Cissy Hillwood. You've always been boy crazy."

"I'll be careful," Cissy promised. She paused before giving Mama the best reason of all. "And don't forget, I can go to church and worship without having everyone in the congregation judging something that wasn't my fault."

Mama dropped her napkin onto the table and faced Cissy. "It's gonna hurt me way more than I ever thought, but I must admit this is probably the best thing you can do."

"I wonder what Daddy will say."

"I don't think he'll like it a single solitary bit, but I'll work on him."

Cissy's spirits rose. She couldn't believe how fortunate she was to have this opportunity. After all, how many girls from Hartselle, Alabama, had a job and a place to live in the most exciting city in the whole entire United States of America practically handed to them on a silver platter?

Chapter 2

A WEEK AND A half later Cissy found herself sitting in a window seat of a 747, her hands clammy from a mix of excitement and trepidation. Daddy hadn't said much, but the looks he gave her between when he found out and when she walked out the door just about broke her heart in two. Mama drove her to the airport, lecturing the whole way. "Don't get in a car with anyone you don't know...Make sure you have money for a cab...Find a good church as soon as possible..."

Cissy smiled. Mama said over and over she hadn't really wanted Cissy to leave, but the town's ostracism had bled onto the rest of the family, so she realized there was no other choice if she wanted to maintain even a semblance of acceptability. It would take a while—at least until the next scandal—but over time, without Cissy there to remind everyone, people would eventually move on. She just hoped this whole thing wouldn't affect Mama's weekly standing appointment at the hair salon.

She closed her eyes and allowed her mind to take her to a place she'd only dreamed of in the past but never thought she'd have a chance to actually experience. New York City! Wow! Scary but exciting and filled with possibilities. She settled into her seat. And so many guys to choose from.

Cissy's heart thudded and her knees wobbled as she stepped off the plane at JFK. Uncle Forest said he'd be waiting for her by baggage claim. She sure hoped he had a big trunk. She had the hardest time deciding what to bring, so she tossed into the suitcases everything she thought she might possibly need—or want.

She hadn't seen Uncle Forest in several years, but the instant she spotted the salt-and-pepper-haired man with the same piercing blue eyes she and her mother had, they both broke into smiles. He opened his arms wide and strode toward her, while she practically threw herself into his broad chest. "Whoa there, little girl." He held her at arm's length and gave her a long look. "Actually you're not such a little girl anymore. Where are those cute little pig-tails I remember?"

"And where's that Southern accent I remember?" She gave a jaunty head bob. "You've done become all New York-ified."

He tilted his head back and let out a hearty laugh. "That's the best thing I've ever heard it called. You might not hear the accent, but the folks around here sure do. I don't think a day goes by when someone doesn't call me out on it. Here, let me take your carry-on, and we'll go get your other bag."

"*Bags*. I have several."

Uncle Forest shook his head. "Sounds like you're already New York-ified. Good thing Bootsie made me get all the product samples out of the trunk."

It took some serious maneuvering to get all her bags in his car, but a half hour later they were on their way into the city. Cissy remained speechless for most of the trip as she gawked at the tall buildings, until she couldn't hold back anymore. "This is so incredible. It's just like on TV."

He lifted an eyebrow and gave her a look she didn't understand as they sat at a stoplight. "Yep. Maybe even more so."

"What?"

He grinned and patted her hand. "Just wait. You'll see. Oh, by the way, we're stopping off at the office before I take you home. I want you to meet some of my employees, your coworkers."

Cissy's heart continued to thud as they got closer to the heart of the garment district where Uncle Forest's company was located. She'd always envisioned it being in a tall, shiny building with a doorman and a super-modern elevator with chic women breezing past her. Instead she found herself walking into a very old building with a musty smell, then stepping onto a rickety elevator with a door that took forever to close. She wasn't about to let Uncle Forest see her disappointment, so she forced the smile she'd learned back when she was on the homecoming court at Hartselle High School.

"You're gonna love everyone. I have the best staff in the city."

The elevator shook as its door opened right smack dab in the middle of an office filled with cluttered desks, boxes everywhere, and people dressed in various fades of black. Uncle Forest stepped out and gestured for her to join him.

"Where are we?" She took a tentative step toward the closest desk as everyone stopped what they were doing and stared.

Uncle Forest clapped his hands. "Hey, everyone, this is Cissy, the niece I was telling you about. She's gonna be one of our new sales reps."

A couple of the people grunted their greetings. Several of them gave her a cursory glance but went back to whatever they'd been doing. Only one person—a guy with longish sandy brown hair, skinny pants, a tight bomber jacket, and boat shoes—took the initiative to approach.

"Hi, Cissy. I'm Dave, and your uncle has asked me to

show you the ropes." He wiped his hand on his black pants and extended it.

Cissy wasn't about to be rude, so she accepted the handshake but pulled back as quickly as possible. "So this is Zippers Plus, huh?"

Beaming proudly, Uncle Forest opened his arms wide. "Yep. This is it. So how do you like it so far?"

Cissy scanned the big warehouse-looking room with metal desks and open shelving, took a deep breath, and looked her uncle directly in the eye. "I absolutely love it." If she said that often enough, she was certain she'd start to believe it.

"I put together some things you might want to take a look at tonight." Dave handed her a bulging three-ring binder. "It's an overview and explanation of what we offer. I jotted down some notes on each page, but if you have any questions, I'll be glad to answer them." The look he gave Uncle Forest let her know he'd done it more for brownie points than for her, but that was okay.

She took the binder. "Thank you. I'll look at it tonight."

"Come on, Cissy." Uncle Forest gestured toward the elevator. "We need to get all your stuff unpacked at the house. Bootsie is dying to see you." He punched the elevator button with one hand and waved with the other. "Get back to work, everyone. Don't forget I want you all here bright and early for a meeting tomorrow."

Dave grinned at Cissy. "See you then."

As soon as they had stepped onto the elevator, Uncle Forest started in on how difficult of a time he'd had when he first arrived in New York. "New York takes some getting used to." He placed a hand on her shoulder. "It's not easy for outsiders to get started here, but after a couple of years and a few bumpy seasons—well, that and a serious setback that took me forever to recover from—I'm doing as well as anyone else in sewing notions."

"That's nice." Cissy gulped. "So who will I be selling to and where will I go to sell?" She wanted to ask when she'd get her company car, but this didn't seem like the right time.

"There's an empty desk in the corner...or there will be as soon as we clear some of the files off of it. That'll be where you'll make your phone calls."

"So I'll be a phone salesperson?"

"That's right." The elevator arrived back on the ground floor.

She had a brief moment of regret, but right when Cissy took her first step outside into the bright sunshine, there was no doubt in her mind she'd made the right decision to come to New York, as she spotted the best-looking man she'd ever seen in her entire life. He was a good foot taller than her, dressed in a charcoal gray business suit, striped tie, and crisp white shirt. She'd seen plenty of men all dressed up on Sunday mornings, but not one of 'em looked as good as this one. His gaze zeroed in on hers, giving her the full impact of the darkness of his eyes, and she felt the earth beneath her shift. A slow smile spread across his lips, but something behind her caught his attention, and his expression instantly went sullen.

Cissy glanced over her shoulder and saw her uncle giving the man the squinty eye. "Who is that man?" she whispered. "He is so good looking. Do you know him?"

"Do I know him? Of course I do. And I suggest you stop ogling him and remember your family loyalties."

"Whatever are you talking about?"

The man stepped up to them. "Hello, Forest. It's good to see you again." He glanced down at Cissy. "And who is this lovely lady? I don't think I've ever seen her here before."

The binder slipped out of her hands and landed at her feet with a thud. She squealed. "Oops-a-daisy."

The guy bent over, picked up the binder, shoved some of the loose papers back in, and locked gazes with her as he handed it to her. "So people really do say that?"

"What?" Her voice squeaked, so she cleared her throat. "People really do say what?"

"Oops-a-daisy." He grinned. "That is very…cute."

Uncle Forest let out a low growl that Cissy could barely hear. She doubted the man heard, but he couldn't possibly miss her uncle's disdain.

"Stay away from my niece, Jenkins. She works for me."

"Your niece?" The man her uncle called Jenkins lifted an eyebrow as he glanced back and forth between Cissy and Uncle Forest.

"You heard me."

The man slowly shook his head. "I mean no harm. All I was hoping for was an introduction."

Cissy couldn't stand it anymore, so she shifted the binder to the crook of one arm and stuck out her other hand. "My name is Cissy Hillwood, and the reason you haven't seen me before is I just got in from Hartselle, Alabama."

He smiled, took her hand, and squeezed it. "I'm Tom Jenkins, and I—"

"Never mind, Jenkins." Uncle Forest wedged himself between Cissy and Tom, gently shoving Cissy away. "Like I said, she works for me. Hands off."

"Nice meeting you, Cissy Hillwood." Tom grinned as a playful expression flashed across his face before walking into the building next to Zippers Plus.

"He's cute," Cissy said. "*Very* cute and polite."

"Maybe so, but he's the competition, and from what I hear, a womanizer, and I don't want you having anything to do with him." He glared at her. "Now call your mama and let her know you're here with me."

Uncle Forest drove in silence, allowing Cissy to day-dream about that good-looking Tom Jenkins. She'd never seen her uncle so agitated. What was that all about? She glanced over at Uncle Forest, whose jaw remained firmly set, his narrowed eyes showing he hadn't forgotten their encounter either. Good thing his mouth was closed, or she feared fire might come spewing out of it.

The tension-filled air in the car prevented her from saying a word. Mama had always said Forest was serious about his business, and if anyone said or did anything he thought might hurt it, that was the end of them as far as he was concerned. Cissy wasn't about to mess anything up for herself right now—not when she needed this job. Granted, it wasn't what she'd expected in New York City— at least not as exciting or glamorous—but at least it gave her something to do while the folks back home cooled off.

As they rode, Cissy watched the scenery change from concrete and massive old buildings to a more neighbor-hoodsy area. Based on the signs she saw along the way, she knew they were in Long Island. Trees lined both sides of the street, and children played in the yards—nothing at all like what she'd expected.

"Are we still in New York City?"

"Long Island's a suburb," he grunted.

Uncle Forest pulled into a driveway, put the car in park, and turned off the ignition but didn't make a move to get out of the car. Instead he remained sitting there staring straight ahead.

Cissy had no idea what to do now. She held her breath and reached out to touch his shoulder. He flinched but turned to look at her.

"I hope I didn't make a mistake by bringing you here." He contorted his mouth and narrowed his eyes.

"You didn't," Cissy said. "I promise."

He held her gaze for a few very squirmy seconds. "Your mama was mighty worried about you, and I couldn't turn my back on my baby sister. She would've done the same thing for me if the situation had been reversed."

Tom Jenkins's image faded as the memory of Mama's face replaced it. Cissy recalled her hand wringing and glistening eyes after they left the diner on the day of Spencer's sentencing. It had to be rough having your only child go from being popular and sought after to having everyone hating on her.

The weight of Uncle Forest's hand on her shoulder brought her back to the moment. "Ready to go in and see Bootsie? She's dyin' to see you. I think she's sad we didn't have any daughters to dote on, so this is her big chance." He grinned for the first time since seeing Tom Jenkins. "Humor her, okay?"

Cissy could use a little doting on after all she'd been through since the trial. "Sounds good to me."

"You go on in, and I'll get your bags. I'm sure Bootsie will show you to your room, but don't expect to spend much time in there. She has all kinds of things she wants to talk to you about."

Cissy headed up the sidewalk, glancing around at the neighborhood as another flood of disappointment washed over her. There was something too familiar about it—too normal. It could have been any of the established neighborhoods in Hartselle. Most of the houses were either two-story or split-level, some with front porches, all with driveways that led to two-car garages. The yards were a glossy, new-spring green. Here and there bright red and yellow tulips dotted yards.

She'd expected something different—more concrete than grass, bright lights, and the sound of horns honking and cabbies hollering. After all, she had moved to New York!

When she got a few feet from the front porch, the door swung open, and out bounced her aunt—looking like she did five years ago, only a little grayer headed and slightly rounder. "Don't you look pretty? Come here and give your old aunt a hug."

Forest had lost most of his Southern accent, but Bootsie sounded as if she'd never left Alabama. "Hey, Aunt Bootsie. Thank you so much for havin' me. I don't know what I would've done if—"

"It's our pleasure. Ever since the boys took off, this house has been way too quiet. I'm countin' on you to liven it up again."

"Not too much livening up," Uncle Forest said from behind her as he lugged her bags into the house. "I don't know why you needed to bring so much stuff. I told your mama we run a casual office. All you need is—"

"Is a black skirt, black pants, and some white or off-white shirts," Cissy said. "But that's just not me. I like a little color in my life."

"Don't get too crazy with the way you dress, Cissy."

"I have to be—"

Aunt Bootsie winked at her. "He's not used to having girls around. Our boys could go a whole week with a pair of jeans and a couple T-shirts." She smiled. "You do realize people here don't dress like they do in Alabama, right?"

Cissy nodded and crinkled her nose. "Looks to me like they don't fully utilize the color wheel. I wonder if any of 'em know about gettin' their colors done."

"Colors done?" The look on Aunt Bootie's face let Cissy know the answer.

"Maybe that's the problem. Everyone my age in Hartselle knows what season they are. I'm a spring." She looked Aunt Bootsie over. "I think you might be an autumn, with your hazel eyes and golden tones in your skin. That's pretty special because most people are winters."

Aunt Bootsie looked even more perplexed now than before. "I have no idea what you're talkin' about, Cissy, but I sure do look forward to findin' out." She sighed. "I think I've missed a lot not havin' daughters."

Cissy planted her fist on her hip. "You've got me now, and I'll tell you everything I know about seasons and how to play up your colors." She held her tongue and refrained from letting her aunt know that the dark shade of purple she was wearing made her look like she'd just come off a nasty bout with the flu. "I think you'd look gorgeous in coral." She squinted and tilted her head. "Yeah, that would look real nice on you."

Aunt Bootsie tilted her head. "Coral, huh?"

Cissy nodded. "Or teal." She grinned. "Or maybe even a print with a full autumn palette."

"I don't believe I have anything that..." she grinned, "that exciting. It'll sure be fun to show you around the city."

A loud snort came from the kitchen doorway as Uncle Forest entered. "Don't tell me you ladies are planning to do a bunch of retail therapy." He managed another smile.

"Sounds like having you here is gonna cost me a whole lot more than your salary and benefits."

"I get benefits too?" Cissy's last job had given her just enough hours to keep her in fashion but not enough to qualify for benefits.

"Yep. All my employees get the best health insurance money can buy." He puffed his chest. "And all I expect is loyalty." His look said more than a month of talking. "Total loyalty."

Chapter 3

TOM SAT AT his desk, stared at the computer screen for a moment, and pondered what to do next. One of the shipments he'd been waiting for was late, and the excuse of a long weekend wouldn't fly for him. Years earlier if someone had told him he'd be this ticked off by a late shipment of sewing notions, he would have laughed.

After Tom had tired of working on Wall Street, he'd started looking at businesses he could purchase. His accountant recommended taking over the only failing company he'd invested in. Although Tom had never had any intention of working in the fashion industry, he saw potential in Sewing Notions Inc. The company purchased most of their notions from other countries, and they'd gotten into some trouble with customs. He decided that since he didn't have anything else lined up, he could at least help get the company back on its feet before moving on to something else. Unfortunately, once he arrived, the former CEO disappeared, and Tom didn't have a choice but to stick around a bit longer. He quickly realized that the notions business wasn't as much about fashion as it was juggling manufacturers, retailers, and demanding designers.

He took another glance at the e-mail before picking up his phone and punching in the number of the distributor. "This is unacceptable. There are plenty of other manufacturers out there that would bend over backward for my business. If you can't deliver on promises…"

He slammed down the phone just as he saw Marianne,

the administrative assistant he had inherited when he took over Sewing Notions Inc. Thankfully she had proved to have more integrity than the previous owner.

Marianne stood at his door, head cocked, assessing him. The gray streaks in her hair gave away her age and the fact that she was too busy to have her hair dyed. She typically wore dark skirts and button-front tops that did nothing for her figure, but today she had on slacks. "Okay, who were you chewing out this time?" Marianne's knowing look gave Tom no room for evading her direct question. His administrative assistant knew him all too well.

He tightened his jaw and shook his head. "These people need to learn to get things right the first time. I can't believe they think they can continue to be late with these big orders and stay in business." He raked his fingers through his hair. "We have people waiting."

"Are we talking about Sew-Biz?" Marianne took a step closer, still holding his gaze.

"That's exactly who I'm talking about."

"They might be late, but they do represent some of the best manufacturers in Korea. Be careful not to burn any bridges."

Tom pinched the bridge of his nose to thwart a headache that threatened when things didn't go according to plan. "Yeah, I know."

Marianne dropped a file on his desk. "When you have a moment, I'd like for you to take a look at these numbers before they go to the accountant." She started toward the door but stopped and turned around to face him. "Try not to get too worked up over the late order. Our customers will understand a slight delay." She tilted her head. "Is there something else?"

Tom pushed aside a file and ran a hand through his hair.

He paused for a second and then nodded. "Did you know that Forest Counts has a niece?" Marianne had worked in the industry twenty years and knew more about the people and personalities than he ever would. He relied on her to keep a finger on the pulse of industry gossip—who was up and coming, who was floundering, who was being hired or fired.

"No, but I'm not surprised. Most people his age have nieces and nephews." Marianne tilted her head. "So tell me about her. What's her name, and where did you meet her?" She gave him a mischievous smile. "And is she young and attractive?"

"Yes, very attractive. I ran into her and her uncle just outside the office."

"And what did Mr. Counts have to say about this meeting?"

"Not much, but he was obviously not thrilled to see me."

To escape Marianne's knowing gaze, Tom picked up a page from the folder Cissy had dropped. If Forest hadn't been so bent on pulling her away, Tom would have handed it back to her. He looked at the page and saw a faded copy of a picture of a zipper with all the different parts labeled and some notes beside it.

In the long silence he could feel Marianne's penetrating glare, and he felt his face flame.

"She must be something special to rattle you like this, but then again you've always been attracted to impossible situations." Marianne held up her index finger. "Just remember that you need to get to know the girl before you get all worked up...or risk facing her uncle's wrath."

"I know." He let out a deep breath. Marianne was right. Because of her uncle, Cissy was definitely what Marianne would call an impossible situation. "It might be worth risking though."

"All righty then!" Marianne shoved her glasses up to her head, leaned back, and folded her arms, still grinning. "So tell me all about her."

Tom welcomed her input. He'd worked with her long enough to know that she had good instincts about people. "Her name is Cissy Hillwood, and she's from Alabama. She will be working for her uncle."

"Interesting." Marianne unfolded her arms and propped her elbow on her desk. "At least you know better than to expect a warm welcome. Everyone in the notions business knows how Forest feels about you. It was bad enough before you got here, and then ever since you won the Mizrahi account, he's done nothing short of dissing you."

"I know, and I can't blame him after I managed to get a few of his best accounts, but it's not like there aren't enough accounts for both of us."

"Tell him that."

"I've tried to, but he's too stubborn to meet with me. Acts like I'm the enemy or something."

"Maybe you are. I think you should try to see things from his perspective." Marianne put her reading glasses back down on her nose and pointed to his desk. "I took several messages while you were out. They're on your desk."

"Thanks." Marianne turned to leave, but he stopped her. "And Marianne?"

"Yes?"

"If you hear anything more about Forest Counts or Cissy Hillwood, let me know, would you?"

She smiled. "Sure. I'll keep my ear to the ground." With that she left his office, chuckling softly.

Tom took a cursory glance at the messages as he thought

about Forest Counts and his grudges. The man was notorious for having started his business, Zippers Plus, on a shoestring and built it to be the thriving business it currently was. Unlike some of the other suppliers of sewing notions companies, he was no-frills, no-nonsense, but he always delivered, and that was what really mattered in the long run. And unlike Sewing Notions Inc. the company that Tom had managed to turn around, Zippers Plus had never had its reputation defiled...just temporarily deflated.

As the morning progressed and orders came pouring in, Tom answered questions from the sales people through e-mail and phone calls. The construction noise coming from his office put a cramp in his professional style, but he didn't have a choice at the moment. Marianne had tried to soundproof his area and make it more private when the remodeling first started, but the heavy blankets she'd strung around his desk left him gasping for air, and he yanked them down before the end of the first day. At least he could look forward to being back in his office that had a large glass window giving him a view outside the four walls.

No matter how hard he tried, Tom couldn't purge the image of Forest's niece's deep blue eyes and honey-brown hair from his mind. She had a blend of Southern belle softness and steely determination he'd seen in the most ambitious women he'd met—only not the aggression he'd come to know and expect. He had a feeling she got what she wanted without having to appear too pushy.

The faded, photocopied image of the labeled zipper kept catching his eye from the corner of his desk. He considered tossing it, but then he wouldn't have any excuse to see this woman named Cissy. Even her name brought a smile to his face.

He'd just hung up from another sales call when

Marianne sauntered over to his desk and picked up the copy of the zipper photo. She snorted. "Looks to me like they don't expect much from their new salespeople." Her eyebrows lifted, as she looked him in the eye. "I mean, who doesn't know the difference between the teeth and the zipper pull?"

"I didn't." Tom met her gaze. "In fact, I'm still learning about some of this stuff, and you know I've never even used what we sell."

"Oh, but you do." She pointed to the carded buttons hanging on the wall behind him. "You use the notions all the time. We all do."

"So I suppose being the consumer I am makes me an expert."

Marianne rolled her eyes as she gave him a dismissive wave. "Why don't you just go on over to Zippers Plus and give that to the pretty girl? You might as well just get it out of your system."

"That's probably a very bad idea."

She leaned over his desk and planted her face less than a foot from his. "Maybe so, but you know you want to. But first figure out how to get past her grumpy uncle who can't forgive you for taking some of his customers away from him."

"I took your advice and thought about trying to see things from his perspective, and I can't say I blame him." He leaned back in his chair and folded his arms. "Business is business. I might not be all that forgiving either if I were in his shoes."

"Oh, you'd forgive him," Marianne argued.

"Not on company time."

Marianne sighed and nodded. "You have a good point. If he did it on personal time, you'd give him the shirt off your back and all the money in your wallet. But when it comes to your business…" She raised her eyebrows, tilted her head toward him, and gave him one of those looks only she dared.

"You know I can't afford to give away the shop. If I did, you'd be out of a job, or worse, working for grumpy old Forest Counts instead of young, charming me."

Marianne let out an exaggerated sigh. "Maybe so. But I still think you should consider being a bit more Christlike in your business dealings."

"What do you mean?" he huffed. "It's not like I lie or cheat or steal…or do anything illegal."

She shrugged. "I don't know. There's much more to it than that. Sometimes it just seems like you pick and choose when you live your faith—like when you're not at the office. On weekdays you just seem to leave your faith at the door." She pointed at the nonexistent door. "Or more recently, curtain."

Tom smiled weakly at the joke. "Look, I've said this before. Business in New York is cutthroat. If I don't play the game, the barracudas will eat me alive. After all this company has been through, I have to play the game."

Marianne shook her head, but doubt still filled her eyes. "I don't agree. You can still be a shrewd businessman without playing the game like the ruthless barracudas." She gave him a chance to digest what she said before continuing. "Look, Tom, I know how tough it was on you growing up, knowing that your dad couldn't make it in business."

"People told him time after time that he was too nice. If he'd—"

"Being nice wasn't what made him lose his business. You need to understand the difference between being a good businessman and being a shark that doesn't care who gets hurt."

She'd cut close to the quick with that comment.

"I really need to get back to work." Tom turned his attention to the computer, further signaling the discussion was closed. Still, out of the corner of his eye he could see Marianne frowning as she left his office. She might have his number, but he didn't have to agree. She was an excellent assistant, but she obviously couldn't understand what he had to do to keep this business viable—and her and everyone else employed. His dad's compassion at the small hardware store he owned in upstate New York had cost him the profit needed for his family, and there were days he overheard his parents arguing about the bills and not having enough money to pay them. The financial stress created a chasm between his parents, and they eventually divorced. Since they were broke, he, his sister, and his mom moved in with his aunt in Queens. He rarely saw his dad, who'd taken a traveling job that kept him on the move. Tom's early life had been rough, so when he became an adult, he vowed to never make the same mistakes his dad had made. Sure, he had a heart for helping others, but once he reached the office, he had to look out for the interests of the business.

Chapter 4

COME ON, GIVE me a break," Uncle Forest grumbled into the phone, making Cissy cringe. "You know good and well I didn't just start this business yesterday. Wholesale prices don't jump 25 percent in two weeks."

Cissy glanced up at Dave, who hovered near her desk after conducting her first lesson on how to make sales calls. She inhaled the scent of his fresh-smelling soap as his amusement-filled gaze made her smile. Long, reddish eyelashes framed his gray-blue eyes, and his smile showed that he either had great genes or an expensive orthodontist to thank. She'd already noticed that he was only a few inches taller than her, but his muscular arms let her know he wasn't a wimp.

Dave leaned over and whispered, "Want to take a break now? This is probably a good time to go to lunch." Even his breath was nice. If she hadn't already seen Tom Jenkins, she might have been attracted to Dave.

It was already almost noon on her first day of work, and since she'd turned Aunt Bootsie down on her offer of bacon, eggs, biscuits, and a side of grits, her stomach had begun to rumble hours ago. "Sure." She started to stand, but Uncle Forest's glare in her direction startled her, so she sat back down. "Maybe we need to ask permission first."

"No need. We can go to lunch whenever we want, as long as there are enough people here."

Since she and Uncle Forest had been the first ones to

arrive and Dave came in a few minutes after them, it made sense to be the first to take lunch. "Okay, if you're sure he won't mind." She looked back over at her uncle.

Uncle Forest appeared at the door of his office, nodded, and gestured for them to go ahead. She let out a sigh of relief.

Cissy and Dave rode the elevator in silence. The second they stepped out on the first floor, he let out a soft laugh. "You realize this is just how he is, right? I mean, since he's your uncle, I'm sure you've seen that he's all bark and no bite."

"I haven't really been around him that much since he moved away from Alabama when I was a little girl, so no, I didn't know that about him." Cissy smiled at her new friend. "So tell me about him."

Dave made a face. "I don't want to get in trouble."

"Anything you say will be kept in the closest confidence."

"Same here. I would appreciate knowing I can say whatever, and it won't get back. I'll do the same for you."

"You got it. I had an office friend back home. She and I used to vent all over the place at lunch, but when we got back, we zipped our lips." She gave him a reassuring look. "So whatever we say stays between us."

"Promise?"

"My word is my promise." She smiled. "So what's it like working for Uncle...er...Forest Counts?"

Dave swallowed hard, glanced away, and then turned back to look her in the eye. "He comes across mad all the time, but he knows what he's doing in business, and he's always ethical, even if it costs him money. There are only two notions distributors in this city that are doing well: Zippers Plus and—"

"Sewing Notions Inc., right?"

Dave squinted. "How did you know?"

"A little birdie...and that very good-looking Tom Jenkins."

"You know Tom?"

Cissy nodded. "Yep. He practically mowed me down yesterday after we left the office. You should have seen Uncle Forest's face."

"Whoa. I can only imagine."

"What do you know about Tom?"

"I know he likes good-looking women." He shot her a glance, and she let out an embarrassed giggle. Dave frowned and took on a big-brother air. "Cissy, I think you need to be very careful. Sewing Notions is our biggest competitor, and there's bad blood between Mr. Counts and Tom, who just happens to own Sewing Notions Inc. Your uncle will protect his business with everything he has, and if he thinks anything is going on between you and Tom, there's no telling what he might do." Dave gave her a sympathetic look. "You might find yourself on a plane back to Alabama."

She thought about that for a moment before nodding. "Thanks for all your help. I don't know what I'd do without you."

"You'd do fine." He chuckled. "And I'm just doing my job."

Cissy laughed. "Mama always said not to bite the hand that feeds me." She glanced around. "Where are we going?"

"There's a fabulous little deli around the corner that serves the best sandwiches in New York." Dave wiggled his eyebrows. "At least that's what the sign in the window says. Anyway, they're cheap, and the food is good."

The sound of "Sweet Home Alabama" erupted from Cissy's handbag, so she pulled out her cell phone, glanced at the screen, and saw that it was Mama. Cissy held up a finger and asked Dave to slow down so she could talk.

"I hear sirens," Mama said. "What happened? Is someone hurt?"

"No, Mama, this is New York. There are cars—and sirens—everywhere." She glanced at Dave, who appeared amused.

"I don't like—"

"Trust me, I'm just fine, but I can't talk now. Dave and I are on our lunch break."

"Who's Dave? Do you know anything about him? How did you meet him? I can't believe you've already—"

Cissy looked at Dave again, who was obviously trying hard to pretend not to listen. "He's another salesman at Uncle Forest's company, and he's training me."

"Oh, I reckon that's okay. Does Forest know you're with him?"

"Yes, of course he does."

Mama let out a breath. "Call me later, okay? I can't help but worry about you, Cissy. You've always been so impetuous and boy crazy."

"Mama!"

"Just be careful, okay?"

"Of course." Cissy hung up and gave Dave an apologetic glance.

He laughed. "My mom still worries about me too, and I'm almost thirty."

As they walked, Cissy relaxed. The tension in the office had been high all morning, with Uncle Forest arguing over wholesale prices and the competition between the salespeople and their competitors. She wanted to talk about anything but work.

"So where are you from?" she asked.

Dave contorted his mouth. "Is it that obvious I'm not from here?"

"Not really," she said. "I just assumed you had to be from somewhere."

"I was born in St. Louis, but my family moved to Indiana when I was a teenager."

"What brought you here?"

He shrugged. "After I graduated from college, I wanted to move to the big city and get a high-powered job. So I threw my résumé up on all the job sites."

"Did Uncle Forest hire you through a job site?" That sure didn't sound like her uncle, but what did she know?

"Are you kidding?" He cast a goofy look in her direction. "No way. I had my first interview on Wall Street, and they pretty much told me I didn't stand a chance of working there...at least not for a few years."

"It's a long way from Wall Street to Zippers Plus," she said.

"Let's just say I took the scenic route getting to my job. Lots and lots of interviews—from the business district to where I am now." He shrugged. "It's a very long story that will take more time than we have for lunch."

"By the way, how much time do we have?"

"As little as possible." Dave stopped in front of a hole-in-the-wall deli and pushed the door open. "After you."

Cissy couldn't believe how many people were crammed in the small space between the display counter and the wall. "It must be good."

Dave nodded. "It's affordable and fast. I'm sure you'll probably want to come back."

The rapid-fire orders from customers and the order-taker's hollering intimidated Cissy, so she hung back and let Dave order for her. As she hovered a few feet from the counter, she took a deep breath and inhaled the blended scent of vinegar, deli meat, and exhaust fumes that wafted in from the street each time someone came in.

To her surprise, they had their order and were out the door in less than five minutes. "Are we taking these back to the office?"

"Are you kidding?" he asked. "No way. We'd never be able to eat with all the calls coming in. Let's find a bench somewhere."

This was all so new to Cissy—from the older-than-dirt buildings, the crazy-busy deli, and the random benches stuck in the middle of grassy, parklike settings half the size of her parents' front lawn. She couldn't help but laugh at the giant button and needle sculpture smack dab in the middle of the fashion district. But in these strange, new surroundings she felt invigorated and liberated.

Dave unwrapped his sandwich and grinned at her before taking a bite. "I know that look."

"What look?" she asked as she carefully removed the onions and repositioned the pickle in her sandwich.

"The one that tells me you're scared half to death to be so far away from home but you wouldn't go back right now because you don't want anyone to say 'I told you so.'"

She looked him directly in the eye and slowly shook her head. "Sorry, Dave, but you got that all wrong."

Dave belted out a belly laugh. "Keep telling yourself that, and you might actually start believing it." He gave her a warm smile of understanding. "Don't be embarrassed. We've all been there."

She glanced down at the remnants of her sandwich and thought about how different things were back home. Instead of sitting on a bench in the middle of the loudest city she'd ever been in, she'd be enjoying a salad in a café with someone she'd known all her life.

Dave shoved the last bite of sandwich into his mouth and crumpled the paper deli bag. "Ready to head on back?"

Cissy hadn't finished half her sandwich, but she stood anyway. "I'll just save the rest of this for later."

Dave made a face. "You need to learn to eat faster, Cissy. You're in New York now."

Considering that Dave was her only point of reference, all she could think to do was nod. "I'll try."

As soon as they rounded the last corner toward the office, Dave slowed way down. "Try to be as inconspicuous as possible."

"What?"

"*Shh!* Look down and keep walking."

Nothing he could have said would have made her more curious than that. She looked around until she spotted a petite woman with shoulder-length honey-colored hair and a big smile coming straight for them. "Do you know that woman?" she asked.

He groaned. "You blew it, Cissy. We're going to have to talk later."

"Hey, Dave." The woman approached, circled around them, and stopped, folding her arms. "So is *she* the reason you've been too busy to call?"

Cissy shook her head. "Dave is showing me the ropes."

"I just bet he is." The woman looked her up and down, a hint of amusement in her eyes. Cissy knew that look and understood Dave had nothing to worry about. She was just having a little fun teasing him.

"My name is Cissy Hillwood." She extended her hand. "I just got into town yesterday."

"It doesn't take long for some people." The woman

grinned at Cissy as they shook hands. "I'm Charlene Pickford, and I'm from Atlanta. How about you?"

"I-I can explain," Dave stuttered. "I—"

"Hartselle, Alabama."

Charlene's eyes lit up. "I know someone from there. Have you ever heard of Jesse Yarborough?"

"Yes!" Cissy couldn't believe this. Here she was, hundreds, maybe thousands of miles from home, and she and this Charlene woman knew someone in common. "He was the assistant principal of my high school until he moved to Atlanta."

"Where he was the *principal* of my high school…long after I graduated, but I met him when I had to help my cousin out of a pickle." Charlene shook her head. "It certainly is a small world. So where are you staying, Cissy Hillwood?"

"With my uncle, Forest Counts. I'm working for him too at Zippers Plus."

"Oh, I get it." A dawning of understanding replaced her amused expression. She turned to Dave. "So is that what you were trying to explain?"

Both women turned and waited for Dave to say something, but he just stood there for an uncomfortable few seconds, clearly perplexed. Finally he shuffled his feet and nodded. "I guess."

Charlene laughed. "C'mon, Dave, lighten up. I was just funnin' ya."

"Huh?"

Charlene playfully jabbed Cissy. "Someone needs to give that boy a lesson in how to talk Southern."

"Oh," Dave finally said, smiling. "Well, maybe so, but we really need to get back to the office."

Charlene dug around in her handbag, pulled out a card,

and handed it to Cissy. "Give me a call sometime, and we can talk. Do you like tea?"

"Of course," Cissy said. She glanced at the card and saw that Charlene was the marketing assistant for Paradise Promotional Products. "Who doesn't?"

"Oh, honey, I'm not talkin' about sweet tea. There's this really cute little tea bar a few blocks from here. They serve all kinds of interesting and exotic teas like you never had before. I'd love to meet there sometime, and we can chat. I sure do miss my friends from Atlanta."

"Sounds good," Cissy said as Dave gently pulled her away. "I'll call you."

Once Charlene was out of hearing distance, Dave mumbled, "I wish you hadn't gotten so chummy with her."

"Why not?"

"She's just using you to get to me."

Cissy chuckled. "Why would you say that?"

"Trust me on this. She works a couple of buildings down from us, and I've been having to get creative with when I come and go so I don't run into her."

Cissy didn't want to burst his bubble of delusion, so she didn't argue. "I'll try to keep that in mind. Do you know everyone in town?"

He made a face. "Hardly."

They finally reached their office building and went inside. Dave had just lifted his hand to punch the elevator button when the door opened and out stepped Tom Jenkins. The second their gazes met, she felt every ounce of breath escape her body.

"Steady there, Cissy," Dave whispered.

Her lips stuck to her teeth as she tried to smile at Tom. He grinned back.

"Something fell out of that folder you dropped, so

I brought it over. I thought you might need it," he said. "Your uncle said you wouldn't be back for a while."

"Thank you," Cissy managed. "What was it?"

"A zipper...a photocopy of a zipper, that is." Tom laughed at himself.

"I could have made her another one," Dave said, clearly uncomfortable with the situation. "You didn't have to bother coming over."

"Oh, but this is so much better." Tom's gaze never left Cissy's. "I'd like to get together sometime...that is, if you can get away some evening."

Her face flamed and her mouth got even dryer as she nodded. "Yes, I would like that."

He handed her a business card. "Call my cell phone anytime, and we can make plans." With a nod toward Dave, he took a step back. "I better let you get back to work."

The instant he left, Dave shook his head. "You've been here one day, and you have plans with two people. That's crazy. I go weeks without a date."

"Maybe you need to make more of an effort." Cissy thought for a moment. "Wait a minute. I thought Charlene was interested in you."

"Yeah, but she's a little too...well..." He made a face. "She's all into God and church and stuff, and I don't really have much time for that."

"Maybe you should make time." Cissy stuck Tom's card into the side pocket of her purse. "People around here sure do like to hand out business cards. I think I need to get me some."

"Yeah." Dave shook his head as they stepped into the elevator. "I can't believe I let you talk to Tom Jenkins. Do you know what your uncle will do if he finds out?"

"Yes, I do, and I won't say anything if you don't." Cissy

held Dave's gaze to make sure he was listening. "Don't worry about *letting* me do anything. I've never been one to *let* others keep me from doing whatever I want." She gave him one of the smiles Daddy always said was her best weapon, and he let out a groan.

Chapter 5

DAVE DIDN'T HAVE to worry about telling Uncle Forest anything. The instant they stepped off the elevator, Uncle Forest met them, waving the zipper diagram around with fiery sparks spewing from his eyes.

"Did you do this on purpose, Cissy? Because if you did, you and I need to have a serious conversation."

Dave scooted away while Cissy remained standing there in a facedown with her uncle. "On purpose? Do what?"

He shoved the paper at her. "Leave this behind?"

Cissy glanced over at Dave, who had managed to slip a few steps away. Where was a friend when she needed one?

She couldn't very well tell her uncle she didn't know what he was talking about. That would be a lie. She took a deep breath and squared her shoulders before turning to look him in the eye.

"I didn't do anything on purpose, but I do think it was nice of Mr. Jenkins to deliver it."

"So you know he came by here." Uncle Forest's eyes got very squinty, reminding her of Mama when she was about to give her the what for.

"Yes." Cissy paused and silently said the fastest prayer ever. "He said it fell out of the training binder, and he thought I might need it." She maintained the glaring gaze with her uncle. If he was anything like Mama, looking away would give him the edge, and she wasn't about to let him get the best of her. Putting her in the guest room and giving her a job didn't give him the right to bully her.

Finally he closed his eyes and shook his head. "Your mama was right. You sure are a handful. Strong willed and determined to do things your own way."

"She said that?"

"Dern tootin' she did." Whoa, he wasn't kidding when he said he still had a Southern accent. "She said that and then some."

So much for Mama's loyalty. "I might be a handful, but I'm honest, loyal, and a hard worker." Cissy folded her arms. "Did Mama tell you that?"

He pursed his lips. "Yes. And she also said I might have to save you from yourself. I should have paid closer attention and read between the lines before I opened my trap."

"What are you saying?" Cissy felt the dreaded rush she experienced right before she lost her job in Hartselle. "Do you want me to go back to Alabama?"

Uncle Forest raked his fingers through his thinning hair. "No, that would be too easy. I'm not giving up on you." To her surprise, he grinned. "Besides, you're not the only one in the family with a stubborn streak. You come by it honestly."

No kidding.

His expression softened a tad as he put his arm around Cissy and led her to her desk. "Your mulishness will either make you a star in this business..." He lifted one eyebrow. "Or break you and send you packing." He pointed to her chair. "Now sit and study. I want you ready to start selling by next week."

He hovered over her desk for a few seconds, so in spite of not wanting to look at him again, she knew that was the only way to get her uncle to leave her alone. "What?" she asked as she met his gaze.

"Jenkins isn't a good guy. He'd send his own mama up the river if he thought it might be good for business."

"Oh, come on, Uncle Forest. I'm sure—"

"Trust me on this." He spun around and left her sitting there pondering their conversation. As the minutes ticked away, she felt her frustration fade.

Cissy did everything she could to concentrate on the attributes of various sewing notions, but the activity in the office was way more interesting. Uncle Forest seemed constantly on the verge of a hissy fit that made hers look like a picnic with butterflies and spring flowers. He'd kept his office door open, so she was in his direct line of vision. One of the other sales reps alternated between making calls and applying makeup to an already very theatrical-looking face. Dave's voice rose as he tried to save a customer. She wanted to tell him to change his tactic to agreeing with the person on the other end of the line. As it was, he created a negative energy that made the caller an adversary. If they were in Alabama, she would have said something about winning people over with sweetness, but she was on different turf now. Give her a week, and she'd have a better feel for the territory. Every now and then she caught even more of a glimpse of Uncle Forest's Southern upbringing. His voice dripped with honey as he spoke to prospective customers, but the harder edge returned during negotiations with a supplier. As annoyed as she was with him, she couldn't miss his fine balance between charm and business acumen.

Toward the end of the workday, as the rest of the employees got ready to leave, Cissy started straightening her desk. Uncle Forest hung up and walked over to her.

"What're you doing?"

She glanced up at him. "Getting ready to go?"

"We're not leaving yet," he said. "I still have another hour's worth of work to do before I can even think about going home."

"But everyone else is—"

He gave her a wicked-looking grin. "We're not everyone else. I own this company, remember?"

Cissy forced a smile. "Yes, of course." She bit her tongue before saying what was really on her mind—that she just might go crazy if she read another word about zippers or buttons or thread or... or anything else about sewing. Until now the only things she knew about sewing were what she'd learned in home ec. And once she finished hemming that A-line skirt back in tenth grade, she vowed she'd never sit in front of a sewing machine again.

By the time Uncle Forest packed his briefcase, Cissy wondered if she'd bitten off more than she could chew with this job. Maybe she should have stayed back in Alabama and ridden out the wrath of Hartselle. She thought for a moment as she followed Uncle Forest to the elevator. Nah, it would be a month of Sundays before folks got past their favorite hero being behind bars.

"So how'd you like your first day on the job?" Uncle Forest asked as he started the car.

"There sure is a lot to learn. How many sewing notions do I have to know about?"

He snorted. "You remind me of your mama right now, answering a question with a question."

"Really? Mama doesn't like when I do that. It annoys her." Cissy sighed. "Come to think of it, everything I do annoys her."

"Your mama adores you, and you know it. I had to talk her into letting you come all the way up here. When I heard what happened to that loser, I knew what you were in for. Did you ever hear about what his daddy did to me?"

"Spencer's daddy?"

Uncle Forest nodded. "Yeah, Spencer's daddy. He was just like Spencer—spoiled rotten just because he could catch a football and make it to the goal line without getting knocked over. The only way he graduated was with the teachers' help and a little bit of cheating that they turned a blind eye to." He shook his head. "He just about destroyed me."

"I didn't realize that," Cissy said. "What did he do to you?"

"I was always pretty good in science, so right before the homecoming game the teacher asked me to tutor him just so he could pass the six-week exam. If he didn't make at least a C, he wouldn't be able to play in the game that would bring the school all the glory they craved." A pensive look crossed his face. "It was futile, though. No matter what I said or how many memory tricks I taught him, I couldn't get through his thick skull. I knew a lot was riding on it because Hartselle High School was in the running for our division's state championship."

Cissy smoothed the front of her shirt. "I think I know where this is going."

"So I let him look at my paper during the exam."

That so wasn't what she expected. "You cheated?"

He grimaced. "Afraid so. But that's not even the worst part. We got caught."

"Ouch." Cissy made a face. "That's terrible."

"And that's not the half of it. I also lied and backed him up, saying I'd copied his paper."

"You didn't." Cissy looked at him in bewilderment. "Why would you say such a thing?"

"I wonder the same thing myself. It really didn't matter anyway. We both got in trouble, and he wasn't able to play in the game."

Cissy offered a sympathetic smile. "Dare I ask who won the championship?"

"We did." He grinned right back at her. "That made things even worse. Spencer's daddy was not only a liar and a cheat; he wasn't even needed to win the game. Nothing was ever the same for either of us after that." He flinched. "From then on he blamed me for everything that went wrong."

"So is that why you came to New York?"

"No, another scandal happened shortly after that, and everyone pretty much forgot what happened—well, except Bubba McCully and me. I came to New York for the opportunity to build an international business."

"Have you seen Mr. McCully since you left?"

Uncle Forest gave her a quick glance. "Nope. And I never heard anything about him either...that is, until your fiasco with his son."

"Sounds to me like his son inherited some bad blood." Cissy turned her attention to the scenery as they made their way to Long Island.

Uncle Forest changed the subject and talked about his sons as he drove. As the house came into view they saw Aunt Bootsie standing on the porch shielding her eyes. Cissy turned to her uncle. "Must be nice to have someone so excited to see you every day."

"I'm not the one she's excited to see." Uncle Forest pulled into the driveway and put the car in park. "You've just breathed new life into our home merely by being here. I don't remember the last time she watched for me."

She noted the sadness in his voice. "What's wrong?"

"Nothing. We just miss the boys." He opened his car door. "Are you going to get out or just sit here and make your aunt worry?" Uncle Forest scooted out of the car and leaned over, looking at her. "I'd be willing to bet anything she's been cooking all afternoon." As he straightened, she heard him mumble, "To think we have to have company to get a decent meal around here anymore."

Something was going on, and it wasn't all rainbows and Skittles.

"Cissy." Aunt Bootsie came toward her with open arms, beaming as though she'd just seen a newborn baby. "So how was your first day at the office?"

Forgive me, Lord, for this little white lie.

Cissy forced a smile. "Wonderful. I have a lot to learn, but Dave is helping me learn the ropes."

Aunt Bootsie scowled at Uncle Forest. "You didn't stick her with Dave."

"I don't know what you're talking about, Bootsie. Dave is one of the finest people I have working at Zippers Plus."

"He's also your least productive salesman."

"You don't think I'd take valuable time from my best salesperson to train her, do you? That would put us out of business."

Whoa. Based on the harshness of his tone, it sounded like there might be more than one issue here. Time for a little intervention.

Cissy dug deep and forced a lilt to her voice. "We had a very productive day. I spent all morning studying the different items we carry. I had no idea there was so much to learn about this business. Dave has been so good about answering my questions." She chattered as quickly as she could, elaborating on some of the minutest details of what she could remember from the manual Dave had made.

Uncle Forest rolled his eyes and walked away. "I'll leave the small talk to you ladies."

"Supper is almost ready," Aunt Bootsie said. "Go wash up."

"Let me know when you want me in the kitchen." With that he disappeared up the stairs, leaving Cissy standing with a very irritated Bootsie.

Aunt Bootsie sighed, shuddered, and forced a smile. "So what do you think of New York?"

Cissy swallowed hard. "It's very big...and old." She scrunched her face before adding, "And smelly."

Aunt Bootsie laughed as she took a step toward the kitchen. "Good observation. C'mon, you can tell me more while I finish gettin' supper cooked."

"What can I do to help?"

"Nothin'. Why don't you just sit down? You've been working hard all day." Aunt Bootsie stopped and looked at something on the table. "On second thought, would you mind straightening up the placemats? Forest left his all catawampus this morning when he got up, and I didn't get around to fixing it." She made a *tsk*-ing sound with her tongue. "I declare, sometimes that man acts like he has a team of servants at his disposal."

Cissy bit her tongue. If Aunt Bootsie said one more thing, she wasn't so sure she could hold back.

"Ever since he recovered from losing his biggest accounts, you'd think his middle name was Zipper. That's all he ever cares about anymore."

That did it. Cissy couldn't keep biting her tongue with World War III about to erupt. "Why are you so mad at Uncle Forest?"

Aunt Bootsie froze, a large stirring spoon poised in

midair above the pot. She slowly turned around and faced Cissy. "Don't tell me he got to you first."

"What are you talking about?"

"Oh, did he tell you how I don't care about the business that puts food on the table? Or that I don't listen to him anymore, when all he does is rattle on and on about zippers this, buttons that? Or about the latest greatest thing in thread?" Her jaw tightened. "I bet he said I desert him every Sunday morning and run off to church when all he wants to do is sit here, chug coffee by the potful, and bury his nose in the newspaper."

Cissy slowly shook her head as she rose from the table. "No, he never said any of that. All he said was—" She stopped herself but realized she'd already said too much.

"What did he say?" Aunt Bootsie had turned all the way around, still holding the spoon like a weapon.

"He just said y'all were excited to have me here when we saw you standing on the porch." Cissy held her breath, hoping that would work. At least it wasn't a lie. It just wasn't the whole truth.

"Well, that's true...at least for me."

Cissy seized the opportunity to turn the tables. "So are you saying he didn't want me here?"

"No, I'm not saying that at all." Aunt Bootsie turned back around a little too quickly. "It's just that—"

"Are you the one who insisted I come?" Cissy asked.

"Well..." Aunt Bootsie's shoulders sagged. "Sort of. I just told your mama that there's no point in you havin' to go through all that scuttlebutt around Hartselle when we have this big old house goin' to waste. Besides, it's time for him to face the fact that what happened to him in Hartselle wasn't his problem. I'm sorry you went through so much with Spencer, but it did serve to let Forest know the problem lies with the McCullys and not him."

Good thing Uncle Forest told her what happened. "But what about the job? Does Uncle Forest not need another salesperson?"

"Oh, he needs another salesperson, all right. In fact he's been interviewing for the past month. Everyone who's any good wants too much money, though, so I told him this was perfect. He could train you his way, and you could stay here in the house with us, so you wouldn't expect such a high salary."

Cissy didn't mind being cheap labor as much as she did being the game piece in whatever was going on between her aunt and uncle. But now wasn't the time to say that.

Silence fell over the kitchen, with the exception of a clanging spoon and the shuffling of Aunt Bootsie across the floor as she filled serving dishes. Cissy straightened the placemats, found the flatware, and arranged it on the table.

When everything appeared almost ready, Cissy went to the door. "I'll let Uncle Forest know supper's ready." Aunt Bootsie didn't say anything, so Cissy scurried out to the living room to get him.

First thing he said when he entered the kitchen was, "Looks good, Bootsie. I sure do miss your good old-fashioned home cooking."

Aunt Bootsie gave him a look that could stop a bear. "Don't expect me to do this every day, Forest. You know what your doctor said."

He waved his hands in dismissal. "What does that doctor know? He's never had good ol' Alabama cookin'."

"Are you sick?" Cissy asked.

"His cholesterol is twice what it should be, so I've started making low-fat meals."

"If a stranger dropped by on a normal day, he'd think we'd gone all vegetarian."

"That's not true, Forest, and you know it. Someone's gotta look after your health." She cleared her throat. "You certainly don't."

One look at the platter of ham and bowls filled with fat-laced veggies let Cissy know that wasn't the case tonight. "I think everyone is trying to cut back the fat," she said slowly. "Even in Alabama."

Uncle Forest sat down and pounded his fist on the edge of the table. "That's ridiculous. People in my family have been eating that way forever, and they live as long as anyone up here."

"That's because you come from a family of farmers. They used to work hard in the fields all day, so they didn't have to worry about all that fat," Aunt Bootsie argued. She glanced over at Cissy. "In case you're wondering, this isn't the first time we've had this conversation."

Obviously. "I understand." Cissy didn't want this to go on, so she decided to take her aunt's side for health's sake, even though she totally understood where her uncle was coming from. "I've been trying to eat healthier too, especially since Aunt Mona had her heart attack." Aunt Mona was the youngest of her grandmother's sisters.

"Aunt Mona is dern near ninety years old," Uncle Forest bellowed.

Okay, so Aunt Mona wasn't the best example, but that was the best Cissy could come up with at the moment. "I still think it's a good idea to do what we can to stay healthy. The good Lord gave us these bodies, so we should take care of them."

"Amen," Aunt Bootsie said as she sat down, still glaring at her husband.

"That's nonsense," he said between clenched teeth. "All those health nuts have poisoned everyone's minds. They're miserable because they munch on cardboard, and they're trying to bring all of us down with them."

"Cissy, honey, go ahead and help yourself." Aunt Bootsie lifted a basket of rolls dripping in butter. "Have some bread."

Even though she loved this kind of food, she knew she'd pay for it later, so she took a roll knowing she wouldn't eat more than one or two bites of it. But she had to be polite and do whatever it took to lower the tension.

Frustration welled in Cissy's chest. It seemed that no matter what she said, it angered her uncle or brought up a rift between him and her aunt. But not saying anything was awkward, so she decided to talk about the only thing she figured was safe.

"Where do y'all go to church?"

"That's it. I'm outta here." Uncle Forest stood up so quickly his chair almost fell over before he caught it. After shoving it back in place, he stormed out of the kitchen.

"Wh-what just happened?" Cissy looked from the doorway back to her aunt.

"I think you just hit on the heart of everything that's gone wrong with your uncle," Aunt Bootsie said. "Ever since Sewing Notions Inc. stole his biggest accounts, he's been a very angry man. And the one he's the angriest at is the Lord for letting it happen."

"But—"

"He hasn't been to church in several years."

That sure explained a lot. "How about you?"

"I go most Sundays, but I sometimes feel like I'm being

rebellious because it seems to bug Forest when I leave him behind." Aunt Bootsie lowered her head. "I pray for him all the time, but it doesn't seem to be working."

Cissy remembered feeling that way not long ago, when she realized she was in a no-win relationship with Spencer. Mama had said the Lord was listening to her prayers, and He would answer them as He saw fit. It wouldn't necessarily be what she expected or even wanted, but it would be what was best for her. And here she was, all the way up in New York City.

Aunt Bootsie cleared her throat, but the tears still lingered in her eyes. "Some of the men from the church even stopped by to talk to him, but he refused to come out of our room. I reckon there's nothin' anyone can do to change his mind."

"I'll pray for him too, but in the meantime I'd like to hear about your church."

A smile crept over her aunt's face as she talked about the energy of the pastor, the loving spirit in the church, and the endless opportunities to get involved in mission work. "We have overseas missions and programs to help the needy right here in our own backyard."

"Sounds good."

A shadow fell over the kitchen, letting them know they weren't alone. A softer expression came over Aunt Bootsie's face. "Hey, Forest. Ready for dessert?"

Cissy heard the quiver in her aunt's voice, but otherwise she appeared normal. As soon as she thought she had things figured out, another element of contention flew into the mix. Maybe the Lord had brought her to New York for more than one reason.

He sat down and nodded but didn't say a word. His silence said more than words would ever be able to.

Cissy looked over at her aunt. "Need help?"

"No, sweetie, it's a one-person job. Why don't you just have a seat, and I'll bring it to you." Aunt Bootsie scurried around pulling out plates, slicing the cake, and putting it on the table.

Cissy was full from supper, but she didn't want to appear rude. She took a small bite of the chocolate cake with buttercream icing. "This is delicious."

The cake really was good. As full as she was, she managed to polish off what was on her plate, and she had to exercise self-restraint when Aunt Bootsie offered more.

After Uncle Forest finished his, he stood up and carried his plate to the sink. "Why don't you ladies go on to the living room? I'll clean up."

Cissy flashed a look in her aunt's direction. Aunt Bootsie nodded and gestured toward the door. "We'll most certainly take you up on that."

Once they were out of hearing range of the kitchen, Cissy stopped. "Does he normally clean up?"

"Only when he feels bad about something." Aunt Bootsie gave her a motherly squeeze. "This is his way of apologizing for acting like such a clod."

Cissy giggled. "You could get a lot of mileage out of that."

"Trust me, I would if I didn't think it would seem like schemin'." Aunt Bootsie sighed. "I don't think the Lord is fond of schemin' and deception, but I can't say I haven't been tempted."

Cissy realized she'd just learned more about her aunt and uncle in the past hour than she'd known all her life. Even the best relationships sure could be complex.

"Why don't you go to bed early tonight?" Aunt Bootsie

said. "I'm sure you're exhausted after your first day, and you'll be gettin' up with the chickens tomorrow."

"I'm fine."

"You are now, but that's only because Forest let you sleep in this morning."

"Sleep in?" Cissy narrowed her eyes. "We were the first ones there."

"Maybe so, but he's normally out of here before the sun comes up." Aunt Bootsie gave her a sympathetic smile. "I don't think he plans on spoilin' you at the risk of missin' out on business."

Cissy groaned.

Chapter 6

CISSY SET THE alarm on her cell phone extra early to prevent upsetting Uncle Forest. Good thing she did too because he'd already finished his breakfast by the time she got to the kitchen. He took one look at her, grunted, shook his head, and left her alone with Aunt Bootsie.

"Is he mad at me?"

"No." Aunt Bootsie leaned around and checked the door. "He's always rather quiet first thing in the morning. Don't let him get you down, Cissy. By the time he gets to the office, he should be just fine." She smiled. "Just try not to say too much on the way in. He likes his quiet time."

"Thanks for letting me know." Cissy's nature would have had her babbling all the way in, like she did yesterday, so now she knew to make a concerted effort to be quiet.

Aunt Bootsie was right. Uncle Forest didn't say more than a half dozen words all the way in. If she hadn't known what to expect, she would have tried to force conversation.

As they left the parking garage, Cissy spotted Tom entering the office building next to Zippers Plus. Uncle Forest shot her a look that let her know he'd seen Tom too, but he didn't say a word. She looked down, pretended not to have noticed, and continued walking.

An hour later Dave walked into the office. The smile on his face beat all. "Good morning, everyone."

"Everyone?" Cissy chuckled. "It's just you, me, and my uncle."

"That's all that really matters." He walked over to Cissy's

desk in the corner, dropped a long-stemmed red rose on it, and with his back to Uncle Forest, ran his fingers over his lips, indicating that she needed to keep hers zipped. "So glad you made it back for your second day at work."

"For me?" Cissy whispered. She looked at the flower but didn't touch it.

"I put it on your desk, didn't I?" He whispered back as he made a face. "Of course it's for you."

"Thank you." Cissy lifted it, took a sniff, and put it back down when she realized it didn't have a smell. She looked up at him and raised her voice. "What are you so happy about?"

He feigned shock. "Are you saying you don't think I'm like this every day?"

Uncle Forest stuck his head around the half-wall that separated him from the bullpen. "That's exactly what she's saying." He got up and joined them. "What's this all about?" Cissy knew exactly the moment her uncle saw the rose when his eyes bulged, and his face turned a fiery shade. "Who gave you that?"

Cissy pointed to Dave. "He did."

"Oh." Uncle Forest let out a sigh. "I guess that's okay." He switched his attention to Dave. "So why the cheery disposition? Did you finally meet a nice girl?"

"Maybe." Dave glanced down at Cissy and gave her a flirty smile.

Uncle Forest pulled back and wagged his finger. "Oh no ya don't. You know I don't allow my employees to date each other."

Cissy started to argue, but Dave made a hand signal to shush that only she could see at his side. "I don't mean to be disrespectful, but if Cissy and I discover that we have something special between us, would you deny us the opportunity to get to know each other better?" Before Uncle Forest could answer, he continued. "She's such a beautiful woman, you can't expect her to sit home every night. And wouldn't it be nice to know something about the person she's with? I just happen to find her extremely attractive." He paused as he looked over at Cissy and then turned back to her uncle. "Can you blame me?"

His comments rendered Cissy totally speechless. She hadn't seen that one coming.

Uncle Forest frowned as he pondered the thought. "I don't know. I'll have to think about it."

"I would never want to do anything against your wishes, Mr. Counts, but I would be honored to take your niece out to dinner one night this week."

"Wait just one minute." Cissy stood, holding her hands up, shushing both men. "No one ever asked me what *I* want."

Dave sat down at his desk that was only a few feet from Cissy's and gave her an exaggerated look of apology. "I'm so sorry, Cissy. It's just that I was overcome with—"

"I suppose I'm okay with one dinner, but that's it until I have a chance to discuss this with my wife...and her mother." Without waiting for another word from Cissy or Dave, Uncle Forest took off toward the elevator, which immediately opened when he pushed the button.

The second they were alone, Cissy widened her eyes and glared at Dave. "What in the world was that all about?"

He pretended to be offended. "Are you saying I'm up to something?"

"I wasn't, but now that you mention it, what *are* you up to?"

Dave pretended to be appalled. "So you think I'm a conniving sort of fella?"

"Stop with the fake Southern accent. You're not very good at it." She glanced down at the rose and then gave him a puzzled look.

"You don't think that flower was from me, do you?" He pointed to the rose on her desk.

"Just tell me what's going on. I hate games."

"Yeah, me too, but sometimes you have to play." Dave leaned forward and whispered, "Tom Jenkins sent you the rose. I intercepted it in the building lobby."

"But why?"

"You know your uncle. He would have the big one if Tom came waltzing in here with a flower."

"That's not what I'm asking. Why would he give me a flower?"

Dave rolled his eyes. "Don't tell me you're dense. I had you pegged for an intelligent woman who likes to act."

"Enough nonsense." She looked back at the flower, felt a tummy flutter, and had to stifle a giggle. "Spill it, Dave."

"The guy likes you. He thinks you're cute, and he would like to date you. He's willing to fight the lions and tigers—and the bear who runs this office—just for the opportunity to get to know you better." Dave made a mock grin. "Is that enough or do I need to explain further?"

"But why did you ask my uncle if I could go to dinner with you?"

"Look, Cissy, I'm just trying to help out a coworker. You and Tom obviously like what you see in each other, and you have an obstacle. I thought I'd make it easier for you two to get together."

"So you want me to lie and say I'm with you when I'm really not?" Cissy had been accused of being strong willed and defiant, but she'd never resorted to outright lies.

"I thought—" Dave closed his eyes and shook his head.

"I don't know what I was thinking. Of course you wouldn't lie. You'd much rather be miserable sitting around the house with your uncle and aunt after spending the entire day in the office listening to his grumbling."

Cissy felt terrible, but she needed to make things clear with Dave. "I appreciate what you tried to do, Dave, and I'm not saying I'm perfect or anything…" She paused and tried to think of the right words to say without making him think she didn't appreciate the gesture.

"Now I'm going to say the same thing you told me." He paused and smiled. "Spill it, Cissy."

"I don't like to lie about stuff, no matter what. It's just wrong and makes me feel terrible about myself when I do it. It's not that I think I'm above it, and I certainly understand why someone would…well, you know, tell an occasional little white lie to get—"

"Do all Southern girls do that?"

Cissy pulled back and scrunched her face as she looked at him. "Do what?"

"You just did the same thing Charlene does."

"I still don't know what you're talking about. It's not that I'm not smart, because I am. Everyone back home says so. But I can't read your mind when—"

"Okay." He held up a hand to stop her. "That's exactly what I'm talking about. You over-explain everything."

"Oh." Cissy glanced down at her desk. Yeah, she could see what he was saying.

"I know you're intelligent, and I get that you don't lie. But in the short time since I've known you, I think you are a very nice person who needs to live her own life without interference from her uncle."

"Yeah, it would be nice to make some decisions on my own."

"If you ever change your mind about Tom, I'll do whatever I can to help, even if it does mean getting on the bad side of your uncle." He offered a warm smile. "Perhaps you and I can actually do something together sometime, since you obviously can't go out with Tom without making your uncle mad. I realize I'd be your second choice…" He glanced down and then back up at her with a shy smile. "You are very cute."

Cissy let out a breath she just realized she'd been holding. "Thank you, Dave. That's very sweet…I think." She held his gaze, hoping for even a hint of what she felt when she saw Tom, but it didn't happen. "Maybe we can go out sometime. But never consider yourself anyone's second choice."

As Dave worked through the morning and she studied the training book, she pondered just how much he was willing to risk—the biggest thing being his job. None of her friends had ever stuck their neck out for her like that before. In spite of the fact that he was willing to be dishonest, she appreciated his offer more than she'd ever be able to express. And he really was cute, even if he did look about ten years younger than he was. Maybe if she spent a little less time thinking about Tom Jenkins and more time thinking about Dave… *Well, that's not gonna happen.*

At eleven thirty Dave got up and stretched. "Want to go to lunch again? I'm meeting some friends at a diner you might like."

"I appreciate your offer, but not today. Aunt Bootsie made me a sack lunch with leftovers, and I thought I'd take it to that little grassy area with the benches behind the building."

"Have a good one." He plucked his jacket off the back of his chair, flung it over his shoulder, and headed for the elevator. Cissy watched as he punched the button and disappeared when the doors closed.

All her life she'd had male friends, but Dave seemed the most willing to take a risk strictly for friendship. Too bad he didn't go to church. She imagined he'd make a mighty fine Christian.

"Now that he's gone, tell me what you want to do."

Cissy had been so deep in thought that the sound of Uncle Forest's voice startled her. "I didn't hear the elevator."

"I came up the back stairs." He leaned against the wall, his arms folded. "Now answer me. What do you want to do?"

"What do I want to do?" She gave him a puzzled look. "About what?"

"Do you like Dave?" He planted a fist on his hip and leaned against the wall.

"Oh, that. Of course I like him. What's not to like?"

Uncle Forest shrugged. "So you do want to date him?"

"He's nice, but I don't think he and I will ever be more than friends. I don't think he goes to church, and my faith is important to me."

He grunted and pulled away from the wall. "You better let him down nicely. He's just now starting to get up to speed with his accounts, and I don't want him leaving the company just because he can't face my niece who jilted him."

Cissy laughed. "Dave is much stronger than that."

"I'm just glad that rose was from Dave and not Tom. I might not like having coworkers in my office dating each other, but I can live with it. Having you steppin' out with a competitor . . ." He shook his head. "That's a whole 'nother thing."

She clamped her teeth down on her tongue so hard she

was certain she'd drawn blood. Rather than respond, she opened her desk drawer, pulled out her lunch cooler, and stood up. "I'll be back in about an hour." Then she took off before he had a chance to say another word.

It was still rather early for the lunch crowd, so the only people who didn't appear to be in a hurry to go somewhere were a woman pushing a stroller with twins and a man wearing baggy clothes and ratty shoes. Unfortunately the man took up most of the bench she'd spotted earlier. She glanced around and saw another one less than twenty feet away. The view wasn't as nice over there, but she wasn't about to ask the man to move.

As she opened the bag inside her cooler, she was amazed by all the food Aunt Bootsie had been able to pack in such a small space. There was enough for at least two people, maybe even three. She smiled as she imagined her aunt putting everything together with loving hands. Bootsie reminded Cissy of her mother.

"Hey, girl. Got room for me?"

Cissy glanced up at the familiar voice and saw Charlene standing there with a brown paper sack in hand. She scooted over and gestured toward the bench. "Have a seat. I thought I'd be alone."

"If you'd rather—" Charlene puckered her lips into a bow shape.

"No, I'm glad you're here. It'll be nice to have someone to talk to." Cissy grinned at Charlene. "How long have you been in New York?"

"A year. Long enough to be homesick." She opened her paper bag, glanced inside, and then looked longingly at Cissy's feast. "They don't make food here like they do back home."

"I know what you mean." Cissy pushed the cooler toward

her new friend. "Help yourself. There's enough for both of us."

Charlene only hesitated for a few seconds before reaching in and pulling out the second ham sandwich. "I kept trying to tell myself the delis here are the best in the world, but there's nothing better than a good, old-fashioned ham and biscuit sandwich with all the fixins. The bread here is so crusty it hurts my mouth."

"You should see what my aunt made for supper last night." Cissy's eyes rolled back. "You would have been in hog heaven."

"Well, if you ever need someone to taste her food, I won't let you down."

Cissy laughed. "I'll have to remember that. It would have been nice to have you there last night."

"Just say the word." Charlene started to laugh, but she caught herself as she studied Cissy. "What's wrong?"

Cissy took a deep breath and made a quick decision to open up just a little. "My uncle is being overly protective of me."

"Does he have a good reason to be that way?"

"I s'pose. I haven't always made the best decisions." Time to change the subject. "So what does a marketing assistant at Paradise Promotional Products do?"

Charlene shrugged. "Everything the marketing manager doesn't want to do. I'm hoping he gets promoted or transferred soon so I can apply for his job."

"Do you live close to the office?"

"I do now." Charlene took a bite of her sandwich and sighed as she chewed. "Delicious." She grinned. "When I first got here, I couldn't believe the prices of apartments in Manhattan, so I found a place about an hour and a half away. That commute got old, so I started looking with something different in mind. Now I have a tiny apartment in the city."

"Must be nice." Cissy sighed. "I haven't been here long enough to even think about moving out of my uncle's house, but when I do..." She smiled. "You said you couldn't believe the price of apartments. Are they that expensive?"

"Oh yeah." Charlene told Cissy how much she paid. "I realize it's way more than anything back home, but I'm getting used to it. Living closer in has a lot of advantages, and I've learned ways to cut other expenses."

"Maybe you can give me some pointers."

"I'll be happy to."

They chatted about their hometowns for the remainder of lunch, but Cissy started imagining herself having her own apartment. Wouldn't that be something? No more having to get up with the chickens only to be stuck in the car with a grumpy uncle. No more tiptoeing around her uncle, trying to hide her attraction to his competitor. She wouldn't have to lie about seeing Tom because she simply wouldn't mention him.

And no more down-home Southern cooking from Aunt Bootsie.

Cissy sighed. Being on her own had its price. But she just might be ready to pay it. Yeah, an apartment closer to the office sure did sound good.

Chapter 7

O N MONDAY, THE start of her second week in New York, Charlene joined her again for lunch. Cissy opened her cooler and offered the other half of the sandwich she was sure her friend would like.

"So how's everything goin' with you and Dave?" Charlene asked.

"Oh, he's been really patient with me at work." She sighed. "This is all so new to me, I'm sure I'm not the easiest person to train. Dave is...well..." She stopped before she blurted anything that might hurt her new friend's feelings.

"He's what?" Charlene's tone implied that she thought something else might be happening.

"Oh, it's nothing. He just said he's not into God like you are, so I didn't want to get into something that wouldn't work." Cissy gave Charlene an apologetic look. "I know you liked him and all, but—"

Charlene let out a chuckle. "Yes, I did like him, but like you said, we found out we're not spiritually compatible. I'm glad you feel the same way about your faith."

"I do." She glanced down at her half-eaten sandwich. "He and I are pretty good buddies, so maybe I'll have some opportunities to witness to him."

Charlene shrugged. "Just don't expect an overnight conversion."

"Oh, I know," Cissy said. "It's up to the Lord to touch someone's heart, so I plan to be available if He wants me in on it."

A low chuckle escaped Charlene's lips before she got serious. "How about church? Did you find a place to go yesterday?"

Cissy nodded. "I went with my aunt. Her church is fine for her, but it seems like the older, married, family-type church. Not exactly the place to meet eligible men." She thought of Tom, and must have gotten a far-off look in her eye, because Charlene nudged her.

"Thinking of someone back home?" Charlene asked.

"Not hardly." She explained what she'd run away from, while Charlene *tsk*-ed and made sympathizing noises.

"Sounds like you got out of there in the nick of time."

"Boy, did I ever." She didn't want to talk about Spencer again, so she changed the subject. "Do you know anything about a guy named Tom Jenkins? The owner of Sewing Notions Inc.?"

Charlene shook her head. "Can't say I do, but isn't Sewing Notions Inc. your uncle's main competition?"

Cissy sighed. "Unfortunately yes. I ran into him my first day here, and he gave me his card and asked to get together, but I thought my uncle would explode. I don't know why, though. Tom seems like a perfectly nice man. And he's very good looking!"

Charlene laughed. "Sounds like the Capulets versus the Montagues." At Cissy's puzzled look, Charlene said, "You know, *Romeo and Juliet*? Okay, you probably studied some other Shakespeare play in high school English. Anyway, maybe you should have a talk with your uncle about this Tom guy. Find out if there's anything you can do to persuade him to give you his blessing."

"I don't think I want to go there." Cissy made a face. "He gets furious any time Tom's name comes up." She sighed.

"I might as well stop thinkin' about a man I'll never be able to see."

"Maybe you should think about getting your own place."

"Need a roommate?" Cissy asked.

"There's barely enough room for me, but I just happen to know there's another apartment that'll be vacant soon. The guy across the hall from me got a job in Chicago, so he's moving out at the end of the month."

"That's next week."

"Yeah. He'd actually like to be out sooner, but the landlord won't let him unless he has someone else who can move in right away." Charlene took another bite. "Interested in taking a look at the place?"

"I couldn't. My aunt and uncle went to so much trouble to make room for me."

"You just asked if I needed a roommate." She narrowed her gaze. "You haven't been here long, but I suspect you'll be looking for your own place soon anyway." She grinned. "Am I right?"

Just then Charlene's attention went to something behind Cissy. Before she had a chance to turn around and see what it was, she heard his voice.

"Cissy? I hope you don't mind my interrupting. Dave said you might be here."

Cissy's heart pounded ninety to nothin', and she had to reach for the side of the bench to reestablish her equilibrium. "Oh, hey there, Tom." Her voice cracked as she glanced up at his smiling face. "Sorry I never got back to you. I've been busy settling into my new job. Where did you see Dave?"

"I didn't. When I didn't hear from you, I thought maybe you'd lost my business card, so I called Dave to get your number. He said you were taking an early lunch and told me that you like to come here."

Charlene scooted to the very edge of the opposite side of the bench. "Well, bless Dave's heart, wasn't that sweet of him." She patted the middle of the bench. "Have a seat."

Cissy gestured to Charlene. "Tom, this is my new friend, Charlene. Charlene, this is Tom Jenkins."

Tom smiled at Charlene before turning his attention back to Cissy. "So how would you like to get together sometime, Cissy?"

He sure didn't beat around the bush, did he? "I—" Cissy cleared her throat.

"I reckon it's time for me to head on back to the office." Charlene picked up her things and stood. "If you change your mind and want to look at that apartment, Cissy, let me know soon."

Tom slid onto the bench beside Cissy as he cast an apologetic smile in Charlene's direction. "I didn't mean to run you off.

Charlene laughed. "Trust me, you're not runnin' me off. I have work pilin' up on my desk, and it won't get done on its own."

After she left, Tom leaned back, still smiling. "Your friend is even more Southern than you."

"I don't think that's possible. She just talks more than I do."

"Maybe that's why you haven't answered my question. Would you be interested in getting together soon?" He gave her an expectant look. "I can't promise excitement, but I'm a good conversationalist."

Her heart hammered, and she found herself speechless.

"So how about it? Would tomorrow or Friday night be better for you?"

Cissy couldn't think of anything she wanted more, but no way would Uncle Forest ever permit it. The temptation to take Dave up on his offer crept back to her mind. She squeezed her eyes shut and said a very short prayer for strength.

"Are you praying?"

Her eyes popped open, and she nodded. No telling what he'd say. From what she'd observed so far, not many people up here seemed big on praying. Either that or they didn't want others to see them doing it.

He smiled. "I didn't know a simple request for a date required a prayer."

She tightened her jaw. Was he condescending to her? Merely the thought of her saying a prayer obviously amused him. "That's what I do, and I don't make excuses, and no one's—"

"Whoa." He held up his hands as if to surrender. "I'm totally fine with praying. I'm a Christian too."

"Really?" The irony of the situation wasn't lost on Cissy. Dave didn't claim to have faith in God, yet her uncle was willing to let her go out with him, while he claimed that this Christian man beside her was the enemy. Then again, Uncle Forest seemed to think Tom was dishonest. Maybe he was just saying he was a Christian to get her to go on a date. She sent him a cautious glance.

Tom leaned forward with his head cocked to the side as he studied her face. "Well? I promise not to bite."

The intensity of his brown-eyed gaze sent a woozy feeling through Cissy, making her insides all rubbery. She finally glanced away and sighed. "Not this week, but maybe next week?"

"Unless this is a kindhearted Southern girl's version of a brush-off, I can accept being put on the back burner for a week." He grinned. "Or longer if necessary. I'm a very patient man."

"Oh, trust me, this isn't a brush-off. I totally want to—" Her face flushed, and she dropped her gaze. "I mean, I would enjoy getting to know you better." She sighed. "Just not this week...I mean, I can't this week."

He gave her a reassuring smile. "I understand. Why don't you call me when you're free?"

She hesitated before nodding. "I can do that."

He stood. "I'll let you get back to your lunch."

He started to walk away when she called, "Thank you for the rose last week. That totally made my day."

"Good. I'll do that again sometime."

"Is that a promise?"

Tom nodded and waved. As he walked away, Cissy's mind started whirling with ideas for a way to get to know him better. Without her uncle finding out, that is.

Once she recovered, she packed up her lunch and headed back to the office. The second Cissy stepped off the elevator Dave confronted her with a silly grin. "So how was lunch?"

"Good. Now I have a question for you." She turned him around and pretended to look at his back. "Where are your wings, bow, and arrow?"

He made a face. "Huh?"

"You know, since you've decided to take up playin' Cupid."

He laughed so hard he snorted. "I always leave them at the door. I'm surprised you didn't trip over them. But seriously did you have a chance to talk to Tom?"

"Yes." She sat down at her desk and dropped her handbag and cooler into the bottom file drawer before slamming it shut.

He lifted an eyebrow. "Is that all I'm getting after all the trouble I went through?"

"All you did was tell him where I was." She reached into her jacket pocket and pulled out her phone. "Now what is Charlene's number? I don't know where I put her card."

Dave stepped back. "Okay, I get it. This is girl-talk stuff. At least you can give me credit for introducing you and Charlene."

"True." Cissy smiled at him. "I like Charlene. She reminds me of some of my old friends."

"So there ya go. I'm helping you learn the ropes here in the office, I brought you a new friend, and I'm helping out with your love life."

"I reckon I do owe ya for two of those things." Cissy glanced around before pulling Dave to the side. "What do you know about the place where Charlene lives?"

He shook his head. "Not much. I've never been there. The few times we got together, we met out."

"Oh." Cissy sighed.

"Why?" Dave's hair flopped over his forehead as he cocked his head to one side.

"I'm seriously thinking about looking at an apartment in her building."

"That should be interesting. Let me know before you tell your uncle. I wouldn't want to be in the same room when you do." He paused. "Or within a one-mile radius."

"Well, you're outta luck, because I'm gonna talk to him about it right now." Before she could have second thoughts, she marched straight up to Uncle Forest's office door and knocked.

"Come in."

She eased the door open and stepped inside. "I...uh...can you talk for a minute?"

Uncle Forest looked up at her and nodded as he pointed to the chair beside his desk. "Sit while I finish up here."

She waited for a couple of minutes as he punched a few numbers into the program and then closed it out. Finally he leaned back and folded his hands behind his head. "What do you need?"

In her nervousness the words tumbled out in a garbled rush. "I have this new friend, Charlene, and she told me about an apartment opening up in her building not far away. I understand that's rare, and I don't want to miss out on this great opportunity, and Charlene—"

"You what?" Uncle Forest stood up from his desk and bellowed so loud her ears rang. "Why on earth would you come all the way up just to live in my house and work at my company and then turn around and move into some ratty apartment?"

"It's not ratty," Cissy said.

"How would you know? Have you seen it?" He placed a hand on his hip and leaned toward her.

She forced herself not to cower. "Um...no, not yet. But I'm sure it's nice since Charlene lives there."

"Don't be so sure. I've seen a few of the apartments around here, and I don't think you have any idea what they're like. How much is it?"

"That's another thing. It's rather pricey, so I'm sure it must be nice."

Uncle Forest howled with laughter. "You sure do have a lot to learn about living in the city, Cissy. Everything is pricey in New York, even shoebox-sized apartments."

Cissy pulled her teeth between her lips to keep from mouthing off. She'd just have to show him to prove he was mistaken.

They had a several-second stare-down before he finally

lifted his hands in surrender. "Okay, Cissy, I know how stubborn you can be. You'll just have to see for yourself. Go look at that apartment, and if it's something you think you can tolerate and afford, move into it. Just don't come crying to me when the four walls close in around you." The look on his face nearly broke her heart.

She looked away so he wouldn't see her raw emotion. "I didn't say I was going to move. I just want to look."

"Then do it." He sat down at his desk and turned to face his computer monitor to let her know that he planned to have the last word in the discussion. "I hate to say 'I told you so,' but you'll see that I'm right. Even if you like the apartment, I doubt you can make it on your own in this city long enough to pay your second month's rent."

She hated when people were so sure they were right when there was no way they'd have any idea. Now, more than ever, Cissy was determined to prove herself. She had to show her uncle, Mama, and everyone else she could stand on her own two feet.

"I'll go look at the place after work," Cissy said. "So I'll take the train to your house when I'm done."

He drummed the desktop with his fingers. "You'll do no such thing. Bootsie would serve my head on a platter if I didn't wait for you."

All the more reason she needed to do this. How could anyone expect her to get around on her own if they kept her on a leash? She wanted to argue, but he'd already turned his gaze back to the computer screen, so she knew it would be futile.

Trying her best to keep her excitement contained, Cissy relayed the conversation to Dave, who congratulated her wryly on her courage. Charlene squealed with delight when Cissy called and told her. "I'll call the landlord right away. There are several other people interested in it, but I think I can get you in if you want it. The landlord likes me, and I think he trusts me to only refer good people who are gainfully employed. It'll be so fun having you down the hall." She paused for a few seconds. "One thing I want to warn you about, though, is this apartment isn't what you're used to back home."

"Of course it's not," Cissy said. "In fact, I'd be disappointed if it was." The image of scenes from *Friends* reruns flitted through her mind. "I can't wait!"

They made arrangements to meet at the Starbucks on the corner after work.

Throughout the rest of the workday bolts of excitement shot through Cissy, and she caught herself grinning.

Dave walked past her and chuckled. "You look like a kid waiting to see what Santa brought. I can't wait to see what you're like during the holidays."

"Oh, but this is so much more exciting. I've shared apartments with friends before, but this is the first time I'll ever do something completely on my own. I can decorate it just like I want to without having to ask someone else's opinion." She let out a sigh of satisfaction. "It's gonna be so cute."

He gave her a warning look. "Don't expect too much."

She made a face. "And don't be so negative. You sound just like Uncle Forest. This is such an exciting adventure. I can't believe only a few weeks ago I thought my life was over." She sighed. "And now I'm happy to announce that it's just getting started." She lifted her hands in the air. "I feel like Mary Tyler Moore." She closed her eyes and envisioned throwing her hat in the sky. When she opened them, she saw Dave staring at her with a look of disbelief. "You do know who Mary Tyler Moore is, right?"

"Of course I do, but Minneapolis is nothing like New York." He placed his palms on her desk and faced her. "And neither are the apartments. I know you're excited about all this, but you really need to be more cautious."

"I've never been cautious in my life," Cissy admitted.

He stood back and tilted his head toward her. "That's exactly why you need to start now. Learn from your past mistakes."

She waved him off. "Don't go spoutin' off old sayings. Mama does that, and it annoys me to no end."

"You're hopeless." Dave's grimace changed to a grin. "But very charming, I have to admit."

Uncle Forest headed toward them, so Dave backed away. "We'd better get back to work."

For the remainder of the workday Cissy glanced up at the wall clock every fifteen minutes. Time crept by so slowly she wondered if the day would ever be over. Finally, when five o'clock rolled around, Uncle Forest walked over to her desk.

"Go on and see about the apartment you're itching to see. I'll be right here when you get back, and then you can tell me all the reasons you can't possibly move out of my nice, spacious, comfortable home in Long Island with meals ready when you arrive." He let out a laugh that made Cissy more determined than ever to follow through with moving out.

Chapter 8

JUST AS PLANNED, Charlene stood in front of the coffee shop, fidgeting with the strap on her handbag, looking at least as nervous as Cissy felt. "Hey, I was afraid you'd changed your mind."

"No way," Cissy said. "When I say I'm gonna do something, you can pretty much count on it."

"Then let's go."

All the way to the apartment building Charlene chattered nervously about how she'd looked for something—anything—close to her office before finding this place. "It's not really all that great, but the location couldn't be better...and at least the utilities are included." She repeated the rent amount. Cissy had done some calculating and wondered if maybe her uncle was right. Now that she was about to actually see the apartment, she'd have to be more practical than she'd ever been before. Could she afford the rent on what he was paying her? She tried to make up a budget in her head but realized she didn't even know what food cost in New York, much less furniture or anything else she'd need.

Charlene suddenly stopped, interrupting Cissy's thoughts.

"What's wrong?" Cissy asked.

"Nothing. We've arrived."

Cissy took a long look around. The neighborhood seemed rather...commercial. The building Charlene gestured toward was older than anything she'd ever lived in.

But Charlene was right. The location was perfect, only a fifteen-minute walk from work.

She took hold of Charlene's arm and tugged her toward the door. "Then let's go inside and see that apartment."

Cissy waited as Charlene punched a code into the box before turning around and shoving the door open. She took a step before turning to Cissy. "It's not as bad as it looks."

The second Cissy walked into the building, the combination of a musty smell and something burning nearly knocked her out. Charlene didn't make eye contact as she led the way down the dark hall covered in ratty old carpet with worn spots and dirt smudges. One of the doors they passed had a bag of very smelly garbage sitting beside it. The dim lighting in the hallway cast an eerie glow.

"He always puts his garbage here before he takes it down to the street on garbage day," she explained. "The carpet is gross, but we've been promised a renovation soon. Once the owner replaces it, the superintendent says he won't be able to do that anymore."

"That's good." Cissy tried really hard to keep her tone level, but she worried her disappointment might have come through.

"Oh, we're getting new lighting too." Charlene stopped in front of the door at the end of the hall and knocked. "This is where the superintendent lives."

Cissy took a deep breath and nodded. This was just a hallway. The apartment had to be better than this.

The superintendent grunted as he answered the door and didn't utter a word as he made his way to the elevator. He wore pleated khakis and a plaid shirt rolled to the elbows, an outfit that didn't fit Cissy's image of a New York City property manager. As the elevator slowly rose, Cissy marveled at how such a rickety machine that groaned until it came to a stop on the third floor still moved.

"Here we are. I'll unlock the door and leave the two of you to look around," the middle-aged man said. "I'll come back later and make sure everything is still intact."

As soon as he walked away, Cissy started to go inside, but Charlene grabbed her arm. "Don't think you have to do this just because I live here."

"What are you talking about?" Cissy said. "You obviously don't know me that well, or you wouldn't even think such a thought. I don't do anything that I don't think is right for me."

"Remember that this isn't like it is back home. Things are different here." Charlene gulped. "Very different."

"Of course." Without waiting for another of Charlene's stalling comments, Cissy went on into the apartment. She glanced around the small room not even as big as the guest room at Uncle Forest and Aunt Bootsie's place and turned toward Charlene. "Where's the door to the bedroom?"

"This is the bedroom...and the living room..." Charlene gestured toward the wall on the left. "And the kitchen."

Along one side of the wall was a two-burner range with an oven that wouldn't even fit a frozen pizza. The fridge was about the size of the one in her college dorm room. Beside the single sink was about a foot of countertop with a cabinet directly below it and one that was the width of the sink above it.

"This is a joke, right?" Cissy resisted the urge to run screaming from the building. "It's not even—"

Charlene shot her an apologetic look. "I told you it was small."

Small wasn't the word for this place. Cissy blinked a few times, walked around the room, and pushed the door to the bathroom open, until it met resistance. She leaned around it and saw that the space was so small the toilet prevented the door from having full clearance. A small shower fit into the room, and the sink was on a pedestal, so it didn't even have a place to store her makeup. She leaned around and looked for a closet or cupboard, but there was none.

She spun around and made eye contact with Charlene. "How big is your apartment?"

"My place is exactly like this, only flip-flopped. Wanna see it?"

"Um...sure." That would give Cissy at least some idea of how a person could live in such a small space.

Charlene was uncharacteristically quiet as they walked a few steps across the hall to her apartment. "I did the best I could with what I had." She unlocked the door and opened it with a sweeping gesture. "Ta da."

Cissy walked inside and looked around. Yep, it still looked just as small, but at least it had some personality. She sniffed. "It smells nice in here."

"That took time," Charlene admitted. "I opened the window and sprayed gallons of air freshener." She motioned for Cissy to follow her to the bathroom. "I went to one of the container stores and got a small shelf with some drawers for the bathroom." She pointed to the shelf she'd wedged beneath the sink between the pipes and the floor.

Cissy was impressed by the way Charlene made use of every inch of space in her bathroom. She had even positioned a small heart-shaped mat. "Cute rug. Where did you get it?"

"It started out rectangular, but it was too big for the floor, so I had to cut it to fit. I figured while I was at it, I might as well have fun with the shape," she explained. "So what do you think?"

Never one to hurt someone's feelings, Cissy bought time by walking back out and looking at all the artwork on the walls. "You've really turned this place into a home."

"Okay, Cissy, stop beatin' around the bush. I know it's not as nice as anything you've had back home, but this is the best you'll get for the price in this prime location in New York City. In fact, when I spoke to the superintendent, he said he already showed it to a couple people. One was even ready to put a deposit on it."

"So that means I have to make a decision soon?"

Charlene nodded. "Yes, like today."

Cissy gestured aimlessly. "It's just that... well, I have to talk to Uncle Forest and figure out if I can afford it. Besides, I don't even have a bed."

"At least it's so small you won't have to buy much furniture."

"Well, there is that," Cissy conceded as they went back down in the shaky elevator.

"I can take you curb shopping."

Cissy shot Charlene a puzzled look. "Curb shopping?"

"Other people's trash can be your treasure." Charlene stood at the door. "I'll try to stall the superintendent and say you have to get everything in order before you sign a lease."

"Thanks, Charlene. I'll call you in the morning, okay?"

As Cissy walked back to the office, she had a hard time pushing the image of Charlene's look of dejection out of her mind. There was no way she could even consider moving into such a tiny apartment. And that smell. Hoo-eey, that place reeked. How could Charlene even suggest curb shopping? Somehow that just seemed all wrong. She was so deep in thought as she passed the building right before her destination she nearly bumped right smack dab into a rock-hard chest clad in a business suit.

"Whoa, nice to run into you again so soon, Cissy."

Cissy looked up into the eyes of Tom Jenkins. Her breath caught in her throat. "I'm sorry. I had a lot on my mind."

"Like our date next week?" He grinned. "I'll be waiting for your call."

Cissy wanted more than anything to set up their date, but Uncle Forest's image popped into her head. She looked down at the sidewalk.

"If you don't want to go after all, I certainly understand," he said softly. "I haven't exactly given you the opportunity to tell me to get lost."

She jerked her head back up and looked him in the eye. "I want to go."

His slight grin widened to a big ol' smile, showing off his gorgeous teeth with a slight overlap in the front. *Man oh man oh man, he sure is good looking.*

"Then you will call?"

"Um…" What could she do short of lie to her uncle? He'd never agree to letting her go out with the man he called his enemy.

"Will you?" he asked, his voice lowering almost to a whisper.

Cissy knew exactly what she had to do, and it didn't exactly involve an out-and-out lie. If Charlene could be happy in such a tiny apartment, so could she. She'd figure out a way to make that space work, and of course she'd do what Charlene did to get rid of the musty smell. "Yes, of course I will."

Seeing the look on his face made the stench and all the

mac 'n cheese dinners she'd have to eat for the next year in order to pay the exorbitant rent for the hole-in-the-wall apartment worthwhile.

"I should be getting back to Uncle Forest." She looked up at his office, wondering if he could see them talking on the street.

He hesitated then nodded. "I would like to have a talk with your uncle soon. It's long overdue, and I want to explain a few things to him."

Cissy thought about Uncle Forest and the way he'd warned her away from Tom. "That might be difficult. He can be rather…stubborn."

"And he obviously holds grudges," Tom added. "I can't say I blame him after what happened."

"What exactly happened?"

The smile faded from Tom's face. "Just business."

Cissy tilted her head. "What do you mean by that?"

"I had to do what was necessary to turn my company around." He frowned. "I took over a failing business, and I don't like to lose money."

Alarm bells sounded in Cissy's head, but she forced herself to ignore them.

He shrugged. "That was about four years ago, and we've both recovered. He needs to get over it."

So that explained her uncle's attitude. "So you bought the company that almost put him out of business."

"Basically, yes, that's pretty much it."

"Sorry, I'm sticking my nose where it doesn't belong." She tilted her head. "But I'm still curious. How did you get into selling sewing notions?"

"I was working on Wall Street, and the stress started getting to me. I decided to get out, but since I was about to lose money on Sewing Notions Inc., one of my investments,

I had a choice of staying on Wall Street or taking over and turning the business around."

This was a lot of information for Cissy to process. She decided not to pursue the conversation any longer for fear she might say too much or something she'd later regret.

Tom glanced at his watch. "I have to run."

"I have to go too. Uncle Forest is waiting for me."

She lifted her chin and tried her best to adopt the sophisticated expression she'd seen on so many women over the past few days. However, one glance at her image in the window of her office building let her know it wasn't working. She sighed. Did she have what it took to be an uptown belle, or would she forever feel like a ditzy chick from Dixie?

Chapter 9

W HAT TOOK YOU so long?" Uncle Forest asked when she arrived back at the office. "How bad was the apartment? Was it a dive?" He laughed. "I'm glad you got to see how expensive the city was so you could get that silly notion of moving out of your mind."

"It might seem silly to you, but..." She inhaled and let out a shaky breath that she tried to disguise with a smile. "I'd like to take the apartment."

His eyes bulged. "What?"

Cissy nodded. "It's really not that bad, and it's close enough to the office to walk. Charlene lives across the hall, so I'll have someone to hang out with."

"Do you have any idea what your monthly expenses will be?"

She mentioned the amount. "I know it's a lot, but I think I can make it." She swallowed hard. "What do you think?"

"It's about time you asked my opinion." He looked thoughtful as his expression softened. "It will be tight. You won't have a lot of wiggle room for extras, so if you were counting on adding to your collection of shoes and out-fits, I'm afraid you'll be mighty disappointed." He paused. "And I hope you can live on rice and beans."

She nodded. "I don't really eat that much."

"You know you can always come to our house. Your aunt Bootsie and I won't let you starve to death." He chuckled. "So you're seriously considering taking the apartment?"

"I think so."

"But—" He stopped himself. This was the first time she'd

ever seen her uncle speechless. It broke her heart to be the one to make it happen, after what he'd done for her.

"It's really small, but that's probably a good thing. I won't be able to get all my clothes in the closet, so I'm hoping you and Aunt Bootsie don't mind if I keep some of my stuff at your place."

Uncle Forest shook his head but didn't say another word about the apartment. "Let's go home and talk it over with Bootsie. I'm sure she'll have plenty to say about it. She always does."

As they rode down in the elevator and walked to the parking garage, Cissy noticed the downward slope of his shoulders. He looked as though he carried the weight of the world.

"It'll be good for all of us," Cissy said, hoping to lighten the mood. "I'll come for visits, and we'll still see each other every day." She paused as a thought occurred to her. "That is, if you still want me working for you."

He opened her car door with one hand and ran his fingers through his hair with the other. "Of course I do. Your mama would never forgive me if I changed my mind. I just hope she doesn't think I made you move out... or did anything to push you out."

"Oh trust me, she won't. I've done this before, even when she tried to talk me out of it."

"I know." He smiled as he slid into the driver's seat. "She told me all about it. Let's change the subject."

Cissy was familiar with avoidance. She'd practiced it for as long as she could remember. "That's fine."

"I wonder what Bootsie cooked for supper tonight. She wants me back on a low-fat diet, so it's probably something healthy." He made a face that elicited a giggle from Cissy.

"You know it's because she loves you."

"Yeah, I know." He let out a heavy sigh. "Sometimes I wish she didn't love me so much."

Even though their conversation took a different turn, there was no doubt the weight of her moving out hung heavy in the back of their minds. Cissy hated confrontation, which was odd because she found herself the subject of so many battles. Maybe Mama was right. Trouble did have a way of finding her. She wished it didn't overflow to others she cared about.

Aunt Bootsie stood at the stove, holding a spoon but not moving as they entered the kitchen. Uncle Forest went up and gave her a gentle squeeze and a kiss on the cheek. "What's for supper?"

"Baked cod, steamed mixed vegetables, and brown rice. Cissy, could you set the table?" Disappointment tinged her voice. Had Uncle Forest already told her about the apartment?

"Okay. Do we need spoons?"

"No."

Oh, wow. That totally wasn't like Aunt Bootsie. She never gave short answers.

Cissy turned to Uncle Forest, who glanced away just as quickly. "I'm gonna go wash up. I'll be back in a few minutes."

As soon as he left, Aunt Bootsie spun around, still gripping the spoon. "So is it true?"

"Is what true?"

"Forest called me and said y'all would be a little late on account of some apartment you wanted to see."

Cissy slowly nodded. "Yes, it's true." She put down the flatware and closed the distance between herself and her aunt. "But it has nothing to do with y'all. I love both of you very much, and I appreciate what you've done for me, but I'm sure you understand that I need this."

"Sweetie, aren't you being kind of hasty? You've only been in town a week. You've barely had a chance to adjust to your job, much less living in New York City." She tipped her head to one side and held Cissy's gaze. "I'm not so sure you have any idea how expensive and lonely it can be."

Cissy didn't see how she could possibly be lonely with so many people around, but she wanted to carefully choose her words and only answer the objection she was already familiar with. "I know it's expensive, but I don't have a lot of financial needs. I'll be able to walk to work, and I already have plenty of clothes."

"You most certainly do," Aunt Bootsie agreed.

"And it's close to the office." Even to her own ears, Cissy's words sounded rather weak compared to her aunt's reasonable tone.

Aunt Bootsie allowed a faint smile to play on her lips. "That is one good thing. You can sleep an extra hour in the morning."

"And I'll get home an hour earlier."

"More than that, since you won't have to stick around and wait for Forest."

Cissy nodded. "My friend Charlene and I can walk to and from work together every day."

"I wouldn't count on that to continue forever. One of you will meet someone or get a job elsewhere." Aunt Bootsie put down the spoon and held Cissy's gaze. "At least you know you'll have a place to go if things get unbearable. We'll always be here for you."

Tears sprang to Cissy's eyes. She had no doubt one of the reasons she'd been so fearless all her adult life was knowing she had a safety net. Mama and Daddy would never abandon her, and now that she was here, she knew she could count on her aunt and uncle for the same.

Uncle Forest strode into the kitchen, pulled out his chair, and plopped down without saying a word. He picked up his napkin and placed it in his lap.

"How much longer before supper's ready?" he asked.

"It's ready now." Aunt Bootsie pointed to the stack of plates. "Cissy, why don't you give me a hand with this?"

After they had everyone's plate filled, Cissy sat down in her chair. She bowed her head and started to say a private blessing. Uncle Forest cleared his throat. With her head still lowered, she glanced at him from the corner of her eyes.

"I might as well say the blessing," he mumbled. "I don't want my two favorite girls thinking I'm a heathen."

"I never said—" Aunt Bootsie started before Uncle Forest cut her off. She cast a quick glance at Cissy and offered a hint of a smile.

"You don't have to say a word. I can tell what you're thinking." He motioned for them to bow their heads. "Let's get this show on the road so the food doesn't get cold."

Cissy had to bite her bottom lip to keep from laughing. As he said the blessing, she sensed his discomfort, yet he continued all the way to "Amen." When she looked up, she saw the mist in Aunt Bootsie's eyes. It must have been a very long time since he'd led the prayer.

After dinner Cissy offered to do the dishes so her aunt and uncle could watch the news. Cissy was dying to talk to her uncle about some of the details about the apartment, but she wasn't sure how to broach the subject. The superintendent wanted a two-month deposit, and all she had was what was left in her checking account—not nearly enough to move out and buy food, and she didn't want to have to choose one or the other.

"Um, Uncle Forest?"

"Yes?" His tone was neutral, but the look he gave her still showed hurt feelings.

Cissy's palms became damp. She hated asking for money, but she didn't see that she had a choice. At least she wasn't requesting something she wouldn't earn…eventually.

"What is it, Cissy? I know I've been hard on you, but I want you to know that I have faith in you and your ability. You've always been a smart girl…er, young woman. Hasn't she, Bootsie?"

Aunt Bootsie nodded vigorously.

"Thank you." Cissy glanced back down at her hands as she tried to think of how to put her request into words.

Uncle Forest cleared his throat. "I'm really sorry if I came across so harsh earlier. It's just that—"

"You don't have to apologize." Cissy lowered her head and asked the Lord to give her a hand before looking back up. "It's just I'm trying so hard to be independent, and it's all but impossible with so many people doing everything for me."

"I understand." He smiled. "Bootsie and I have been talking, and she reminded me that we forgot your last several birthdays. We wanted to do something nice for you." She met his gaze as he picked up a rectangular piece of paper and handed it to her. "So I wrote you a check. I figured you could buy yourself something nice with it since I have no idea what an almost twenty-four-year-old girl would want."

She picked up the check and looked at it. Her eyes popped wide open. This was even more than what she needed to rent the apartment.

"That's a lot of money." Her voice came out in a hoarse whisper.

He grinned as he leaned over his hands that were folded on his stomach. "This is New York, where everything costs more. Remember?" He gave her a few seconds to recover. "And I figured you might need a piece of furniture or two for your new apartment. Now what was it you wanted to discuss?"

Cissy looked around the room, hoping she could think of something. Her gaze settled on a framed photo of Uncle Forest, Aunt Bootsie, and their adult sons. "I just want you to know how bad I feel that this came up so soon. I never expected it to happen so fast. What you did for me by having me come up here and—"

He held up a hand to stop her. "You're family, and that's all there is to it. Now enjoy your apartment, work hard, and make me proud."

Thankful for the dismissal, she hopped up out of her seat and started for the door. Before she left the room, she spun back around. "Thank you so much, Uncle Forest. I'll do everything I can to make you proud. I'll be the best salesperson you ever had."

Uncle Forest chuckled. "I'm sure you will. Now you'd better start packing, don't you think?"

Cissy pocketed the check and returned to her room. The future appeared much brighter than it had fifteen minutes ago. Now all she had to do was call the Charlene and the superintendent, then break the news to her mother. Good thing she was almost a thousand miles away, but now that she thought about it, even that might be too close.

Chapter 10

THE NEXT MORNING Uncle Forest greeted her with a smile and a bear hug. He was overly nice, making her uncomfortable, but she did appreciate his efforts. All the way in he talked about ways she could save money and how he'd have someone come in to help with decorating if she needed it. She wanted to tell him she wanted to do all that herself, but she didn't want to be rude after the concessions he'd already made.

Once they arrived at work, Uncle Forest went into his office, leaving Cissy in the bullpen with the other employees. Dave arrived as she booted up her computer. He crooked a finger for Cissy to join him by the window. She got up and went around the desks to see what he was looking at.

"It's him," he whispered. "Prince Charming." He pointed down the street. Sure enough, Tom was just arriving for the day.

Cissy snickered and playfully swatted at him. Uncle Forest chose that moment to come out of his office.

"Quit flirting, you two. If you're going to act all lovey dovey, do it on your own time. This is a place of business."

A snort escaped Dave's mouth, but he quickly recovered. "Mr. Counts, I think Cissy is ready to make a few calls on her own now."

Uncle Forest stopped in his tracks, spun around, and looked at Cissy. "Well, young lady, how do you feel about that? Do you think you can handle a sales call?"

She nervously glanced back and forth between Uncle

Forest and Dave before squaring her shoulders and nodding. "Yes, I can do it. I know all the parts of a zipper, and I can tell the difference between a flat button and a shank button."

Amusement played on the lips of both men. Uncle Forest held out a hand toward the phone. "Well then, since you're now an expert, go ahead and make a few calls." He looked at Dave. "Let's start her on getting orders from established clients, and we can slowly move her over to new sales."

Cissy's heart pounded at the thought of making sales calls. She didn't want anyone to know, but she was afraid she'd mess up and cost the company a bundle of money.

After Uncle Forest left, Dave grinned at her. "Ready?"

She swallowed hard, hoping Dave didn't see her hand shaking. "As much as I'll ever be."

Dave spent the next few minutes making sure she understood how the call was supposed to go. He answered her questions about filling out the orders on the computer and gave her a few helpful hints to make it run smoothly.

"Here's a list of existing accounts. Any of them look good to you?"

"How about the Olson account?"

Dave shot her a skeptical look but scooted his chair closer to her desk. She'd already pulled up the file on her computer, so he pointed to some things and explained what they regularly ordered, what they needed periodically, and the items they purchased from another company.

"We carry all of that stuff," she said. "Why don't they just buy everything from us? Wouldn't it be a lot simpler?"

"Good questions," Dave said. "If you figure out the answers, let me know. I've been working on them, hoping they'll eventually make the switch, but in the meantime, let's just try to maintain what we have."

She asked him a few more pointed questions until she had a better idea of how to handle the phone call. Finally Dave moved back to his desk. "You're on your own now, Cissy. Let's see what you can do. Remember I'm right here if you get stuck."

She nodded. Now was her chance to show what she was made of and make Uncle Forest proud. The only thing she wished was that she didn't have an audience listening and scrutinizing every word out of her mouth.

After jotting more notes and pondering an opening, she picked up the phone and punched in the Olson account contact number. She started out with her script, but as she became more confident that she wouldn't botch it, she veered into territory Dave had told her to avoid. She saw him flailing his arms, but she turned her chair away to prevent the distraction. When she hung up, she was absolutely giddy.

"Look what I just did." She pointed to the computer screen that showed the additional items sold.

Dave stood up and walked over to her. As he stared at the screen, he shook his head. "Are you sure about that? They've always said they were happy with their source for snaps and hooks. Every time I bring it up, I get cut off."

"Positive. In fact, she said it made sense to have everything with us, and I just happened to ask at the right time." Cissy leaned back in her chair. "When was the last time you actually asked for the order?"

Dave's cheeks turned pink, and he folded his arms, but he didn't say anything for a few seconds. He glanced back at the order form on the computer screen and slowly shook his head. "Good job, Cissy."

"By the way, what was all that arm waving about?" She

cocked her head to one side and gave him a teasing look. "It was really distracting."

His shoulders slumped. "I was trying to tell you they didn't want to order snaps and hooks from us."

Cissy laughed. "Good thing I didn't pay attention to you."

"Yeah, good thing." He swiveled his chair around to face his computer. "I have work to do, and so do you. Getting an order from an existing client is a cinch. Getting a new sale is where the real work begins."

"I know." She knew she'd hurt his feelings, and based on her history of being in his shoes, she also knew that nothing she could say would make him feel better. But she had to at least try. "Dave, I appreciate everything you've done to help me. I don't know what I would have done if you hadn't been so thorough...and put together that training binder."

"Someone else would have done it." His clipped tone let her know he wasn't in the mood to talk.

Cissy got back to work. Talking to clients was a blast compared to the long hours of staring at the notions manual, reading about what each item did, and learning how to answer various objections the accounts might have. And success right off the bat sure was nice. It gave her the confidence she sorely needed. Besides, it was fun chatting with someone. She just might wind up enjoying this job.

Lunchtime finally arrived. As she dug through her handbag for some sandwich money, she found Tom Jenkins's business card. She pulled it out and stared at it for a moment. The background of the card was stark white, and the lettering was crisp. Very neat and attractive, just like the man. Goose bumps ran up her arm as she read the words. *Tom Jenkins. President and CEO. Sewing*

Notions Inc. She stared a moment at the small white card. She pulled out her cell phone, got up, and made her way to the corner of the room to make sure no one could hear her. Then she punched the number on the card into her cell phone.

"Hello?"

Her heart hammered at the sound of the familiar masculine voice.

"Hello, is—is this Tom Jenkins?" she asked, even though she knew the answer.

"Yes."

"This is Cissy Hillwood. You asked me to call…"

"Yes. Cissy. I thought I recognized your voice." His voice softened, warming her, and she found herself relaxing.

"It's lunchtime, and well, I was wondering…"

He cut in smoothly. "How would you like to have lunch with me? I know a nice restaurant just a few blocks away. I could meet you there in half an hour." He gave directions, and they disconnected. Her stomach fluttered. Was she really doing this? Having lunch with the gorgeous Tom Jenkins, arch rival of her uncle?

Um…yes. And she was absolutely giddy with delight.

A half hour later she found herself outside Keens Chophouse. As soon as she stepped inside, the luxurious décor enveloped her and let her know she was having lunch with someone of means. From the rich, dark paneling and hand-painted murals to the Oriental rugs and white tablecloths, everything about this room screamed elegance.

"Cissy?"

She spun around toward the sound of Tom's voice and spotted him standing about ten feet away, grinning. Yeah, baby, this was what New York City was all about. Her lips quivered as she smiled back at him. "This place is nice."

His grin widened. "I thought you might like it." He gestured toward the dining room. "After you."

After ordering, Tom leaned toward her and looked into her eyes, making her lightheaded. She gripped the napkin in her lap and willed herself to relax, but it was hard with this man sitting so close.

"Does your uncle know you're here with me?"

She slowly shook her head. "I didn't tell him."

He flinched. "I don't want you to lie."

"Oh, I didn't lie. I just didn't say anything."

Tom pursed his lips and nodded. "So how do you like the city so far?"

Starting the moment she stepped foot into Keens, it became the best experience of her life. "I like it." She gestured around the dining room. "And this is super nice."

He laughed. "Yes, I agree. So do you think you might be in New York a while?"

"I hope so." If this were any indication of what living in the city would be like, she'd be here forever. "As long as I have a job, I will."

Tom took a sip of his water and smiled. She sure did wish she knew what he was thinking.

After their food came, she picked up her fork but paused when she saw that he'd bowed his head. She put down the fork, bowed her head, and thanked the Lord for the food she was about to eat and for the man sitting next to her. When she opened her eyes, she saw the look of satisfaction on Tom's face.

Today had been such a banner day so far Cissy couldn't hold everything in. After they placed their order, she found herself gushing about how she'd gotten the apartment and her upsell to the Olson account.

"I've only been here a week, and I've gotten more accomplished today than..." She raised her hands to her sides. "Than I did all last year." *Not to mention having lunch with a super handsome man*, she silently added to her tally.

Tom chuckled. "Sounds like you've been very busy."

"Well, I'm not one to brag, but I think I'm pretty good at sales." She stopped for a moment and thought. "Oh, I'm sorry. I hate when people do that."

"What?" He didn't even bother trying to hide his amusement.

"I said I didn't brag, and then I went and bragged." She feigned a look of regret before a grin erupted. "I'm sorry, but I just can't help myself. This is all so exciting and new for me." He'd been a wonderful listener, that's for sure. She'd always been a chatterbox, but she couldn't remember a time when she'd talked this much on a first date.

He smiled. "It's not bragging when it's the truth. Sounds like you're quite a salesperson. If you weren't working for your uncle, I'd try to hire you to work for me."

She couldn't help but beam even more. "That's sweet. I have to admit, I plan to study the books even more to see where I can increase business with the accounts we already have." She lowered her voice and leaned toward him. "Uncle Forest isn't letting me loose on new accounts yet, but I figure if I can prove myself by building on existing ones, he'll eventually let me at 'em."

"Oh, I'm sure." Tom laughed.

"Anyway, it really wasn't all that hard to get the snaps and hooks business from Olson." As she spoke she found herself on autopilot until she needed to catch a breath. "I'm so sorry, Tom. You must be bored to tears."

"No, actually, I'm quite fascinated."

He grinned. "That account you just increased closed out my account with them."

"Wha—?" Suddenly it dawned on her. "You had their hooks and snaps?"

He nodded. "Yup."

She felt as though someone had knocked the wind out of her. "Oh, Tom. I don't know what to say. Here I am, talkin' a mile a minute, while you're probably sittin' there fumin' about losing business. Should I say I'm sorry when I'm so happy about it?"

"You shouldn't do anything other than what you're doing, Cissy. That business hardly brought enough revenue to worry about. I was just holding on to the account to do the exact same thing you did…only you beat me to it."

She issued what she hoped he saw as an apologetic grin. "Can we still be friends?"

He nodded as a grin slowly made its way across his lips. "Absolutely."

Cissy basked in the presence of the best-looking man she'd ever seen in her life. She wanted more than friendship, and she fully intended to do everything she could to make it happen, but this could be more complicated than she'd bargained for. What if she continued to take away sales from Tom? Would *he* want to date the competition?

He lifted an eyebrow. "So tell me more about your apartment."

That was all she needed to go off on another tangent, until she caught herself. "See? I'm doin' it again. That's why my friends back home used to call me Motor Mouth."

Tom burst into laughter. "Motor Mouth? How cute!"

"And true, I'm afraid. If I don't learn to keep my mouth shut, I'll get myself into all kinds of trouble again."

"Don't worry about that with me. If you say something that bothers me, I'll let you know...but I don't see that happening. I enjoy listening to you." He dipped his chin. "How does your uncle feel about your moving out so soon?"

Her throat constricted as she remembered the anguished look on his face. "I know he really didn't want me to move out of his house, but he's pretty awesome about understanding why I need to do this." She paused. "He says I'm a lot like him. The family didn't want him to leave Alabama, but he wanted something different, and he had to go for it. That's how I am."

Tom smiled but didn't say anything.

"But now I really do need to get back, and since I need to drop off the deposit at my apartment..." She grinned. "It feels so good to say that."

"When are you moving?"

"On Saturday. Uncle Forest is helping me with my suitcases, and he's getting me a daybed. I still have to find a table—a very small table—and a couple of chairs."

"I would offer to help, but I doubt your uncle would allow that." His smile was rueful. "Maybe one of these days I'll talk to him. Clear the air."

A hint of shyness washed over Cissy. "That would be nice," she said softly.

"That number you called me from, was that your cell?"

"Yes," she admitted.

"May I call you again? Or text?"

She nodded. "Yes, either is fine."

Her lunch hour had flown by way too fast. After they finished eating, he walked her to the corner and took her hand in his. "I'm very happy you called, Cissy, and I look forward to next time we can be together."

Giddiness washed over her. No one had ever looked at her the way Tom did.

Her mind raced, and her heart danced all the way to her new apartment. This was turning out to be the best day of her life... ever.

Chapter 11

ISSY FELT AS though she was walking on air as she floated into the elevator leading to the Zippers Plus office. She had just finished signing her lease, and committed a huge chunk of her future salary. Her apartment might be expensive and small and musty, but it was hers. All hers. Never in her life had she done something so...well...so grown up.

Charlene promised to help her get rid of the bad smells, and she planned to decorate the boring walls to liven them up. This was the first apartment that she would have without roommates, so she could decorate it any way she pleased.

The second the elevator door opened to the office, she saw the look change on Dave's face when he glanced her way. Uh, oh. Something wasn't good. She sure hoped he hadn't gotten into trouble because of her sale. Dave had that account for quite a while, and she'd managed to do something on her first try that he hadn't since he'd been there.

As she approached Dave, she put on her best, practiced smile, hoping to lighten things up a bit. "I got the apartment! I am so excited."

"We need to talk," he said through clenched teeth.

"Aren't you happy for me?" The little-girl voice came through, so she cleared her throat. "I know you tried really hard, but sometimes it takes someone with a new perspective to make changes."

Dave gestured toward her chair. "I need to warn you before you step into the lion's den."

"Huh?" She sat down, wondering why on earth he would want to dampen her enthusiasm. Even professional jealousy had its limits.

Dave sat on the corner of her desk and held out a sheet of paper that had red marks all over it. "Cissy, after you left, I checked on your sale to the Olson account. You just sold a bunch of stuff to them for less than wholesale. We're losing money on this deal."

"What are you talking about, Dave?" She took the paper and looked it over. "We have the entire account now. That's a good thing, right?"

"Only if we're making a profit. If you continue doing this, you'll put us out of business."

Cissy sighed. She had no idea what he was talking about, so she went along with him. "If I did something wrong, I'll fix it."

A sardonic smile spread across his lips. "I don't think anyone can fix this, Cissy."

"I can try." She waved the paper in his face. "If I messed up, I'll just call and tell them I made a humongous mistake. That happens, and I'm sure they'll understand."

"I don't know..."

"Thanks for telling me first." Cissy forced a grin. "Let me go do it now before Uncle Forest catches wind of this."

"Too late. He knows."

Her shoulders slumped. "And I just signed the lease on that apartment."

He shrugged and offered a look of apology. Too bad it didn't appear real.

She straightened her shoulders and lifted her chin. "I refuse to let anything stop me from doing what's right.

Before I talk to my uncle, I'm gonna go make a phone call and try to fix this. It's my fault, so I'll tell them not to hold it against Uncle Forest."

Dave gestured toward her phone. "You do that. Meanwhile, I think I'll go find some earplugs so I won't have to listen to your uncle after you make an even bigger mess of things."

He took off before she had a chance to reply. Cissy looked down at the paper and tried to figure out what had happened and how she had made the mistake that would probably cost her job. She still didn't see the problem, so she went to her desk, pulled up the wholesale numbers, and compared them. As she went down the line and saw that the cost of some items was per item and not per dozen, it became apparent how she'd managed to majorly mess up. A sense of dread came over her, but she wasn't about to let that paralyze her. Uncle Forest had been too good to her to cost him money on one of his big accounts.

With a shaky hand, she lifted the phone and punched in the number of her contact at Olson. "Um…this is one of the most difficult things I've ever done in my life, but I need to cancel that order we talked about earlier." Her heart sank deeper with every word. "I gave you some incorrect information, and if we go through with this sale, Zippers Plus will lose money, and I might lose my job. I mean, I'm new and all, and I'm sure you understand. I don't want to do that to my boss because he's my uncle, and he gave me a chance when no one else would. I am so sorry, and if you give me a chance, I'll find a way to make it up to you."

Her contact at Olson remained mostly quiet as she listened to Cissy's explanation. One thing that helped was that her contact sounded like a young woman too, someone named Jenna, who seemed laid back and nice. Occasionally Cissy heard a slight giggle that confused her, but she kept plowing forward. Finally, when she finished explaining and apologizing up one side and down the other, she sighed and said, "So I'm sure you understand that this was all my fault and my uncle had nothing to do with it."

Jenna replied, "Yes, Cissy, we already knew that, which is why we've adjusted the numbers to what we would normally pay Zippers Plus."

"You what?" Now Cissy was really confused.

"We know the wholesale prices, and I understand that with you being new, everything is probably somewhat of a blur. As you were talking, I followed the numbers in the book and made corrections as we went."

"Okay, let me get this straight. You knew I was pricing stuff too low, but you weren't going to tell me?" Cissy slumped down in her chair. The folks at Olson must think she was the biggest loser ever.

"I figured someone at Zippers Plus would let you know."

Now Cissy felt as though she had never left Hartselle, where everyone knew what a mess she was but patted her on the head and smiled anyway. "Do you want to redo the order?"

"Tell you what. When you fax the agreement, include the correct prices, and we'll forget this ever happened."

"You will? I mean, are you saying—?"

"I'm saying that we're still turning all of our business over to Zippers Plus. We were planning to do that anyway to keep things simple, but you just happened to call at the right time. What happened to Dave anyway? He's been wanting us to consolidate for months, and after we discussed it at the last meeting, we agreed that we'd be better off with Zippers Plus."

Cissy let out a deep sigh of relief. "Oh, he's here. In fact, he's been training me. But don't blame this on him either! It was all my doing."

Jenna laughed softly. "I hope he's not too hard on you. We all make mistakes."

"But I think I make more than most people." Cissy wanted to kick herself in the backside for admitting too much too soon. Even she knew she talked too much, but sometimes she couldn't help it.

"Maybe so, but you'll do just fine as long as you continue being honest and taking responsibility for your mistakes. Not everyone does that, ya know?"

"Thanks, Jenna. I owe you big time." After Cissy hung up, she leaned back and stared at her desk. Now Uncle Forest wouldn't have to take the hit on his bottom line, but she also couldn't continue taking credit for a sale that was about to happen anyway.

She lowered her head in prayer, thanked the Lord for saving her from herself, and asked for His guidance in fixing things with her uncle. Finally she opened her eyes to see Dave staring at her. She smiled. He didn't.

Hoo boy, this wasn't going to be easy. Cissy took a deep breath, swallowed hard, and stood up. She took a couple of steps until she stood right next to Dave.

"So how'd it go?" he asked, clearly trying to hide a smirk.

She understood his frustration with her, so she couldn't be too angry about his change in demeanor. "Jenna knew I'd made a mistake."

He lifted an eyebrow. "So she was going to let us take the hit on the sale?"

Cissy shook her head. "No, in fact, she said that they

were not only going to pay the wholesale prices, but you would have gotten the business anyway, next time she spoke with you. I just happened to call at the right time."

A look of confusion washed over Dave's face. "What are you talking about?"

"Her relationship with you is what sealed the deal. She said you're such a good salesman they were already convinced to place all their business with Zippers Plus. It had nothing to do with me."

"Oh." Dave glanced down at his desk, but not before she noticed the flicker of satisfaction on his face.

"So now I need to go tell Uncle Forest."

He looked back up at her and blinked. "Tell him what? That you corrected your mistake?"

"Yes, and that you are a great salesman who got the whole Olson account."

His demeanor instantly changed back to how he'd been when she first met him. "So what are you saying?"

"I just said it." He grinned. "I want to hear you say it again."

"Okay." She rolled her eyes. "You're a great salesman, and I plan to tell Uncle Forest just that."

"Thanks, Cissy. I owe you lunch."

"No, I'm the one who owes you lunch." She grinned.

Dave lifted his hands. "I won't argue with you. Just name the day and time."

"How about tomorrow?"

"Sounds good."

She took a step back. "Say a prayer for—" She cleared her throat as she remembered Dave's comments about Charlene. "I'll be back."

She'd barely lifted her fist to knock on Uncle Forest's office door when she heard him bellow, "Come in and close the door behind you." That was starting to sound like a mantra with them.

As she entered his office, her heart hammered. This would be one of the most difficult things she'd ever done, but she knew it was the right thing to do.

"I don't have much time, Cissy." He looked up at her over his discount store readers. "Sit down."

She perched lightly on the edge of the chair. His no-nonsense glare made this even more difficult than she'd imagined.

"Before you say anything, Uncle Forest, I wanted to explain."

He folded his hands on his desk and leaned toward her, his scowl making her sweat. "So explain."

"I wanted to talk to you about the Olson account. I made a huge mistake."

"Yes, I know what happened. Dave already told me, and we went over the numbers." He rubbed the bridge of his nose, letting his glasses slip off and onto the desk. "You obviously need more training before I let you loose on any more accounts. I can't afford to take that kind of hit every day."

"Um . . . you're not going to take a hit," she said.

He snickered. "Are you saying you want me to take it out of your salary?"

That thought hadn't even occurred to her. "No, sir. I just called Jenna and told her I messed up. She said she knew that, and they didn't plan to hold you to the numbers I gave."

His eyebrows practically slammed together as he looked at her in confusion. "What?"

Cissy explained how she got the numbers confused and what she'd said to Jenna. "She said she was adjusting the numbers before signing the agreement."

He leaned back in his chair as a grin slowly spread across his face. "So you are a decent salesperson, after all."

"That's another thing." Cissy bit her bottom lip. "I'm not the one they bought from. Jenna said they'd planned to turn over all their business to Zippers Plus next time Dave called. They like him...and of course Zippers Plus. I just happened to make the call at the right time."

Uncle Forest's smile faded a bit, but he nodded. "Thanks, Cissy. Why don't you go back to your desk and study the packaging sizes before you make another sales call?"

She stood up and walked to the door. "Thank you for not firing me."

"You know I couldn't do that. Your mother would be furious, and losing a few bucks is nothing compared to her when she gets mad."

Cissy giggled. "Yes, I know."

"Send Dave in."

The instant Cissy told Dave her uncle wanted to see him, he hopped up and went without a word. As she sat down, the cell phone in her pocket chimed, letting her know she had a text message.

Do you have time for lunch tomorrow? My treat.

She paused, wishing she hadn't offered to treat Dave to lunch. Surely he'd understand. She started to send a message that she'd love to join him, but she stopped. That would be acting like the old Cissy. She tightened her jaw as she typed a reply.

Sorry, other plans. Business lunch. Some other time?

He sent back a happy face. What did he mean by that?

Before she had time to ask him, Dave came waltzing—no, more like *floating*—out of Uncle Forest's office, grinning like he'd just discovered Bubba Pyle's All-You-Can-Eat Catfish House.

"I take it Uncle Forest is happy with you?"

He nodded and burst into chatter as he sat back down at his desk. "Thank you so much for coming clean about your sale…I mean, telling Mr. Counts that I was the one who…well, you know, established the rapport." He clamped his mouth shut, but he was still grinning.

Cissy held up her hands. "I only did what I was supposed to do." She looked him straight in the eye. "What Jesus would have wanted me to do."

"Whatever." He squirmed in his chair. "He's letting me have a couple of the bigger accounts to see what I can do with them. If I'm able to increase business again, he'll promote me to senior salesman."

"That's wonderful." She remembered lunch. "All the more reason to celebrate at lunch tomorrow."

He grimaced. "About lunch…Mr. Counts asked me to have lunch with him, and I couldn't very well—"

"Say no more. I totally understand." Cissy grabbed her phone and jumped up from her desk. "I need to run to the powder room. Be right back."

The instant she got behind the closed door of the ladies' room, she punched out a new text to Tom.

Plans have changed. Can have lunch now.

Tom didn't get back right away, so she worried that his plans might have changed as well. As the minutes passed, so did her hope that she'd get to do what she really wanted to do all along.

On her way back to her desk, her phone chimed again. *Hey. Sorry it took so long. Had to make a quick call. How's 11:30 at Porter's Deli?*

Perfect. She thought for a second. *Where is Porter's Deli?*

Chapter 12

As soon as Tom got Cissy's message with her change of plans, he had to call Marianne, who'd left early to pick up her sick teenager from school. She didn't hesitate to tell him to go to lunch with Cissy. The next morning, Wednesday, she came in with the paisley cooler he'd gotten her for Christmas.

"How's Mackenzie?" Tom asked. He'd met Marianne's daughter a few times and was amazed at how similar she was to her mother. Very astute and no-nonsense, even at age sixteen.

"Much better. It must have been a twenty-four-hour bug that's been going around. I hope I don't get it." She opened a drawer and dropped her lunch into it. "So where are you taking Cissy?"

"Porter's Deli. They have the best corned beef."

Marianne raised her eyebrows. "You sure do know how to woo a girl. Corned beef on rye at a stand-up counter. Move over, Casanova."

"Hardly." Tom patted his heart. "I'm just a simple man who has a lot of love to give the right woman."

Marianne cracked up. "And you think she might be the right woman?" She finally settled down. "Seriously, I'm glad you've finally decided to have a social life. I was starting to worry about you. It's not healthy to be an all-work-and-no-play kind of guy."

"I'm not all work. I have church."

Marianne tilted her head forward and gave him one of her maternal looks. "You know what I mean. You need more than paid work and mission work. There are thousands of single women in New York. I'm glad you finally found one that meets your requirements..." She gave him a stern look. "Requirements that seem mighty rigid and unrealistic to me."

He laughed. "Thanks for understanding."

Marianne smiled at Tom. "No problem. I'd much rather have lunch in the office than watch you mope around all afternoon." She changed the subject. "By the way, I forgot to tell you yesterday that I got a call from the Olson account. Seems they have decided to move all their business over to Zippers Plus."

"I know." He busied himself with some papers, trying not to meet her eye.

She leaned against the wall with her arms crossed, an expression of amusement playing on her face. "Does a cute little Southern belle have anything to do with this?"

"Maybe." He grinned back. "That cute little Southern belle obviously knows how to charm clients."

"So you're not going to follow up with the Olson account?" She looked aghast.

"Nah. I think we can let that one go."

"Miracle of all miracles."

"And I'm sure that won't be the last one." He glanced away. "I have a feeling Cissy has more surprises in store for me, and I look forward to seeing what they are."

"That is, if her uncle doesn't get in the way."

"I'm thinking it's time to make peace with him. We can be competitors without being adversaries. He's a smart, honest man who has done amazing things in this industry."

He heard her mumbling something about romance making people say and do the strangest things. She was right. If anyone but Cissy Hillwood had been involved, he would have done whatever was needed to save the account. It was small, but he liked having an "in" with every designer, with hopes of expanding. That was how he'd salvaged the company, starting with one or two small items with each account and building as the clients' confidence grew.

Marianne shook her head. "And here I thought you were all business."

He felt himself grow defensive. "What do you mean?"

She cleared her throat. "You know how you always say that when you step into the office, it's all business?"

He nodded. "Yes, of course, that's the way it has to be."

"Not really." She gave him an apologetic look. "If you keep seeing this girl, you're going to have more conflicts with your business, you know."

"I've already said I think I can work things out with her uncle."

She hesitated. "Besides that. What if Cissy does end up affecting your business, and in a major way? Tom, I know you have faith and integrity in most things, but what if she leaks some information about Zippers Plus or—"

"I have an appointment, and I can't afford to be late." He knew his tone was clipped, but he didn't need a lecture. As it was, guilt plagued him every time he did something in his business that he suspected wouldn't please God. But how could his business survive otherwise? Not just his own well-being was at stake; he held the fates of dozens of workers and their families as well. He didn't want to let them down, but most of them didn't seem to understand the pressures facing small business owners. *Surely the Lord would understand.* As soon as that thought crossed his mind, even more guilt weighed heavily on his heart.

"Tom?"

He blinked a couple of times before looking directly at Marianne. "What do you need?"

"If you tell me where their files are, I'll pull them and stack them on your desk," Marianne said. "That should save you some time." Her tone had changed, so he could tell he'd hurt her feelings.

"What would I do without you?"

She shrugged and left to pick up the ringing phone. Tom waited a few seconds to make sure it wasn't for him before leaving the office. He had to stop off at one of the men's suit designers before meeting Cissy. They needed some custom-designed notions, and he promised to look at their drawings to see if he could find them. Since most of the notions were manufactured offshore, he'd been struggling with quality-control issues. Most notions were made quite well, but he had little recourse when they came in substandard. Sure, he could cancel orders with manu-facturers that were consistently bad, but he'd still be stuck with bad merchandise. He wished he had a stateside fac-tory to create the more complex pieces.

After a long meeting with the designer Tom headed for Porter's Deli. If he had a lunch meeting with anyone else, he would have canceled to take care of business. He hated putting things off, but since meeting Cissy, she'd jumped to the top of his list of priorities.

When he rounded the corner near Porter's Deli, he spotted Cissy waiting for him before she spotted him. Then almost as though someone had tapped her on the shoulder to announce his arrival, she spun around and faced him. The brightness of her smile and obvious delight at seeing him warmed his heart. He could get used to this.

They went inside, ordered, and carried their food to the closest bench. "I'm glad the weather is holding up," he said.

She nodded. "Yeah, can you imagine all those people in the deli fighting for the same four tables?"

"I've seen it happen, and it isn't a pretty sight." He paused. "So how is it, now that you've had a little more time in New York? Do you like working for your uncle?"

"It's okay. Good thing Uncle Forest is my mom's brother, or I'd probably have to worry about him sending me packing for seeing you. I'll get in trouble, but I'm pretty sure my job is safe."

"I don't want to cause a problem for you with your family," Tom said. "If—"

Her eyes popped open wide in horror. "No!" She looked down and fidgeted with the sandwich wrapper before looking back up at him. "I mean, I'm sure he doesn't want me hanging out with you, but I'm sure once he gets to know you, that'll change...I mean, that is, if we..." She gave him a look of helplessness.

Tom nodded. "I know what you're saying, but I'm not so sure he'll give me a chance."

She gave him a flirty look that warmed his heart even more. "Would you like for him to?"

Tom placed what remained of his sandwich on the bag and took her free hand in his. "Yes, I would very much like to get to know you and your family."

She instantly stilled. After what seemed like forever, she let out a long breath. "Where do you go to church?"

He recognized the diversion tactic, but he accepted the fact that she wasn't ready to talk about his meeting her family. "Inner City Outreach Church. Why?"

She shrugged. "I just wondered. Is it close to your house?"

Now he understood. "No, actually it's closer to your apartment than my house. Would you like to go with me this Sunday? Our pastor is a powerful speaker, and we have quite a few members and leaders who have hearts for the Lord. I think you'd like it."

She shook her head. "I promised my aunt I'd go to church with her in Long Island." Her voice was laced with disappointment. "Sorry. My aunt has been so good to me, I can't let her down."

"That's too bad for me, but I understand. So tell me how you like living in the best city in the world so far." His teasing expression made her giggle.

She started out telling him how much more exciting the big city was after living in a small town all her life. She moved on to talking about the apartment that she couldn't wait to move into.

"I don't know what I expected, but I have to admit I was disappointed when I first saw the apartment." She scrunched her cute little nose. "It's so small and...old."

"A lot of things in New York are old, but that doesn't mean they're not as good as something newer."

"Oh, I know that. In fact, the more I think about it, the more I realize it's probably good for me to be in a smaller space. There's not as much to take care of."

He nodded. "I agree. Now that I'm in a house, I see that I had it made when I lived in an apartment."

She gave him a questioning look. "Don't you like having a house?"

"Oh, I like it, but it's a handful to maintain. Fortunately there are plenty of folks around who know more about fixing broken plumbing and replacing wiring than I'll ever know."

"My daddy always did that kind of thing," Cissy said. "He always said a real man didn't have to call someone in to fix everything that's broken. He should learn—" She visibly gulped. "Oops. There I go again, sticking my foot in my mouth. I didn't mean anything by that. I didn't mean to offend you."

"No offense taken. I actually do know the basics of home repair, and I've done my fair share of it, but at this point in my life, I don't have the time."

"I'm sure." She squirmed, letting him know she was still very uncomfortable, so he decided it was time to change the subject.

He leaned back in his chair. "How are you feeling about your job now?"

"There's quite a bit more to sewing notions than I ever imagined," she said. "Just this morning we found out that one of our suppliers in China is about to raise their prices, so one of the executives who just happens to live in San Francisco is starting his own company." She leaned back and grinned. "Uncle Forest is hoping for an exclusive distribution right. He's meeting with the man next week. It's supposed to be—"

He gently placed a finger over her lips. "I think we should change subjects now. This conversation is going somewhere that I don't think your uncle would like."

Her eyebrows shot up as she clearly realized what she'd done. "I want to crawl right under this bench. I can't believe I just did that." A pained expression replaced her shock at the monumental mistake she'd just made. "Can you try to forget what I just told you?"

He wouldn't be able to forget, but for the first time in business he could push it to the back of his mind and not act on it. Marianne's words played in his mind, and guilt swelled in his heart.

"This is your lunch hour," he said softly. "Let's stop talking about work."

"Sorry."

"No need for an apology."

He studied her features as she nibbled on the edge of her sandwich. Her wide blue eyes sparkled above high cheekbones that gave her a distinctive modelesque look. However, she carried slightly more weight, making her curvier than most of the models he knew, and he thought she looked much healthier for it. Every now and then as she tossed her shoulder-length brown hair back, he caught a glimmer of reddish highlights. This girl was a stunner, and even more so since she didn't appear to realize how gorgeous she was.

She stopped nibbling and faced him head-on. "What are you looking at? Do I have mustard on my face or something?" She dabbed her lips with the paper napkin from the deli.

"No," he said as he continued staring at her. "All I see is a very pretty face."

Her chin dropped, and her cheeks reddened as she blinked. With twitching lips, she dipped her head and smiled. "Thank you."

"Not only are you very pretty, there's something else about you that I find immensely attractive."

"There is?" She dropped all pretense of trying to eat as she looked back at him. "Like what?"

He nodded as he took both of her hands in his. "Like your ability to talk about anything."

Cissy leaned back and laughed. "Yeah, I do have a motor mouth."

"So you said." He laughed.

"That's only one of the things they call me." She shrugged.

"Oh yeah?"

"Well, that and 'Mouth of the South.'"

He laughed. "At least you're giving me a couple of choices."

Her eyes widened. "You wouldn't dare."

"Maybe after I get to know you better." He tapped his chin. "Mouth of the South has quite a nice ring to it, but I sort of like Motor Mouth too."

She frowned. "I need to stop talking so much."

"No, that would be a travesty. I love your enthusiasm."

"Mama says I'm too enthusiastic for my own good." She contorted her mouth in a humorous twist. "She says I shouldn't be so excited about so many things."

"But I like that." He grinned.

A serious look took the place of her comical expression. "Do you think I act like a country bumpkin?"

A laugh escaped before he caught himself. "No, of course not. In fact, I think the opposite. You're a very charming Southern lady who delights me with the most unexpected things."

"Really?"

He nodded. "Yes, really. Plus you have such a cute way of putting things...Motor Mouth."

She cringed. "I really don't like to be called that."

"Would you like for me to come up with a different nickname for you?"

She gave him a dubious glance. "Like what?"

"Cupcake, maybe?"

She laughed. "Cupcake? What kind of name is that?"

He tapped his finger on her nose. "You're very sweet."

Once again her face turned a deep shade of crimson. "Thank you."

He glanced at his watch, stood, and pulled her to her feet. "We better get back to our offices before they send someone out looking for us."

"Yeah, I better run. I need to get back to the office before my uncle and Dave get back from their business lunch."

"I'm sure that's probably a very good idea," he agreed.

"Charlene and I will be coming up with decorating ideas tonight. Want to stop by to see my new place, say, around sixish?"

"I'd love to."

He jotted down her address and placed his hand on her shoulder. An overwhelming urge to kiss her came over him, so he pulled away and took a step back. She gave him an odd look but didn't say anything.

"See you then."

Conflicting emotions took over as he watched her walk away. She'd said something about the Chinese manufacturer that he'd heard buzz about but hadn't acted on yet because he wasn't sure. Knowing what he now knew could certainly put him in a more solid business position, but taking advantage of it now could jeopardize his relationship with Cissy. The magnitude of the turmoil his relationship with Cissy could cause slammed him hard. Which should come first—business or Cissy?

Chapter 13

THE INSTANT TOM turned the corner, Cissy took off in a run. She was already ten minutes late.

Uncle Forest gave her a stern look as she walked out of the elevator. "You're late."

"Sorry, but you know how time can get away—"

He held up a finger. "We'll talk later. Don't go anywhere."

Dave waved as the elevator doors closed between them. When she got to her seat, she let out a sigh. One of these days she'd do everything right...well, maybe not everything, but at least something. Hopefully it would happen before she messed up one time too many at Zippers Plus. The last thing she wanted right now was to get fired and sent back to Hartselle.

Speaking of which, everything was quiet, and there were a couple other people in the office right now, so she pulled out her cell phone and punched in her parents' number. Uncle Forest had called about the apartment before she did. Good thing too because he managed to soften Mama's anger by reassuring her that he'd keep a close eye on Cissy. Mama still lectured, but it was nothing like what she would have done if she hadn't already known.

Mama answered.

"Hey. How's everything at home?" Cissy asked.

Mama ignored her question and cut to the chase. "Forest called me last night and told me about your mess-up on the job. Why can't you be more careful?"

Her heart sank. "I'm trying...really I am." She pinched the bridge of her nose with frustration. Why would Uncle

Forest feel like he had to tell Mama everything? All the more reason for her to move out and have a private life of her own.

Mama clicked her tongue. "I reckon I can't expect a hen to lay an ostrich egg."

"Mama."

"I know. It's just that you keep making the same mistakes over and over. Seems you'd learn something by now. We're all beside ourselves about you moving into that apartment all by yourself. Forest said it's gonna cost you half your salary, and it's no bigger than a shoebox."

"How would he know? He hasn't even seen it yet."

"Well?"

"Okay, so he's right. It's small. But it'll be mine." Cissy realized her voice had gotten shrill, so she lowered it. "I need this, Mama. You know good and well that until I get out completely on my own, I'll never figure out how to totally take care of myself."

"Like when Spencer came after you? What would you have done if I hadn't been there to call the police?"

Mama was right, but Cissy couldn't admit it—at least not now. "I don't know, but I'm sure I would've figured something out."

"Just remember that you're in a bigger jungle now, and there are plenty of wildcats on the loose."

An image of Tom popped into Cissy's mind. Was he a wildcat? She giggled at the thought of a real wildcat wearing a tailored suit, tie, and dress shoes.

"What's so funny?" Mama demanded.

Cissy coughed to cover her laughter. "Mama, I've only met nice people so far. I already know one of my neighbors. Her name is Charlene, and she's super sweet. She's the one who told me about the apartment, and we plan to do a lot of things together. She knows all the best places to shop and eat and…"

Mama snorted. "Shop and eat? Honey, at those prices you might have to stand on a corner somewhere with your hand out." She paused. "Forget I said that. I don't want to give you any ideas."

"You know I'm not—"

One of the office phones started ringing. Cissy used it as an excuse to get off the phone with Mama. "I gotta run. I'll call you after I'm settled in my new apartment."

Between answering phones and pretending to study the notions manual, Cissy managed to stay busy until Uncle Forest and Dave returned. Uncle Forest blew right past her with merely a head nod. He obviously had something on his mind. Dave, on the other hand, couldn't stop grinning.

"Must have been a good lunch," she said.

He nodded. "It was."

"That's nice." She lifted the manual and stared at the types of closures.

Dave's shadow lingered over her desk, so she looked up and saw that his grin had only widened. "Aren't you going to ask me about it?"

She stifled a smile as she lowered the manual. "What would you like for me to ask?"

He held out his hands. "Anything."

"What did you have for lunch?"

Dave rolled his eyes, slammed his palms on the desk, and planted his face about a foot from hers. "Not that. Ask me about what Mr. Counts and I discussed."

With as much drama as she could manage sitting at a metal desk in a pleather chair, Cissy widened her eyes and leaned a couple more inches closer to Dave, hoping he'd back off a bit. "What did you and *Mr. Counts* discuss?"

Dave pulled back. "He's decided to go ahead and take action. As soon as you've completed your training, I'm getting a promotion."

"Oh, yeah?" Cissy offered a closed mouth smile and bobbed her head. "Who's to say I'll ever finish my training?"

Dave rolled his eyes. "Ha ha, very funny."

"Maybe..." She playfully bobbed her head. She liked teasing Dave. "Don't count on anything."

"You're not going anywhere."

"Okay, you're right." She folded her arms. "So what will you be promoted to?"

Lifting his chin, he replied, "I already told you. Senior salesman."

She started to make a face and let out one of her signature sarcastic remarks, but she caught herself. Dave didn't know her well enough to see the depth of her kidding around, and she certainly didn't want to spoil his day.

"That's awesome. What are you now?"

"Just a salesman, which is what you'll be after you're fully trained."

"Wait a minute." Cissy stood up. "What am I now?"

"Sales trainee."

Cissy shook her head as she lowered herself back into her chair. "This place is too caught up in titles."

Dave folded his arms and leaned back, the smug look more subtle but still there. "So tell me all about your lunch."

"It was good. I had my first corned beef sandwich."

One corner of his lip twitched. "Did you eat alone?"

It took every ounce of self-restraint not to bob her head. "What do you think?"

"What do I think?" He tapped his finger on his chin. "You need to be ultra-cautious when it comes to Tom Jenkins."

"Wait a minute. You didn't seem to mind bringing me that flower from Tom."

"I know, but that was before I was in management." Dave pursed his lips and gave her a look that she was sure he intended to be authoritative, but it came across more comical than anything. She stifled another giggle. "He's your direct competitor, so you need to understand that some business people are unscrupulous enough to use romance to get company secrets." He paused. "Has he pressed for any company secrets yet?"

"I don't think—" Her cell phone chimed, letting her know she was receiving a text message. She lifted a finger. "Hold that thought."

The message was from Charlene asking if she needed help getting the apartment ready to move into. Cissy texted back to ask what she was talking about. While she waited for Charlene's response, she turned back to Dave. "You don't think Tom is using me, do you?"

He lifted one shoulder but quickly caught himself. "You never know about people in this town, Cissy. He's done some stuff in the past, so you never know."

She blinked as thoughts of Spencer flashed through her mind. "Not just this town. You never know about anyone, anywhere."

This time he went through with the shrug. "Be careful. I know you can't wait to get out on your own, but if you don't watch your backside, New York City will eat you alive."

"You sound like Mama." Thank goodness her phone chimed again. Dave was starting to annoy her.

Cleaning. That was all Charlene's message said.

"Dave, before you start making calls, I do have a question about this apartment I'm about to move into."

He lifted both eyebrows. "What's that?"

"Doesn't the property management company take care of cleaning, or is that something I have to do?"

He burst into laughter. "It's not exactly like you can afford an apartment at The Plaza. If you want it clean, you have to do it yourself. They don't provide maid service, at least not in your price range."

"That's not what I'm talking about. I know I'll have to clean it once I'm there. Charlene asked if I wanted help getting it ready. I thought the building superintendent would arrange for that so everything would be fresh and clean for me when I move in."

Dave slowly shook his head. "Afraid not. Things don't work like that here in New York…at least not in a place either of us can afford. And if anything breaks…" He closed his eyes and slowly opened them. "Don't count on someone coming if you call."

Cissy had lived in apartments before, but she and her friends always rented from apartment complexes. With pools. And a tennis court. And a maintenance staff that made sure everything worked and was clean before she moved in.

She swallowed hard and texted Charlene back, letting her know she'd appreciate any help she was willing to give. Then she went to her uncle's office and knocked.

"Better make it quick, Cissy. I have a phone conference in ten minutes."

"Okay. I just wanted to let you know that I'm going to the apartment after work to clean, so I'll be a little late getting home tonight."

He rubbed his temple. "Do you realize Bootsie is expecting us at the normal dinner hour? Besides, do you expect to clean in that outfit?" He looked her up and down, taking in her little black pencil skirt and silk blouse. Then he glanced down at her pumps and shook his head.

"I'll borrow something from Charlene. I need to get it ready to move into, and it's not like I have days and days."

Uncle Forest clasped his hands behind his head as he leaned back in his chair. "All right. Tell you what. Leave at four thirty and do whatever you need to do as fast as possible. I'll let Bootsie know we'll be home around eight or so."

"Okay, thanks."

She'd made it to the door when he said her name. She turned around. "You'll be back here by seven. Understood?"

"Understood." Cissy returned to her desk feeling just like she did as a teenager when Mama scolded her for leaving her makeup all over the bathroom vanity.

She could tell Dave was staring at her, but she refused to look back at him. Instead she pulled out her cell phone and texted Charlene to ask if she could borrow some clothes and let her know she needed to leave by six forty-five. Charlene got back with her immediately and said it wouldn't take all that long since the apartment was basically only two rooms, and neither of them was very big.

What an understatement, Cissy thought as she tried to get back into studying. Doubts had begun to creep into her thoughts once again, and no matter what she did to push them away, they remained. That wasn't all. She was already getting sick of the sewing notions business. If she never had to look at another picture of a zipper, snap, hook, or spool of thread, she'd be perfectly fine. For the first time since she'd arrived in New York, she felt a pang of homesickness.

Chapter 14

THE WHOLE AFTERNOON seemed long, but the last hour really dragged. The time finally arrived so she could leave.

Fifteen minutes later, Cissy was knocking at Charlene's door.

Charlene flung the door open and opened her arms wide for a hug. "Hey, neighbor, ready to get started on your new digs?"

"I am." Cissy waved her hand in front of her outfit. "But Uncle Forest reminded me that I'm not exactly dressed for manual labor."

Charlene lifted a finger. "I've got the perfect cleaning clothes ready and waiting." She glanced down at Cissy's shoes. "But I don't think you'll fit into my shoes."

Cissy stepped out of her high heels. "I'm used to goin' barefoot."

"Then take these things..." Charlene lifted some sweatpants and a T-shirt from her sofa bed. "You can change in the bathroom."

The pants were a couple of inches too short, and the T-shirt hung loose, but that didn't matter. Cissy planned to change back before leaving anyway.

She bounded out of the bathroom with flourish. "Ta-da! Say hi to Washerwoman Cissy."

Charlene chuckled. "Let's get this show on the road. I don't think it'll take long if we get right to it." She pointed to a bucket on the floor. "You grab that, and I'll get the broom and mop."

Cissy shoved the key into the door of her brand-new apartment. It took a few jiggles, but she finally got it to turn. As the door creaked open, the stench overtook her. Whoa. It was even worse than she remembered.

"Why don't we open the window and let it air out for a few minutes before we get started?" Charlene crossed the room and tugged at the window. After a brief struggle the window yielded, and outdoor air began to drift in.

Cissy set down her bucket filled with cleaning supplies. "I don't even know where to begin." She stood in the middle of the room looking around.

"Here," Charlene crossed the room and stooped down to get a sponge and a can of scrubbing foam. "You start in the bathroom, and I'll tackle the kitchen. Then we can meet out here and finish up."

Cissy nodded. She had had some dirty roommates in her time; cleaning here shouldn't be much different. She went into the bathroom, sprayed the foam all over the shower, took a deep breath, and began to scrub. An hour later, reeling from the cleaner fumes, she took a step out of the bathroom and looked at her work. It didn't exactly sparkle, but it did look and smell a thousand times better.

"I did the kitchen already, so all we have left is the rest of the room." Charlene tossed a rag onto the side of the bucket and pulled out a clean one.

She and Charlene cleaned the windowsill, baseboards, and hardwood floor together. "So how was work today?" Charlene asked. "Getting the hang of it yet?"

Cissy told her about her monumental sales error. "I'm not so sure Uncle Forest would have asked me to come here if he'd known how much of a flub-up I am."

"That's nonsense. You're just as competent as the next person. You just need proper training, that's all."

"You really think so?"

"Of course." Charlene straightened up and looked Cissy in the eye. "You are a Southern belle, Cissy, and I mean that in the best sense of the word. You are just as smart as you are pretty, and you are strong without being abrupt or crass."

Cissy studied Charlene. "Do you ever get homesick?"

"Boy howdy, do I ever." Charlene grinned. "But maybe things will get better now that you're here. When I hear you talk, I can almost pretend I'm back home."

The sound of footsteps in the hallway silenced them. Cissy expected them to go past her apartment, but they stopped and a knock sounded. Cissy jumped and sent Charlene a slightly guilty look.

She'd forgotten about Tom until now. "That would be Tom. I told him he could stop by to see my new place, but I didn't even think about seeing him in…" She glanced down at the too-short sweatpants and oversized T-shirt.

Charlene laughed. "Don't worry. You look cute, no matter what you wear." She jumped up and followed behind Cissy as she opened the door.

"Need help?" Tom asked, gesturing at the dust rags still clutched in their hands.

Charlene scooted out the door, waving. "I'll be at my apartment if you need me. Leave the cleaning supplies outside my door on your way out."

Dropping her cleaning cloth, Cissy turned back to Tom and gave him a goofy grin. "I got all dressed up just for you."

He looked her over and gave her a thumbs-up. "I see that. Very nice and…cleaning lady chic."

"That's what I'm going for." She motioned for him to

follow her. "Thanks for coming. We just finished cleaning, so it will be fun to show off my new place. Interested?"

"Absolutely." She gestured grandly, giggling. "You are now in my foyer. Don't blink, or you'll miss it." He took another step. "And now you're in my kitchen." One more step, and her giggles erupted into snorting laughter. "Welcome to my living-room-slash-bedroom."

"Very nice. Compact but clean."

"Don't laugh."

He lifted his hands as he took a step toward her. "I'm not laughing. In fact, I think you're doing great, considering you haven't been in town long."

"Really?" Her cheeks flamed hotter than ever as she studied his face and tried to see if he was serious. And safe. Dave's warning about the competition still rang in her ears.

"Absolutely. It takes some people months of being on waiting lists before they're able to settle in. Apartments so close to everything are in high demand. I've known people to commute two hours each way until something came open."

"I thought Charlene was exaggerating." Cissy relaxed a little and glanced around with a new appreciation. "I reckon I have her to thank. She's the one who told me about it."

"And she must have pulled some strings to make it happen for you."

Her breath became shaky as she realized how close he stood to her. If she'd been back home, she would have assumed he was getting ready to put a move on her, but she wasn't sure about big-city people. Maybe they just liked to stand close.

Cissy started to turn away from him when she felt his

hand on her shoulder. When she spun around, the look in his eyes spoke a language she knew. He liked her. A lot.

Heart hammering, she forced a smile. "Thanks for letting me know how fortunate I am." Oh, she sure did want to kiss those perfect lips, but she needed to keep her wits about her. "I'll have to pick up a little something for Charlene to show my appreciation." She had to stop and lick her lips before they stuck to her teeth. "She and I will probably hang out a lot." Her mouth was on autopilot. What was she saying?

Tom removed his hand, but he continued grinning down at her. "I can't get over how cute you are."

With a quivering hand, she tucked a hank of hair behind one ear. "Why, thank you, Tom. That's very sweet. I'm sure you're just being nice, though, since I'm a mess after working all day, and—"

He laughed. "You always have something to say. What was that phrase you used before?"

She took a deep breath, held it long enough to get a little more oxygen to her brain but not long enough to pass out, and slowly exhaled. "Motor Mouth?"

"Yes, that's what I'm talking about." His gaze moved from her to the tiny kitchenette along the wall. "Do you need any more help here?"

"No thanks. Like I said, Charlene and I got it all done." She reached for her cell phone and glanced at the time. "I better be getting on back to the office. I don't want Uncle Forest wondering where I am or what I'm up to."

Tom nodded. "Let me know if you need anything." He took a couple steps toward the door before turning around. "When will you start staying here?"

"I was hoping Saturday night, but since I'm going to

church with Aunt Bootsie on Sunday morning, probably not until that night."

"Interested in a short walking tour late Sunday afternoon?" he asked.

Giddiness overwhelmed her until she remembered how long Aunt Bootsie's Sunday dinners could last. "What time?"

"Whenever you get back. Just call me when you get home."

Home. His words echoed through her head as she took another look around her apartment. This was now her home. "I'll do that."

"I wish I could help you move in, but there's no point in antagonizing your uncle."

She twirled a piece of hair. "I know. But I don't think it'll take all that long since we don't have much room for stuff. As it is, I think I'm going to have to store some of my clothes in their house."

He headed for the door. "I look forward to your call on Sunday."

"Thanks for stopping by," Cissy said, waving. A smile twitched her lips, and when Charlene stuck her head out of her apartment door with a questioning look, Cissy grinned back at her so wide her cheeks burned.

Charlene waved her toward her apartment, grabbed her by the arm when she got close enough, pulled her inside, then pushed her into a chair. "What did he say?" she demanded.

"I don't have long. Uncle Forest—"

Charlene waved her index finger back and forth. "You're not gettin' away with leaving until you at least give me some kind of details. Does he like your apartment? Did he kiss you?"

Cissy laughed. "At least let me change back into my work clothes, and then I'll talk."

"Yeah, don't think you're gonna scoot out on me...not after the way I saw him lookin' at you."

It took Cissy about three minutes to take off the cleaning clothes and put her work outfit back on. When she came out, she saw Charlene standing there still waiting, arms folded, eyebrows raised, toe tapping.

"Want something to drink?" Charlene asked.

"Sure." She sat on one of the two chairs at the tiny table. "But I have to make it quick. He said he thought the place looked clean and said I was fortunate to have found this place and that you must have pulled a few strings since these places are hard to come by."

"Yeah, well..." Charlene put a glass down in front of Cissy and sat across from her. "What else did he say?"

"He's taking me on a walking tour late Sunday afternoon."

"Look at you! I've been here almost a year, and nothin' like this has ever happened to me, but you're here a week, and you have guys waitin' in line."

Cissy tilted her head back and laughed. "Guys? I don't think so. More like one guy who is somewhat interested and wants to get to know me better."

"Honey, that's how it all starts."

Cissy stood, carried her glass over to the sink, and turned around to face Charlene. "I have to admit, I'm a little nervous about this thing with Tom."

"I know you are, but relax. It's not like you have to marry the guy. Go out with him, let him buy you dinner, have a little fun..." She tilted her head as a few seconds of silence fell between them. "When you're with him, ask questions. If you don't like his answers, you can stop seeing him at any time. However…" She paused and wiggled her eyebrows. "If you like what you hear, you're still in the game."

"But my uncle—"

"The fact that he and your uncle are competitors can be a challenge, but as long as the Lord is in charge, you might be amazed by how things can work out. I've seen some miracles and changed hearts in my life."

Cissy took in everything Charlene said and finally nodded. "I've only known you a little while, but you've given me some of the best advice I've ever heard."

Charlene chuckled. "Now if I could learn to take my own advice, we'll both be set." She pointed to the door. "You better scoot on outta here so your uncle won't be mad."

Cissy gave Charlene another hug before leaving. All the way back to the office she rehashed seeing Tom and then her conversation with Charlene afterward. She'd take Charlene's advice and pray that she would let the Lord be in charge of whatever happened.

Chapter 15

NOTHING MAJOR HAPPENED on Thursday or Friday, which in Cissy's mind was a miracle, considering what had been going on lately.

Cissy's eyes popped open early Saturday morning, and her mind started racing right away. A momentary twinge of regret made her wonder at the logic behind her decision to throw away half her salary for independence just to be able to go out with her uncle's biggest competitor without having to answer questions and face Uncle Forest's angry scowls. But deep down Cissy knew her decision was based on much more than being able to see a cute guy. She needed to prove to herself and everyone who knew her that she wasn't nearly as flighty as everyone thought. She needed to make it on her own, and doing it in New York was the ultimate test.

After lying there, staring up at the ceiling for a while, she finally forced herself to roll out of bed. Time to start packing her clothes. As she carefully placed everything in her suitcase, her conviction that this was something she had to do grew stronger. In the past she relied on the safety net that someone was always there to catch her, even when she made monumental mistakes from her impulsive actions. Now she'd be forced to think things through because she only had herself to answer to. Then she thought about how her safety net was still there with Uncle Forest and Aunt Bootsie nearby, only now she was determined not to use it.

A gleam of sunlight crept into her room, and she crossed

to the curtains, lifting them to peer outside. The sky was clear and showed no signs of rain. *Thank you, Lord!* Moving would be difficult enough without bad weather. She forced herself to sit back down on the edge of the bed to say a longer, more detailed prayer of thanks.

When she opened her eyes, she felt her burden fade and her mood lighten. With a smile on her lips and joy in her heart, Cissy made her bed, changed into jeans and a T-shirt, and skipped down the stairs to join her aunt and uncle for breakfast. Uncle Forest glanced up from his newspaper and watched her as she poured a cup of coffee.

"Happy about the move?"

"I'm so excited I can't stand it," she said. And it was true. Excitement had replaced the trepidation that crept into her head every once in a while since she'd made her decision to take the apartment.

"We have a lot of work to do." He folded the pages he'd been reading and placed them with the rest of the newspaper. "Do you have everything ready to go?"

She nodded. "I just finished up, and my bags are waiting outside the guest room."

"Then go ahead and eat so we can get your things loaded in the car. We're supposed to meet the furniture guy at ten thirty."

Cissy nibbled a piece of toast, but she was too excited to eat a big breakfast. She got up from her chair, rinsed her dish, and stuck it in the dishwasher before hugging her aunt. "Thank you so much for everything. You have been the most amazing person ever."

"You'll be back tonight, right?" Aunt Bootsie said. "I have a big Sunday dinner planned and—"

"Yes, of course I'm coming back. I wouldn't miss going

to church with you for anything, much less miss out on the best food in New York."

Aunt Bootsie smiled as she tried to hide her relief by tossing the dish towel over her shoulder. "I'll have a nice supper waiting for you and Forest when y'all get back."

It took Cissy and Uncle Forest less than half an hour to get everything loaded. Even with so few things, she worried about where they would fit in her apartment.

"I hope this all fits," Uncle Forest said as she slid into the passenger seat beside him. Had he read her thoughts? "If not, you can leave some stuff in the guest room for a month or two, but after that..." He shook his head. "You'll have to find a place to put it."

She had no idea what she'd do with it, but she nodded her agreement. "Don't worry. I'll figure something out. I only left a few things behind. As soon as I find a place to put what I've already packed, I'll get the rest."

He reached over and turned on the radio. As classical music filled the air, she settled back in her seat and thought about the new life she was about to begin. It had happened so quickly, but she'd never been one to drag things out once she made up her mind to do something.

In less than half an hour she was knocking on Charlene's door. Charlene stuck her head out of her apartment. "I'll be right out to help y'all," she said.

It took the three of them two trips each to get all of Cissy's belongings into the apartment. Uncle Forest remained silent as the two women chattered nonstop. Every now and then Cissy glanced at him and wondered if what she saw was disapproval.

"Well, what do you think?" she finally asked.

He took another look around, but his expression was devoid of emotion. "It's small."

Charlene took over. "It may be small, but there's so much she can do with this space. My place is just like it, and I love it."

He grunted. Cissy resisted the urge to try to convince him she was fine with it. She was tired of explaining.

"I'll go get us some coffee while we wait," Charlene said. "I would invite y'all in, but my place is a mess."

Uncle Forest pursed his lips. "That's quite all right. I'm not sticking around long anyway."

The furniture guys arrived with the daybed in pieces. It took them all of fifteen minutes to assemble it. Cissy stood back and looked at the twin-sized bed-slash-couch and marveled at how humongous it looked in this tiny room.

Once the guys were gone, Uncle Forest looked at Cissy without smiling. "Are you sure you don't need a ride back to the house?"

"Positive. I can ride the train and bus."

"I'll be in the office for a couple of hours if you change your mind."

Cissy stood on tiptoe, gave her uncle a kiss on the cheek, and walked him to the elevator, where he turned back to face her with a look of concern. "Do you really want to do this? It's not too late to change your mind. I'm sure there are plenty of other people who can take over your lease if you—"

"Really, Uncle Forest, I'll be just fine. Don't worry about me so much."

Without another word he stepped on the elevator and left her staring at the closed door. She knew Charlene was right behind her, watching.

"He's a very sweet man," Charlene finally said. "He really cares about you."

"Yes, I know, but he's just like my mother. Controlling."

DEBBY MAYNE

Charlene laughed. "All parents are like that, especially when they remember how they were at your age. They seem to forget that they learned better from mistakes than from lectures."

"It makes me feel really bad, though, ya know?"

"Yes, I do know." Charlene took hold of her arm and pulled her back to the apartment. "C'mon, let's get all your stuff unpacked. Then we can go shopping to fill your fridge."

"That won't take long," Cissy said. "I've never seen such a small refrigerator."

"You'll be surprised how much stuff you can cram in there." Charlene held the door for Cissy. "We'll get you set up in no time."

Together they put the sheets and coverlet on the bed. Then they unpacked the boxes of dishes, pots, utensils, and flatware that her aunt had packed for her. While Charlene hung clothes in the closet, Cissy unpacked her books into a small bookcase her uncle had pulled out of the attic and topped it with a reading lamp Aunt Bootsie had given her. She found herself looking forward to cozy nights reading in her new apartment.

Now the closet was packed so tight she wasn't sure she could get another thing in there. She'd have to get rid of a few things in order to fit the rest of her clothes and shoes, which were still at her aunt and uncle's house. Charlene brushed her hands together and walked around the room. "You need some pictures on the walls and stuff to make it feel more like home, but at least now it's livable. Ready to go check out some of the markets?"

Cissy lifted the last box and carried it toward the bathroom. "Let me hang these towels first."

Aunt Bootsie had given her a stack of mismatched

138

towels, but that didn't matter to Cissy. Nothing in her life matched or made a lick of sense, but it was her life, and she intended to make things work. As she pulled out the last towel, she spotted an envelope with her name on it in the bottom of the box. She pulled it out and opened it to find five twenty-dollar bills and a note from Aunt Bootsie, instructing her to pick up a few things for herself. Tears sprang to her eyes.

When she came out of the bathroom, Charlene stood there, arms folded over her chest. "I thought you were just hanging towels. What took you so long?"

Cissy waved the envelope in the air. "My aunt snuck me some money."

"That's about the sweetest thing ever." Charlene tilted her head and narrowed her eyes. "Have you said any prayers today?"

"Um...yeah, when I first got up."

"C'mere, girl. You sure look like you could use a prayer right now, and I intend to make sure you get one."

The two of them held hands as they bowed their heads in the middle of the room. Charlene started out by asking the Lord to watch over Cissy and protect her in the new apartment.

Cissy squeezed one of Charlene's hands and opened one eye. "Do I need protecting?"

"Of course, silly. We all do. Now close your eyes so I can finish, and then you can say a few words."

After Charlene finished, Cissy thanked the Lord for the apartment, Charlene, Uncle Forest, Aunt Bootsie, and her job. She was about to open her eyes when Charlene added, "And thank you, Father, for bringing such a sweet, good-looking man into Cissy's life. Amen."

Cissy sighed and mumbled, "Amen," before opening her eyes to see the look of amusement on Charlene's face.

"Ready to go shopping and spend some of your aunt's money?"

"Of course. I'm always ready to shop." Cissy chuckled. "I have to admit this is the first time I've been excited about shopping for food."

A trip to the produce shop and tiny market around the corner took a huge bite out of the money Aunt Bootsie had given her, but at least she'd have something to eat when she returned.

"I heard New York was expensive, but I cannot believe just how much."

"I know." Charlene smiled. "But you'll learn how to make your money stretch. I've found that day-old bread isn't so bad, especially if you toast it."

"But I don't have a toaster."

"We can watch for a sale."

After they left the market, Charlene nudged Cissy. "What?" Cissy said.

"You didn't even notice the men? From the moment we stepped outside our apartment building, guys have been ogling you."

Cissy tilted her head and gave a teasing smile. "How do you know they weren't ogling you?"

Charlene shrugged. "Oh, I get my fair share of lookers, but this was different. They were younger, and their eyes weren't fixed on me."

"Well, I didn't pay any of 'em a single solitary bit of attention because this is a girls' day out."

"You're hilarious." Charlene pushed the door to the building open. "So what else do you want to do before you head back to your aunt and uncle's?"

Cissy thought about the trip to Long Island, all the money she'd already spent that day, and how even using public transportation could nickel and dime her to death. "I probably need to get going soon," she said. "I've decided to catch a ride with my uncle, and I need to go before he leaves the office."

She managed to put everything away and catch Uncle Forest as he was coming out of the building. He blinked as though he didn't believe what he saw, and then he smiled. "Good girl. No point in riding those smelly trains when you've got me to chauffeur you."

As soon as they got to the house, Cissy ran to the kitchen and flung herself at her aunt. "Thank you so much for the money."

Aunt Bootsie's cheeks flushed. "Your mama would have done that for you if she was here. It's the least I could do. I'll pack some leftovers for you to take to your place when you go back tomorrow."

"I don't have much room left in my refrigerator," Cissy admitted. "Charlene and I picked up a few things, and it's already almost full."

"Then I reckon you'll just have to eat it for supper." Aunt Bootsie gave her a motherly smile. "I never let my own young'uns go hungry, and I don't intend for you to either."

It sure was nice to know she wouldn't starve to death. With the tiny refrigerator and two-burner stove, it might be a tad difficult to fix the kind of meals she was used to.

Uncle Forest joined them in the kitchen. "Your friend Charlene seems like a nice girl. How on earth did you find her in this crazy town?"

"She knew Dave."

A light of understanding flashed across his face. "Ah,

yes, now I remember. She's the holy-roller girl who chased him."

"Forest!" Aunt Bootsie scowled at him. "I'm sure she's just a sweet girl who loves the Lord."

Cissy watched the unspoken communication between them and knew that this must be part of an ongoing discussion about church. "She does. Before we even started, she reminded me that we needed to pray."

"Now that's a good friend to have." Aunt Bootsie stirred something in the pot. "Now go get cleaned up. I'll have supper ready in no time."

Uncle Forest started to go with Cissy, but Aunt Bootsie called him back. He grumbled but did as he was told.

As Cissy washed her hands and freshened up, she wondered what Aunt Bootsie wanted to talk to her uncle about. As gruff as he could be, it was obvious that he deferred to his wife about some things.

Throughout dinner Cissy noticed the looks her aunt and uncle kept exchanging. She suspected there might be some kicking action beneath the table, based on how she noticed him jumping every now and then, particularly whenever the subject of God or church came up.

"Eat up, Cissy," Aunt Bootsie said as she passed the cornbread for a third time. "I don't want you gettin' all skinny like so many of those city girls."

"Trust me, I won't. I like food too much." Cissy took a piece of cornbread and placed the basket on the table before she reached for the butter. "I don't know how those girls can get through the day eating not much more than a leaf of lettuce and a baby carrot."

"Ask your friend Charlene," Uncle Forest said. "That girl's skinny too."

Cissy swallowed the bit of cornbread as she slowly shook

her head and admired the next buttered bite. "Maybe she's just naturally that way. She eats plenty when I'm with her." She glanced over at Aunt Bootsie and noticed that she'd barely touched the food on her plate. "You're not on a diet, are you?"

"Oh, heavens no, Cissy." Her aunt lifted her fork and stabbed a piece of meatloaf but didn't bring it to her mouth. Instead, she shoved it around her plate and then put down the fork. She sighed and turned to Uncle Forest. "Would you mind cleaning up while Cissy and I go for a walk?"

Cissy stopped and stared at her aunt and uncle. This was odd. This was the first time she'd seen Aunt Bootsie delegating housework to Uncle Forest.

"Sure." He stood. "You two run along. I'll have this place sparkling by the time you get back."

A sense of dread washed over Cissy as she put on her walking shoes. Aunt Bootsie *never* wanted to go outdoors. She said it was too hot or too cold or too windy or too dirty or too something. All Cissy could imagine was that she was about to be scolded. But for what? She hadn't done anything…if you didn't count moving out, that is.

"Cissy, you ready?" Aunt Bootsie's voice was right on the other side of the door.

"Go on downstairs. I'll be down in a minute."

As soon as she heard her aunt's footsteps, she stood in front of the mirror, practiced several expressions—surprise, innocence, joy, and confusion without guilt. She'd had to use all of them before. Before she placed her hand on the doorknob, she bowed her head.

Lord, You know how much I'd rather be beaten with a switch than get a lecture. I promise I'll do my best to behave, but You know how hard that is for me sometimes.

Cissy opened her eyes and blinked a couple of times

before turning the knob. She took a deep breath and forged ahead.

Aunt Bootsie had changed into some blue jeans, sneakers, a T-shirt, and a hoodie. "You look cute," Cissy said.

"I don't feel so cute." She zipped up her hoodie. "You don't think I look ridiculous, do you? I don't want anyone thinking I'm trying to act like something I'm not."

"I already said you look cute. Come on, let's go for our walk." Cissy forced a smile. They might as well move along and get this thing over with.

They were halfway down the block before Aunt Bootsie started. "I promised Forest I would to talk to you about living on your own. You do realize he's been beating himself up about this, don't you?"

"Then why did he make it so easy for me?"

Aunt Bootsie shrugged. "We noticed with our own young'uns that when we argued with them they fought harder. If we went along with whatever they wanted to do, no matter how silly we thought it was, they might rebel for a little while, but they eventually came around. It happened even faster if we helped them."

Cissy stopped. "Is that what you think of my getting an apartment? Do you think it's silly?"

With a slow grin, Aunt Bootsie shook her head. "No, not at all. In fact, if I were you, I probably would have wanted to do the exact same thing. There's something sort of exciting about living on your own in New York."

"Then why are we talking about this?"

"I told Forest I would. You see, he made a promise to your mother that he'd look after you, and with you out of the house, it's gonna be all that much harder."

"We've already talked about this. He'll see me every day, unless..." Cissy frowned. "He's not thinking about firing me, is he? He said he wasn't, but I would understand if he changed his mind. I mean, I did mess up majorly, and—"

"No, of course not. Everyone messes up every now and then, even Forest. He's just worried about you getting in with the wrong people and getting into trouble."

"I'm twenty-three—almost twenty-four. I know how to stay out of trouble."

"Well, there is the Spencer thing, and your mama—"

"Oh, that." Cissy reflected for a few seconds. "I totally learned my lesson, and I plan to be very careful with men in the future."

"I understand Tom Jenkins from Sewing Notions is sweet on you."

Cissy smiled at the mere mention of Tom's name. "He's nothing like Spencer." *At least, not that I can tell. I hope.*

Aunt Bootsie let out a soft chuckle. "To hear Forest talk about him, he's the devil incarnate."

"I know, but that's just because he hasn't gotten to know Tom."

"Cissy, there is something you need to know about Tom. He's a shark in business, and he just about cost us ours. Forest had to scramble for quite a while after Tom and his company stole what we'd worked so hard to get. That sure was a rough time for him...for us." Aunt Bootsie's pained smile showed just how rough. "We weren't sure if we'd manage to weather the storm, but the Lord was good and showed us how to get through it."

As Aunt Bootsie talked more about what they'd been through, Cissy thought about Tom. What if her aunt was right? What if he was nothing but a ruthless businessman who stopped at nothing? Maybe she was part of his plan, and he hoped to use her to advance his own company. She shivered at the thought that some of her fears might be accurate. Spencer had been bad enough, but at least he was a little dim in the intelligence department. She was sure she couldn't say the same about Tom. Getting him to show his true colors might take some time. Could she trust herself not to fall for his charm? She closed her eyes and remembered the way he looked at her. He definitely had charm.

Aunt Bootsie finished her story. "Forest was going great guns with Zippers Plus, but when the sharks over at Sewing Notions got finished with us, we essentially had to start over with just a few loyal accounts. We even had to let all but one salesman go. I started working in the office, and we basically rebuilt our business from the ground up. That was one of the most difficult times in our marriage, since we were never sure from one day to the next if we could keep going."

"Is it better now than before?"

Aunt Bootsie's smile widened. "Yes, much better."

"So why is he still angry at Tom...and God?"

Aunt Bootsie sighed. "I'm afraid your uncle is the best grudge carrier around. Thankfully I cured him of carrying grudges toward me quite early in our marriage, but he still has that tendency."

"What about your church?" Cissy asked. "Does anyone ever ask about why he hasn't been coming?"

"I spoke to the pastor about it, and he said that God understands people's hurt and anger. Sometimes they just need to take a step back and lick their wounds. Forest might have put up a shield, but I don't think he has totally shut God out of his life. At least he still prays."

"But church..." Cissy waved at the air. "Even during the worst of times, I didn't miss."

"Why didn't you miss? Was it habit, or did you expect

something to happen if you didn't go?" Aunt Bootsie seemed genuinely interested.

"I'm not sure." Cissy kicked at a stone with the tip of her shoe. "That's just what people do. They go to church."

"If you ever did stop going—and I pray you won't— I think you'd find yourself drifting, losing your purpose, your reason for living, your vital connection to God." Bootsie sighed. "Your uncle is upset and angry, but for him to direct it toward God shows that he still knows Who is still and always will be in charge."

"Well, I suppose that's a good way of looking at it."

"Look, Cissy, I don't like it a bit that he hasn't gone to church with me much over the past few years, but he does bow his head for the blessing, and I think I've caught him talking to the Lord when he doesn't think I'm listening. Your uncle is full of pride, and that's something I'm praying about."

Cissy thought about Uncle Forest's reaction to Tom. "I'll pray about it too."

"Good girl." Aunt Bootsie lowered her arm and lengthened her stride. "Let's do some power walking. I need the exercise."

Cissy laughed and mimicked her aunt's swinging arms and long strides. They giggled like schoolgirls as they finished their lap around the block.

Chapter 16

CISSY LISTENED TO Aunt Bootsie's nervous chatter all the way home from church. She knew that her aunt was worried about her uncle and that nothing she could say would change that. Going to church alone on Sundays must have been difficult for Aunt Bootsie, but she did it anyway. Cissy knew that her aunt never gave up on her uncle, something she wasn't sure she'd be able to do under the same circumstances.

When they rounded the corner to the house and saw Uncle Forest's car in the driveway, silence fell between them. She wondered what her aunt was thinking.

The door opened, and Uncle Forest stepped outside, a wide grin on his face. She tilted her head and squinted her eyes as she tried to figure out what was going on. He opened his arms for Aunt Bootsie. As she tentatively walked toward him, Cissy hung back and observed. He was different—the obvious being the joy on his face, but there was something else she couldn't put her finger on. Something different.

"Lunch is almost ready," he announced.

"But I—"

He lifted a finger to Aunt Bootsie's lips. "You had everything ready in the pots on the stove, so I turned the burners on low to heat it back up."

Cissy watched as Bootsie's bewilderment dissipated and unspoken communication and love flowed between her aunt and uncle. She wanted that—someone who would love her, even through differences and disagreements.

Aunt Bootsie blushed as she backed away and cast a flustered glance at Cissy before turning back to him. "Let's just hope you didn't burn anything. There's a limit to how long something can be heated up."

The meal was delicious. Uncle Forest leaned back in his chair, blew on his fingernails, and playfully rubbed them on his shirt. "I'm a mighty good heater-upper, if I must say so myself."

"You just did," Aunt Bootsie shot back. "And yes, you did a good job, even with the salad you made from scratch."

He pretended humility. "Aw, it was nothin'."

Cissy glanced down at the lettuce that had been cut into bite-size pieces—for a giant—and tomato wedges that needed to be cut into thirds. He hadn't done much, but Aunt Bootsie glowed with appreciation. Cissy knew this was a learning moment, so she took mental notes on how to accept less-than-stellar efforts. When Daddy tried to do something in the kitchen, Mama either did it over or criticized his efforts. In fact, she did the same thing to Cissy, which made her wonder if that might have been part of her problem with wanting to do anything responsible. Mama's unspoken motto had always been, "If you can't do it right the first time, then get out of my way, and I'll do it." Cissy spent most of her time getting out of the way.

When Uncle Forest stood up to clean the kitchen, Aunt Bootsie shooed him away. "You and Cissy run on into the living room and chat. I'll take care of all this."

"I want to help," Cissy said.

Aunt Bootsie tilted her head toward Cissy and smiled. "You've helped more than you'll probably ever realize. I appreciate everything."

Since Uncle Forest had sat down with the Sunday newspaper, Cissy decided this was a good time for a Sunday nap. She didn't want to wait too long to go to her apartment, but all the excitement of the last week—not to mention yesterday's move—had worn her out. She could use a snooze.

Even after she closed her eyes, her mind raced with everything she had coming up. Between seeing Tom and actually being in her apartment, the excitement was almost too much to bear. She managed to fall asleep for a few minutes, but her thoughts became a dream, and she woke up a few minutes later with a start. No way would she be able to get restful sleep, so she figured she might as well get started on her new life.

She sat up, slipped into her shoes, and headed downstairs. As she rounded the corner toward the family room, she took a deep breath and forced a smile, hoping Uncle Forest wouldn't be able to see her fear.

Uncle Forest glanced over at her as she approached. "Don't tell me you're ready to go now."

"Whenever you are."

He nodded. "Why don't you go tell Bootsie we're leaving soon?"

Cissy did as she was told. Her aunt had just finished wiping off the counter and was hanging up the dish towel when she entered the kitchen.

When Aunt Bootsie turned around, Cissy saw the tears glistening in her eyes. Cissy's heart twisted, and she had that recurring niggling of doubt about her decision to move out, but she couldn't let emotion keep her from doing something she wanted so badly—and now knew for certain was the right thing for her.

"You're leaving now, aren't you?"

Cissy nodded and bit her lip to keep from crying. She cleared her throat and glanced down at the floor.

"Then come over here and give me a hug."

Without a moment's hesitation, Cissy walked straight into her aunt's arms. "I love you, Aunt Bootsie. I hope you know this has nothing to do with you... or Uncle Forest."

"Yes, I understand." Aunt Bootsie let go and pulled a tissue from her pocket. "I was young once, and I remember what it felt like to want my independence. Just remember that if it ever gets to be more than you can handle, you're always welcome back here."

Cissy smiled. "You are so sweet. No wonder Uncle Forest is so crazy about you."

"I'm crazy about him too. In spite of his rather crusty demeanor he's a sweet man, and he loves you too."

"I know."

"C'mon, let's get this over with." Aunt Bootsie took her by the hand and led her out to the living room. "The longer you wait the harder it'll be for both of us."

When they walked into the living room, Uncle Forest stood, shook his head, and made a clicking sound with his tongue. "You girls act like you'll never see each other again. That's just silly. Even before you moved up here, we saw you twice a year."

"I know," Cissy said. "It's just that this seems so... I don't know..."

"Grown up?" Uncle Forest said. He swung an arm around her shoulder and squeezed. "I'll still see you every day, and there's no doubt in my mind that you'll stop by every now and then for some of Bootsie's homemade biscuits."

"I'll send food to work with Forest every once in a while, and you know you're always welcome to come home with him. I don't want you to go hungry, and I certainly never want you to be lonely." Aunt Bootsie kissed her on the cheek and stood on the front lawn as they left. Cissy studied her uncle until he pulled up to a light and frowned at her.

He flashed a quick glance in her direction. "What are you staring at, Cissy?"

"Something is different." She'd noticed a softness today that she hadn't seen before. "What's going on?"

He made a face and accelerated when the light turned green. "I have no idea what you're talking about. So tell me what all you and your friend Charlene have planned."

"Nothing that I know of."

He reached out and patted her arm. "If you're anything like I was at your age, you'll be out the door, exploring the town, and seeing what all you can get into before I have a chance to get back on the parkway."

Cissy didn't want to mention her real plans or be tempted to lie outright, so she smiled and went with his comment. "I can only imagine what you were like at my age. How old were you the first time you came to New York?"

"Younger than you. Didn't your mama ever tell you about the time our family took a trip up to the Big Apple?"

Cissy thought for a moment and slowly shook her head. "No, she never said anything about it. I didn't realize she'd ever been up here."

"Maybe I should keep my big mouth shut, or I'll wind up telling you a secret she doesn't want you to know." He cut a glance in her direction, his eyes all squinty, before he turned back to the road. "Some people know how to keep their mouths shut."

With a pang Cissy remembered her conversation with Tom. In her excitement and nervousness had she told him a secret he shouldn't know? She pushed the thought out of her mind and faced her uncle. "Now you gotta tell me. What secrets do you have about Mama?"

"Well..." He shot a quick grin in her direction. "When we came to New York, she and I snuck out of the hotel room in the middle of the night."

"Are you kidding me? What did y'all do?"

He sighed and made a goofy face. "That's just it. Nothing. We were young and too green around the gills to know what all this city offered, or I'm sure we could have gotten ourselves into all sorts of trouble if we'd known what all we could do."

Cissy laughed. "I'm old enough to know how to stay out of trouble."

A concerned expression washed over his face. "I'm not so sure about that. Just remember why you had to get out of Hartselle."

She lowered her head. "I'll never forget that."

"You may think you know someone, but—"

"Please, Uncle Forest, I really don't want a lecture. I'll be super careful, and I promise I'll stay away from anyone who even remotely seems dangerous." She thought about Tom and wondered if her uncle had been referring to him. But she wasn't about to bring up his name. "Charlene has been here a while. I'm sure she'll warn me if she thinks I'm entering a danger zone."

"And don't forget about me. I might not be able to give you advice every time you want it, but if you need me, you know I'm there early, and I leave late." He patted his pocket. "And I'm only a phone call away."

She nodded. "Yes, I know."

They rode in silence for a while, until they were just a few blocks from her building. "I hope there's a parking spot on the street," he said. At one point he slowed down and leaned over to look at something out her window, so she turned to see what it was. The sign above the door read Inner City Outreach Church. That was where Tom said he went. When she looked back at her uncle, she saw a contemplative look on his face. How odd.

They were at her apartment building less than two minutes later. "We're in luck. There's a spot right out front. Mind if I come up and take another look around to see how you've arranged your place?"

"Of course not!" Cissy was happy to have his company, and it put off the loneliness she was afraid she might experience—at least in the beginning.

He pulled her suitcase from the trunk, and together they headed for her new apartment.

As soon as they got to her floor, she spotted a bunch of things outside her door—a bouquet of flowers and a box filled to overflowing with bakery items. Her heart hammered as she thought about the possibility of Tom sending them. "Who could've sent all that stuff?"

Uncle Forest grinned. "Hmm. I wonder."

She dropped her suitcase, unlocked the door, and picked up the bouquet to read the card. "Enjoy your new apartment, but don't forget about us. Love, Aunt Bootsie and Uncle Forest."

Uncle Forest had already walked inside the apartment. She ran in behind him, flung her arms around him and gave him a huge hug. "Thank you so much!"

He spun around and looked out toward the hallway. "We sent the flowers, but I have no idea who sent that box of goodies. Aren't you going to look?"

She'd assumed they were from him, but now she worried he'd be upset if Tom had sent them. A lemon-yellow envelope stuck out from one side of the box. "Um..."

Before she had a chance to say another word, Uncle Forest had lifted the box, carried it inside and placed it on the small counter by the stove. "You can read the card later. Let me give you another hug and say good-bye so I can leave you to do whatever you've been itching to do all day."

He squeezed her tightly, kissed her on the cheek, told her to be on time for work tomorrow, and left.

Cissy sank down on the edge of her daybed and looked around at the tiny apartment, unsure of what to do next. She'd flipped back and forth between exuberance and fear the last few days, but now that she was here, the fear outweighed everything else.

She stood up on wobbly legs and walked the four steps to the box Uncle Forest had placed beside the table. As she pulled the card from the envelope, she whispered a prayer. "Lord, You know how I am. I pray that You'll watch over me and keep me from messing up. Help me make good decisions, and please don't let me get caught up in stupid drama with any guy, not even if he's super cute." She took a deep breath and slowly let it out. "Amen."

Then she looked down at the card. *I thought you might enjoy some tasty treats in your new apartment. See you at work tomorrow. Dave.*

Her heart sank. She'd hoped for something from Tom.

The sound of a knock at her door quickened her pulse. Maybe that was him. She didn't waste a second before flinging open the door.

"Oh, hi, Charlene."

Charlene raised her eyebrows as she leaned back. "Sorry to disappoint you. I heard you and your uncle when y'all got here, so I just thought I'd see how you were doing."

Cissy stepped to the side and made a sweeping gesture. "Come on in."

"Are you sure? I mean if this is a bad time—"

"No, it's not a bad time. I'm just…I don't know…"

"Having second thoughts?"

Cissy slowly nodded. "Yeah, sort of. A lot has happened in just a few days, and I'm not sure I'm doing the right thing."

"Maybe you are, and maybe you're not. Just remember that nothing you've done is permanent. If you hate this apartment, there are dozens of people who would love to have it, and you can go back to live with your aunt and uncle as if this didn't even happen." Charlene squinted. "Something else is going on, isn't it?"

Cissy tried really hard not to pout. "When I saw that stuff in front of my door, I thought surely Tom—" She shrugged. "I mean, I thought if I moved, things would be better for him and me…well, you know."

Charlene's eyes widened as she lifted her hands to stop Cissy. "Whoa there, wait just a minute, girly. Don't tell me you moved out of that big ol' cushy house with free meals and cleaning just for Tom. No woman should ever do anything for a man unless she has a commitment from him."

"Well…" Cissy fought back the tears that threatened. "It's not just for Tom, even though he did have something to do with my decision so soon. It's just that I…" Her shoulders slumped as she realized she wouldn't have done this if she hadn't met Tom. Until now she didn't want to admit it, even to herself. "Yeah, I'm afraid it has everything to do with Tom."

"Oh, Cissy." Charlene closed the distance between them and took Cissy's hands. "I'm only six and a half years older than you, so I understand. But when you have a few more years under your belt, you'll understand why that's not such a good idea."

"So now what do I do?"

Charlene's gaze darted to something behind Cissy, and she smiled. "Maybe we should talk about this later." She nodded toward the door. "You have company."

Cissy turned around and spotted Tom standing at the door grinning. "Come on in."

"Looks like you've been busy." He turned to Charlene. "Enjoying your new neighbor?"

Charlene laughed. "Of course. We're Southerning up this place. How did you get in the building?"

"One of your neighbors held the door."

Charlene shook her head. "I'm gonna have to talk to the superintendent about that. We're not supposed to hold the door for anyone." She scooted toward the door. "I better get on outta here. See ya." With a wave she disappeared down the hall.

Seconds later Cissy found herself alone with Tom. "I hope I didn't come by too soon. Looks like I interrupted something important, and you probably have some settling in to do."

Cissy forced herself to hold back her exuberance. "Well, I did just get here a little while ago, but that's okay."

"Want me to leave and come back?"

"No!" The word escaped before she had a chance to stop it. She inhaled deeply and tried to gather her thoughts, but with Tom Jenkins standing there watching her that was all but impossible. "I mean, I can do everything later."

His grin widened. "Good. Are you up for a walking tour of your new neighborhood?"

She nodded, not even bothering to pretend she wasn't delighted. "Sounds great. Let me change shoes."

"Yeah, now that you live in the heart of the city, you need to think of comfort first."

Cissy wasn't sure about a lot of things, but one thing she did know was that her high heel shoe collection didn't do her feet a bit of good with all this walking. She'd spent days prior to flying up to New York watching reruns of TV shows set in the city. How those girls ran around town in those stilts was a mystery to her. As it was, she had a bunion starting to form on her left foot, and the ball of her right foot burned like fire.

As she changed her shoes, he pointed to the bouquet. "Nice flowers."

"My aunt and uncle sent them. They were here when I arrived."

"So how was church with your aunt?"

Tom folded his arms and widened his stance as his gaze melted her from the inside out…again. She shrugged and forced herself to glance away. "It was nice, but I think Aunt Bootsie would have liked it better if Uncle Forest had been with us. She says he hasn't been to church in a while. He got really mad at God when your company—" She grimaced. "Oops. I did it again." She shook her head. "It's that motor-mouth thing. I can't seem to stop it. Somebody shoot me."

Tom looked serious. "What do you mean, your uncle got mad at God?"

"I'm not sure I should—"

His jaw tightened as he held her gaze. "Cissy, you know I think you're cute and fun, but I think it's time we got to know each other a little better." His expression softened as he added, "I'd like to know more about you and what makes you the way you are."

She swallowed hard as she realized she was afraid that once he really got to know her he might not like her as much. But he was right. It was time to open up…at least a little.

"Okay, so what do you want to know?"

"About you, your family, how you feel about things."

"Okay, I'm twenty-three, almost twenty-four, and I love—"

"What's the deal with your uncle? Why do you think he's mad at God?"

"You just interrupted me."

"Yes, I know." He paused. "You were still holding me at arm's length with facts and figures."

She let out a nervous laugh. "Isn't that what businessmen like?"

He shook his head. "This is not a business relationship. I want to get to know the real Cissy." He tapped his chest over his heart. "And obviously your family is very important to you."

Cissy glanced down and sighed before looking back up at him. "I never want to betray my uncle's confidence."

"I would never ask you to do that." He tilted his head toward her and gently placed his hand on hers. "Can you at least let me get to know the real Cissy and not just the cute Southern girl I met on the street?"

She held his gaze for a few seconds before slowly nodding. "I'll try my best."

He smiled. "That's all I can ask. Ready to get started on our tour?"

"More than ready."

As they walked down the city streets, Tom took her hand in his as though it was the most natural thing in the world. This simple gesture totally made her day. She resisted the urge to sigh her contentment. No point in scaring Tom.

As they walked, Tom pointed out some things she might not have paid much attention to on her own—from a tiny hole-in-the-wall deli to a produce vendor standing outside a meat market. "You can get some of the best buys from those places," he said. "They don't have much, if any, overhead."

He also showed her several historical landmarks. "Everything here seems so old." She left out the rest of her thought—that it also seemed dirty. Particles from exhaust floated through the air, leaving a hazy film on windows and walls. The buildings were discolored where cleaning crews had removed graffiti.

"That's because it *is* old. This town is rich with history."

Cissy nodded. She'd never been very good at history in school, but maybe it wasn't too late to learn. She asked question after question, and Tom answered most of them without too much trouble. Finally he laughed.

"Cissy Hillwood, you've asked me a lot of questions, and now it's my turn to ask you a few."

"Okay," she said slowly. "But remember that I've never been big on history... until now."

"Forget history." His eyes crinkled as he smiled. "Remember what I said earlier. I just want to know more about you."

At first the questions were standard, like what she did in her spare time, how many siblings she had, and whether or not she missed her friends. Then he started digging a little deeper, making her squirm.

"Why the sudden move to New York?" he asked.

For the first time she could remember, Cissy was speechless. She looked down as she pondered how much to tell him. The ordeal with Spencer was bad enough, but reliving it once again only to have the situation turn Tom away from her seemed downright cruel. Then she thought about how a lie could snowball and get worse. Since this was an impossible question to evade, she decided to entrust him with a brief explanation of the situation and see how he responded. If he didn't like what he heard, at least he'd know the truth, and she would never have to cover anything up. Plus his reaction would give her a chance to see more about his character.

After she finished talking, he blew out a long breath. "No wonder your uncle is so protective. I had no idea how bad it was. No man should ever threaten a woman for any reason whatsoever. I'm glad you stood up to him and gave him what he deserved."

Her heart swelled as she saw that he meant what he'd said. "That wasn't even the worse part of it," she admitted. "What really got my goose was how everyone in Hartselle acted afterward—like it was my fault that the golden boy of Hartselle got locked away."

"How sad for Hartselle." Tom squeezed her hand and turned her around to face him. "But good for New York." He grinned. "And me."

The way he looked at her gave her a tummy tickle, and that always revved her speech engine. "I'm not so sure Uncle Forest would agree with you. He's probably regretting the invitation, but he'd never actually come right out and say that. He's such a sweet man, even though he comes across as a grouch most of the time." She continued on and on, describing her aunt and uncle, and all Tom did was nod or let out a single-word comment letting her know he was listening.

Finally, after a good fifteen minutes she realized what was happening. She lifted her hand to her mouth.

"What's wrong?" he asked.

The concern in Tom's voice, combined with a humongous case of nerves, made her laugh. And it wasn't just a simple ha-ha type laugh. It came out normal at first but quickly erupted into a diabolical laugh that she'd frightened many old boyfriends with in the past.

Once again Tom stopped and stared down at her. "Are you okay, Cissy? Something seems to have happened here. Something I don't understand."

"I have said entirely too much, and sometimes that makes me laugh...from nerves." She grimaced. "Sorry about that."

"Sometimes we just need to talk." He placed his hand around her shoulders. "And I'm a pretty good listener, if you'll just give me a chance."

"Thank you." No matter what he said or how comforting he tried to be, her cheeks still flamed with the embarrassment of not knowing when to keep her trap shut until it was too late.

She was relieved when he changed the subject. "Hungry?"

"Sort of."

"Let's get something to eat while we're out. I'm starving."

She gave him a jaunty head-toss followed by a flirty grin. "So where should we go?"

"I could come up with a list of possibilities for you to choose from." He held up a hand and tapped each finger as he named the types of restaurants. "Chinese, Indian, Thai, Mexican, French..." He put down his hand. "I've run out of fingers, but there's also a great Greek restaurant not far from here."

"Aren't there any normal places like where we can get fried chicken or pork chops or meat loaf?"

He feigned shock. "Normal? Here in New York City? How dare you even suggest such a thing."

She playfully swatted at him. "You know what I mean.

I don't know anything about Indian, Thai, or Greek. I like Chinese and Mexican, but I'm not in the mood for either."

Tom pondered that for a few seconds. "There is a decent little café that offers a nice variety of American food."

"Variety sounds good." His smile warmed her from the inside out. "Especially when it's American."

"Then let's go there."

Throughout dinner and afterward on their walk back to her place, Cissy flip-flopped back and forth between letting down her guard and biting her tongue. Would she ever be able to relax completely in Tom's presence without worrying about giving up the shop? Only time would tell.

Chapter 17

THE NEXT MORNING Cissy got ready in her tiny apartment. The bathroom was so small she didn't have room for all her cosmetics, so she had them arranged on a TV tray right outside the bathroom door. She made a mental note to ask Charlene about the container store where she found her little cabinet because this simply wouldn't do. She also needed better lighting; the single dim bulb above the bathroom mirror didn't help matters any.

With all her clothes crammed into the tiny closet, she had a difficult time picking out something to wear. Tonight she'd pull something out for tomorrow so she wouldn't have the hassle first thing in the morning while trying to get ready. Fortunately Aunt Bootsie had packed a steamer and said she could keep it as long as she needed to. Everything was rumpled and needed freshening, but it was pointless to do anything about it before shoving it into the closet. She sure did miss her walk-in closet back home.

Feeling somewhat bedraggled, she took one last look around her apartment, stepped out into the hallway, and locked the door. Good thing her apartment was close to the office. She barely made it in on time.

Dave glanced up and did a double take. "You might want to check yourself in the mirror," he whispered.

She dropped her jacket on the back of her chair and headed straight for the ladies' room. When she glanced in the mirror, she saw lipstick smeared over her chin and a huge smudge of mascara beneath one eye. One side of her collar was turned in, creating an awkward bulge at her neckline. She straightened her shirt and then grabbed a paper towel to wipe the makeup smears. It took her several minutes to fix everything. Her next purchase needed to be a lighted makeup mirror for the bathroom and after that a full-length mirror that she could hang over the door.

When she walked back to her desk, Dave gave her a thumbs-up and nodded. "So how's the apartment?"

"Good." So far, besides the freedom, the only thing good about it was the comfortable bed, but she didn't want to say those words aloud.

"I bet I know what to get you for a housewarming gift." Dave grinned. "A good light. Some of these old apartments are pretty dark."

"You don't need to give me anything. Oh, and thanks for the food."

"Charlene said you'd appreciate it." He stacked some papers and tapped them. "Mr. Counts is having a meeting in an hour. Need help getting ready for it?"

"Do you think I do?" She forced a smile. "Never mind. I know the answer to that question." She lifted her hands. "I have no idea where to start."

Over the next half hour Dave helped her gather some information to present at the meeting. "He likes everyone to contribute something," Dave explained. "You're actually doing just fine."

"Yeah, after giving away the farm."

"It was nothing that couldn't be fixed," he reminded her with a smugness she knew she deserved. "Actually I think everyone is relieved that the owner's niece made that mistake and not them."

"Are people talking about me?"

He bobbed his head side to side. "What do you think?"

She sighed. "I think they probably all see me as a loser."

"Not a loser. Just someone who doesn't know a thing about this business but got the job because of connections."

"Okay, I know, but you didn't have to come right out and say that."

Dave shrugged. "I thought you liked the truth."

"I do, but sometimes it's painful." Cissy grimaced, seeing again that her ties to her uncle had pluses and minuses. But she'd show them—and herself—that she wasn't a total flake. She actually had brains in her head, and she fully intended to use them in this job.

When they finally sat down in the meeting room, Cissy felt good about what she'd prepared. Even Uncle Forest seemed pleasantly surprised that she contributed. When no one was looking, she mouthed, "Thank you," to Dave. He smiled and turned his attention back to the meeting. She was relieved when the meeting finally came to an end. She'd gone through the entire hour without making any mistakes or saying something that left others rolling their eyes.

After work that night Charlene stopped by. "Why don't we grab some dinner on the street and see what kind of free entertainment we can find?"

"That's what I'm talkin' about." Excitement coursed through Cissy. "Let's go."

They ate chicken on a stick from a street vendor and an apple from a small produce stand as they walked the streets. After watching a mime on one corner, a flautist on another, and a small band on another street corner, Charlene motioned toward a bench.

"So when will you see Tom again?" Charlene asked as they sat down.

Cissy shrugged. "I'm not sure. We didn't talk about it last night."

Charlene tilted her head as she studied Cissy. "I still can't believe you actually went to all that trouble and expense just for Tom."

"I've thought about that. It wasn't just for him." Cissy glanced down.

Charlene touched her arm. "You've already confessed, remember?"

"I know." Cissy hated to admit it, but Tom had been a big motivator. However, now that she was out, she planned to make the most of it, Tom or no Tom. "I think it was time for me to do this, regardless of Tom."

Charlene gave her a look of apology. "I feel bad—like I somehow contributed to something you might regret. I really egged you on, didn't I?"

"No, don't feel bad. It was my decision and mine alone. You didn't make me do anything."

"Of course I didn't *make* you, but I did twist your arm with the temptation of an available apartment."

The rest of their evening together was more subdued. Charlene didn't say much, and Cissy felt that the spark of excitement had long since gone out.

Later that night as she lay in bed listening to the sirens below, Cissy pondered some of her decisions over the past few years. Most of them had been made impulsively, and this was no different. However, in spite of her misgivings over the tiny apartment, she felt that until she had to deal with things on her own, she'd never learn total self-sufficiency. She'd learned how to swim by being given a few basic lessons then jumping off the deep end. And that's exactly what she was doing now. What scarier place to be on her own than New York City? Could she get any deeper than that? One thing about it—she'd either sink or swim. There was no in between in this town.

On her way home from work Tuesday her cell phone rang. When she glanced down and saw that it was Tom, her pulse quickened.

"We're having a coffee shop talent show at my church tomorrow," he said. "Would you like to go?"

"Would I ever!" She took a deep breath and forced herself to calm down. "I mean, yes, I would be delighted."

He laughed. "I like your first response better. I'll pick you up at six thirty at your apartment. It's casual, so wear jeans and sneakers."

Wednesday seemed to drag, but the end of the workday finally came, and she didn't waste a second gathering her things and heading for the elevator. Now that Dave had been promoted, he stayed a little longer. As she passed his desk, he smiled.

"Got a date?"

She grinned back. "Do I look like I have a date?"

"Have fun." He held up a paper. "This report is a bear, but I'm not complaining. Maybe I'll get out of here in time to eat dinner and go to bed at a decent time tonight."

"See you tomorrow."

As Cissy walked to her apartment, she thought about Dave and how much energy he was putting into his work. She understood his ambition, but she felt bad that he neglected his social life. A single man living in the big city shouldn't be cooped up in an office from sunup to sundown.

Thoughts of Dave faded quickly as she pulled on her most flattering pair of jeans. It took her a little longer to choose a top, but she finally settled on a retro muslin peasant style that seemed somewhat coffee-shoppish. One look from Tom let her know she'd made the right choice.

Tom tried to describe some of the people as they walked toward the storefront church. "They're from all over the country, and we even have some international members, which makes it quite a bit different from what you're probably used to."

As soon as they walked into the building with the glass door, she realized what an understatement his last comment was. The room wasn't terribly wide, but it was deep, with folding tables and chairs on both sides of a center aisle.

"We use folding chairs so we can reconfigure the room according to the program." Tom glanced down at her. "The chairs are in rows for Sunday services, and sometimes it's hard to find a seat we're so packed. We're thinking about having two services, but we don't want to rush into that until we're sure it makes sense."

Cissy continued looking around the room and noticed the plain white walls on either side and band equipment on the platform at the front. "This doesn't look anything like a church," she said.

"Since we minister to a wide variety of people, including some who didn't like traditional churches, we thought it would be best to keep all the focus on the services rather than the building and furnishings."

That made sense to Cissy.

Tom led her to the refreshment station, where they got coffee and pastries, and found a seat near the front. Tom started out introducing the acts, but halfway through the night, one of the assistant pastors took over. Cissy found herself sighing with contentment throughout the night as she realized she was finally living her dream. She couldn't have planned a more perfect evening.

As they walked to her apartment afterward, Tom alternated between holding her hand and putting his arm around her. She loved the hand-holding, but when he rested his arm on her shoulder or middle of her back, she felt protected. When they got to her apartment door, she invited him in.

"Not tonight. I have an early morning tomorrow, so I need to go home and get some rest."

Disappointment pulled her shoulders down, and she had to dig deep to keep the lilt in her voice. "Maybe some other time?"

"Of course. Would you like to go with me to hand out sandwiches in the subway on Saturday?"

"I would love to." She frowned. "Who do you hand sandwiches to and why?"

A peaceful expression covered his face. "We find people who look like they could use a meal and a message of hope."

"And you give them both." Cissy looked up at him, and he took her breath away as they locked gazes. At that moment she knew he was about to kiss her.

As his face closed in on hers, her lips tingled with anticipation. She let out a deep sigh as they made contact. She instinctively placed her hand behind his head, and the kiss grew deeper.

He finally pulled away with his eyes at half-mast. "Cissy, you are an amazing woman. Not only are you sweet and pretty, I love the fact that you love the Lord. I can see something really special forming between us."

That was all Cissy needed to hear. "Me too."

"Good." He leaned over, gave her a kiss on the forehead, and took a step back. "I'll call you Friday."

As Cissy closed the door behind her, she practically melted into the floor. There was no way she'd let this one get away. Even Mama would love him, and that was rare.

Now the only thing she needed to work on was her professional life. Training and studying had gotten old after the first week, and now it was really getting under her skin. Cissy had pushed hard to do more on her own, but Dave kept telling her that Uncle Forest still didn't feel that she was ready. By Friday she had decided it was ridiculous for him to hold her first mistake against her, so she marched right up to his open door and knocked.

Grinning, he motioned for her to come on in. "What do you need, Cissy?"

"I've been studying for—like—ever, and I'm ready to make some sales. I know you're all worried after what I did, but I learned my lesson and I won't ever do that again and—"

He held up both hands and belted out a deep laugh. "I know, I know. I'm surprised it took you so long to do this."

"I beg your pardon?"

Uncle Forest pointed to the chair across from his desk. "Sit down. I have a plan to ease you into sales, only this time I'll make sure you're more prepared."

By the time she left his office, she had a short list of small clients and a plan to increase their orders, with follow-up from Dave. Now Cissy couldn't think of anything that would make her life better.

She expected Tom to call, so she was surprised to see him standing outside her apartment building when she arrived. "Hey," she said, trying to keep from throwing herself into his arms.

"I wanted to catch you before you made plans for dinner. A group of us is meeting at the church for a potluck." He paused. "You don't have to bring anything. I'll stop off at a deli on the way."

"I would love to go, and I want to bring something." She shifted from one foot to the other. "What time do you want me there?"

He glanced at his watch. "I'll pick you up at six. We can walk over there together."

As soon as he turned around and left, Cissy took off for the tiny grocery store on the corner. She picked up some overpriced pasta, mayonnaise, and pickles and carried them back to her apartment to make a pasta salad. She had no idea what else she could fix on such short notice.

Tom showed up at precisely six o'clock, holding a bagful of food. "You really didn't have to make anything. I have enough in here for both of us."

"You obviously don't understand Southern girls," she said, pouring on the thickest accent she could. "Our mamas teach us early that we can't show up empty-handed at a potluck, or we'll be considered downright tacky."

"Tacky, huh?" He chuckled. "I wouldn't want you to be called that...would I?"

"Nuh-uh." She shook her head. "That would be really bad." She nodded her head toward the bag. "What all did you get?"

"Sliced cold cuts, olives, and some pasta salad."

"Uh oh." She made a face. "That's what I made."

"I'm sure yours is better than anything you can get around here." They'd arrived at the Inner City Outreach Church, and he opened the door for her and followed her inside.

A half hour later Tom pulled Cissy away from the crowd. "Looks like your pasta salad is a hit."

She smiled and nodded. "Now I understand why Mama gets all worked up over her potato salad recipe. It sure feels good to know people like my cookin'."

By the time they got to the buffet table, there was only one small scoop of her pasta salad left. Cissy gestured with her free hand. "You go on and get some. I can make it anytime."

"Okay, I'll do that." He plopped the last spoonful onto his plate.

Cissy held her breath as she watched him lift the fork filled with her pasta salad to his mouth. When he sighed with contentment and said, "Man, is this delicious," she exhaled. When he added, "I've never tasted anything like it," she was over the moon.

After everyone ate, they said another prayer before the meeting to discuss strategy to feed as many people as possible the next day. Tom and some of his pals had managed to get several bakeries and delis to donate the food, so all they had to do was pick it up and distribute it.

Tom led her out of the church and toward her apartment. "I am so glad you're doing this with me. It's such an important part of my life, and I love sharing it with you."

Nothing he could have said would have pleased her more. "Thank you."

When they arrived at her building, she invited him in. "I have to get up before daylight to pick up the bread, so I need to get home. I'll pick you up at eight." With a quick peck on her cheek, he was gone.

Charlene was just leaving as she got off the elevator. "I'm meeting some people for a movie. Wanna join us?"

Cissy shook her head as she thought about what Tom

said. "I have to get up before daylight, so I think I'll turn in now."

Charlene narrowed her eyes and gave her a curious look. "Okaaaay." She reached out and felt Cissy's forehead. "Are you feelin' sick or somethin'?"

"No." Cissy swatted at Charlene's hand. "I just need to get some rest so I can help hand out sandwiches with Tom."

"Oh, I should have known. It's about Tom." She pursed her lips. "Remember, don't let a man take over your whole life until he's ready to make a commitment."

"I know, I know."

"Be careful."

"I will." Cissy crossed her heart. "I promise."

"Fine. I'll see you later." Charlene waved good-bye as she took off for the elevator.

Once Cissy was inside her apartment, she leaned against the door. Charlene was right. She did have a tendency to put all her energy into whatever guy she happened to be dating. Maybe she'd try something different on Sunday...unless Tom wanted to do something after church.

Mama called. "Where have you been? I thought you had your phone with you all the time."

"I was at church," Cissy replied. "I did have my phone with me, but it was so noisy I didn't hear it."

"Church? On a Friday night? What kind of church meets on Friday night?"

Cissy sank down on the edge of her daybed and kicked off her shoes. "It was a meeting to discuss a mission I'm doing tomorrow."

"What kind of mission?"

"A sandwich mission."

Mama made a strange grunting sound. "I reckon that

makes sense to someone. Anyway, I just wanted to call to find out how you're doing. Forest says you're catching on fast now and that you haven't made any more big mistakes."

"He said that?" Cissy sat up straighter. "Yes, I guess I am catchin' on pretty fast." It pleased her to no end to hear that someone, especially Uncle Forest, was finally saying something good about her behind her back.

"I talked to Bootsie too. She told me that their door is always open if you come to your senses and decide to move back in with them."

"Did she put it like that?" Cissy asked.

"Well, no. But she wants to make sure you know they'll let you back in."

Cissy sighed. "So how are you doin', Mama? Anything new in Hartselle?"

"Not really. I was just callin' to check on you."

"Well, thank you. Now that you know I'm doing just fine, I need to go get ready for bed."

Once Cissy put her phone back in her handbag, she flopped down on her bed. This apartment was still small enough to make her long for her old room back home, but the second she remembered Tom, being here was worth the cramped quarters.

Chapter 18

TOM LOADED UP the church van with as much food as he could cram into the back. Lester Shaw, one of the other volunteers from church, opened the doors to his SUV. "Looks like we have more this week than last."

"Good thing we have a few extra pairs of hands to help out," Tom said. "I invited Cissy, and she agreed to come."

"I hope you told her to leave all her valuables at home."

"I did."

Lester gave him a fake jab in the shoulder. "She's a looker."

"And she loves the Lord."

"Bonus." Lester hoisted the first box of wrapped sandwiches into the SUV. "It's hard to find a woman with everything."

"I know." Tom helped for a few more minutes before going back to the van. "I'm picking her up on the way, so I'll see you later. Any questions about your location?"

"Nope. I have my list right here." He patted his pocket. "See you back at the church this afternoon."

Tom pulled away with a full van, heading toward Cissy's apartment building. He half expected to wait, but to his surprise she was standing outside when he turned the corner. Once he stopped at the curb, she didn't hesitate to open the door and hop in.

"This van smells like pastrami and cheese," she said.

"Hmm. I wonder why." He smiled at her and turned his attention back to the road as he pulled away.

All the way to their designated subway station at 163rd

Street, Cissy asked questions about church and handing out sandwiches. When they got out of the van, Cissy looked around and asked, "Are all the people homeless?"

"Quite a few of them are, but I suspect some live in tenement housing or apartments."

"It's hard to believe that there are so many hungry folks in the United States." She reached out and touched his arm. "I think it's wonderful that our church is reaching out to them."

His throat constricted at the sound of her calling it *our* church. "I agree."

"I'll pray for each and every person I talk to," she said. "I'm sure that if they're hungry enough to accept free sandwiches from strangers, they'll appreciate all the prayers I can give them."

"Yes, it's always good to pray for them, but don't expect a lot of appreciation. And never let down your guard."

"Oh, absolutely." She smiled. "I know that."

She'd no sooner said that than a woman wearing a tattered dress and carrying a canvas bag approached and shoved Cissy into Tom. Cissy turned to the woman, smiled, and said, "Excuse me." The woman snarled back at her and grabbed for Cissy's handbag.

Tom's instincts kicked in. He pulled Cissy around to his other side and turned to the woman. "The only thing we have that you might want is food. If you're not hungry, move on."

His comment didn't faze the woman. She simply turned and left.

"Why don't we call the cops or something?" Cissy asked as she rubbed her arm. "She hurt me."

An overwhelming protective urge washed over Tom as he looked down at her sweet, confused expression. "If I thought it would do any good, I would, but this is nothing compared to what the police are having to deal with in this part of town."

"That's so different from what I'm used to."

"Are you okay, or would you like to leave now?"

Cissy glanced around and turned back to him. "I reckon I shouldn't let that one mean woman ruin it for everyone else. I want to stay and help them."

His heart warmed even more for Cissy as she showed her innate kindness. He didn't know many women who would have wanted to continue after what happened. But he also knew he needed to remain close to protect her from another incident.

"Jenkins?"

The sound of a familiar voice saying Tom's name caused him to turn around. About six feet away stood Mario Perez, one of the few button manufacturers left in New York City. A few months ago Tom had decided to look into manufacturing custom notions himself in order to fill specialized orders he kept getting. Not wanting to divulge his plans, he dropped some of the smaller companies he worked with. When Mario had pressed for an explanation, Tom blew him off.

Mario pointed to the box of sandwiches. "What are you doing?"

Tom's body tensed as he guided Cissy to his other side. "Feeding the hungry."

A roar of laughter erupted from the portly man. "Now that's a sight I never would have expected, but I suppose you would have to do something to make up for your dirty business ethics." He narrowed his eyes as his gaze darted to the food and then back to Tom. "It probably makes you feel even more powerful to give handouts to the poor."

"Power is the last thing on my mind right now." Tom could see Cissy watching him from the corner of his eye. "And my business ethics are perfectly honorable."

"In whose book?" Mario glanced around at Cissy. "Be careful with this guy. He's a shark. He'll use you until he gets what he wants, and then you'll never see him again." With that he turned and walked away.

Tom wished Cissy didn't have to hear that, but it was bound to happen eventually. He'd prided himself on being shrewd in business. He wasn't dishonest, but he did take advantages of others' weaknesses if it was good for Sewing Notions Inc.

"What was that all about?" Cissy asked. "What did he mean by dirty business ethics?"

Tom shook his head. "I didn't need what he sold anymore. Sewing Notions Inc. was one of his biggest accounts."

Cissy looked concerned. "Did you try to talk to him about it before you dumped him?"

"No need to do that. I have my reasons, and they're not open for discussion." He felt bad for keeping her in the dark, but he wasn't ready yet to discuss his business plans.

A look of pain flashed through her eyes, but she quickly recovered. "I would've—"

A small family approached and asked if they still had sandwiches. Tom and Cissy never got to finish their conversation, but it played on Tom's mind for the remainder of the time in the subway station. What must Cissy think of him now?

Cissy trudged up to her apartment, and without stopping, headed straight for the shower. The filthy subway had made her feel grimy from head to toe. Now that she'd witnessed Tom's interaction with that Mario Perez guy, she had some serious thinking to do, but she was too tired to linger on them at the moment.

After she towel-dried her hair and slipped into her comfy yoga pants, her phone rang. Charlene didn't wait a second before pounding the questions.

"How did today go? Did you have a chance to talk with Tom? Are you going out with him again?"

"Whoa, wait a minute." Cissy laughed. "One question at a time."

"I'm just excited and eager to hear how today went. I saw you come in, and when you didn't call, I got worried."

"Today went really well…for the most part anyway, but I'm exhausted. We handed out hundreds of sandwiches to people who looked like they hadn't eaten in days."

"That is so sad," Charlene said. "Here we are in one of the richest cities in the world, and to think there are people who go hungry. It just doesn't seem right, does it?"

"No, and that's why Tom's church has the sandwich mission. Did you know that the subway is the only place some of them can get shelter?"

"I've heard that, but I rarely go to those stations."

"Tom told me it's probably not a good idea for a woman to go there alone, so I probably won't either."

"So tell me more about Tom. Was he all dreamy and romantic?"

Again Cissy forced herself to laugh. She didn't want to mention Tom's reaction to his former business associate. "About as dreamy and romantic as he could be in such a dirty environment."

"But you sound like you enjoyed every minute of it."

"I'm not so sure I enjoyed it as much as I felt that I was

doing something worthwhile." Cissy paused. "It's really nice to be able to help others without someone thinking I have an ulterior motive. No one questioned me. They just accepted the food, and many of them actually thanked me. We stopped and prayed with quite a few of them too."

"That's pretty awesome. I might want to join you sometime."

"I'm sure they can always use more volunteers."

"So what's next on your agenda with Tom? Got any dates lined up for the future?"

Her throat tightened. "I'm going to church with him in the morning."

"What's wrong, Cissy? I'm sensing something you're not tellin' me."

"Nothing. I'm just tired."

"Must be nice to have someone so soon after you got here." Charlene sighed and then grew quiet. "Tom seems like the perfect guy for a Christian girl. I wish I knew someone like him."

Cissy felt bad for Charlene. Maybe she should tell Charlene what happened, and that would make her realize things weren't always as they seemed. She paused for a moment before plunging into as detailed of a recounting of the incident as she could remember.

"So what are you saying?" Charlene asked. "Do you think he's putting on a front for you?"

"I don't know," Cissy replied. "To be honest, I'm confused. If it were just this one situation, I'd probably blow it off, but after what happened to Uncle Forest when Tom took over Sewing Notions Inc., I can't exactly ignore the warning signs."

"You're right, but at least give him a chance to explain."

"Oh, trust me, I will. In fact, I plan to make a list of questions before I see him next."

"You also said he protected you from that woman who shoved you." Charlene sighed. "I don't remember any guy ever protecting me from anything."

"There is that, and I have to admit he made my heart pitter-patter when he did that."

Charlene laughed. "My heart would probably hop right out of my chest if someone did that for me."

"I'm sure someone really nice will come along and sweep you off your feet."

"Wouldn't that be nice?" Charlene's voice tightened. "I better let you go. I'm taking cupcakes for the little kids' Sunday school class tomorrow, and I haven't even started baking them yet."

"Are you teaching Sunday school?" Cissy just now realized that she knew very little about Charlene's church.

"I help out some, but there aren't that many kids left, so I don't have to do much. Our church membership is starting to dwindle, and there's some talk that they might fold soon."

"That's terrible."

"Yeah, I know," Charlene said. "And to make matters worse, our pastor has already accepted another position at a church across town, so after next week, all our services will be conducted by lay leaders."

"If you ever want to…I mean, I don't want to try to pull you away from a church you like, but—"

"If you're inviting me to church with you, I'd love to go. Let's talk about it next week."

After they got off the phone, Cissy fixed herself a cup of herbal tea and sank down on the daybed. The combination of events from the day and her mixed feelings for Tom swirled in her head.

Now that she had some time alone to ponder her current feelings and compare them to her past mistakes, she wondered if she really knew Tom. He'd been such a gentleman with her—charming, fun, and kind. However, now that she'd heard from both her uncle and that man in the subway about how ruthless he was in business, she questioned her own judgment. Now she thought maybe she shouldn't have allowed herself to get so involved with Tom. Mama had always said she felt too much too soon. From early childhood she'd thrown herself into everything she did, from friendships to hobbies, and then as an adult, all her relationships.

"Girls like you get their hearts broken more often," Mama told her. "Why don't you learn to take baby steps until you are sure about what you're getting into?"

Maybe that was what she needed to do with Tom. It wasn't too late to start now. And while she was impressed with his involvement at church and his heart for the homeless and hungry, she couldn't ignore the incident with the man in the subway. What if Tom was one of those after-hours Christians who didn't follow his convictions on company time? She thought of how her aunt and uncle saw Tom, how they viewed him as the enemy. It was hard to believe or to reconcile two such different images of the same man. Who was Tom, anyway? Was he playing a game with her or using her for information to boost his company at the risk of damaging Zippers Plus again? Until she knew more, she'd better keep some distance.

After Cissy finished her tea, she slid beneath the covers of her daybed and picked up a book from the stack on the floor. The irony of the situation wasn't lost on her. Back in Hartselle, she rarely went to bed before midnight on a weekend, but it had become normal here in the city that never sleeps.

Chapter 19

THE NEXT MORNING Tom called as she was getting ready for church. "I'll park at the church and walk to your place," he offered.

"You don't need to do that. I don't mind walking alone." She wanted to go to church with him, but she needed some distance to make it easier to watch for more warning signs.

Silence fell between them for a few seconds before he spoke. "Okay, if that's what you want to do."

"It is."

"I'll see you in a little while. Look for me when you get there."

Cissy was pretty sure that was disappointment she heard in his voice, which pleased her to no end. She finished applying her mascara and took a swipe at her lips with a tube of tinted lip balm. Before she left, she made sure she didn't have anything smeared on her face.

The instant she entered the storefront church, Tom made it to her side. He grinned as he gestured toward the front. "I like to be close to the pulpit so I'm not so distracted."

They passed a row of teenage boys who looked extremely uncomfortable and out of place. She smiled at them, and they jeered back at her. She glanced at Tom, who made it clear he'd noticed. He leaned over and whispered, "I'll explain in a few minutes."

Once they sat down, some of the people around them introduced themselves. Cissy couldn't believe the difference between the ages of these people and the ones at her aunt's church, but she should have expected it based on the location. Not many people her aunt's age lived in this section of the city.

A couple of members of the band had begun to play a soft song. Tom placed his arm around her and leaned toward her, whispering, "We have a ministry to help young kids stay out of trouble. Those guys back there either are or have been members of gangs."

"Oh." Cissy had never met a gang member before. "Are they dangerous?"

"Not here, but I wouldn't want to mess with them when they're with a bunch of their friends."

"How do you find them?" Cissy asked.

He pointed toward a woman sitting a few rows over. "See that woman in the blue shirt? She lives in the neighborhood, and she gives us information."

The church's ministries amazed Cissy. They had nothing like this back home in Alabama. There the ministries consisted of vacation Bible school, canned food drives, and visiting patients in the nursing home.

The music grew louder, and the rest of the band went up on the stage. As the next song began, everyone stood and sang the words that were projected on the white screen at the front of the church.

The whole scenario felt right to Cissy. She loved everything about where she was at the moment—in this fabulous come-as-you-are church amidst a group of unpretentious believers. Her voice quivered with joy as they sang each song. Every now and then Tom glanced down at her with the strangest expression.

When the music ended, before the pastor walked to the center of the stage, Tom leaned over. "I love how you sing with such abandon."

Cissy panicked. She hadn't realized she'd sung loud

enough for him to hear, and that was a very bad thing since she'd never been able to carry a tune in a bucket.

She cringed and gave him an apologetic look. "Sorry about that. I reckon I just got carried away."

He grinned. "That's quite all right. I enjoy hearing your voice."

"It probably makes you feel like an opera singer."

He laughed. "Not exactly. I think you and I harmonize quite well, if you know what I mean."

The pastor lifted his hands, indicating that it was time to pray. Cissy bowed her head and forced herself to concentrate on what she was there for. When the pastor ended his prayer, she silently added, *Lord, show me who Tom really is. Show me if I can trust him.*

After the service Tom took her by the hand and led her to a room behind the stage. "Would you like coffee or something?"

Although Cissy was tempted to stay, she'd already decided she needed a bit of space and time away from Tom in order to slow things down, allow her head to clear, and pray. "I think I'll go on back to my apartment now. I have a lot of things to do, and I haven't seen much of Charlene lately."

The disappointment on his face almost made her change her mind, but she managed to hold back. He nodded his understanding. "Would you like for me to walk you home?"

"No, I think those guys want to speak with you." She started to back away from him until she felt a bump behind her. She spun around and found herself face-to-face with a man-size person with a little boy's face. He had a scar along the side of his jaw, and his scowl let her know he wasn't in the best mood. "Oops. Sorry."

His eyes narrowed as he continued staring at Cissy. Her stomach churned.

"Hey there, Barry," Tom said from behind. "I'm glad you could make it."

The kid turned his attention from her to Tom, but his face never broke into a smile. However, Tom didn't let that sway him or alter his approach. He continued smiling as he took Barry by the arm and led him away from Cissy. They were a good ten feet away when she felt her pulse return to normal.

She took the opportunity to scurry out of the church. When she arrived back at her apartment, she closed the door behind her and leaned against it. A knock made her jump.

The image of Barry's scowl popped into her head. What if he'd followed her home? Then she remembered the code at the door downstairs and let out a shaky breath.

"Who is it?"

"Charlene. Are you gonna let me in, or do I have to spend the rest of the day wondering how church was?"

Cissy opened her apartment door. "Sorry."

"Hey girl, you look like you just saw a ghost. What happened?"

Cissy spent more time telling Charlene about her encounter than the incident lasted. "Tom was amazing, though. He didn't seem fazed in the least by that boy."

"So what are you and Tom doing this afternoon?"

"Nothing," Cissy replied. "I told him I was spending the afternoon with you."

Charlene tilted her head and looked at Cissy with an odd expression. "Oh, but what if I have other plans?"

Cissy shrugged. "Then I reckon I'll be spending the afternoon by my lonesome."

"I was just funnin' ya. I was hoping you'd save a little time for your old-maid friend."

"You're about the last person I'd ever call an old maid. What do you have in mind?"

"I dunno. Maybe we can just walk around and see what moves us. There's always something interesting going on out there."

"Then let's go."

Cissy had a wonderful time walking around the streets of New York City. They rode the subway to Times Square, where they watched tourists until they got hungry. "I'm in the mood for something exotic. How does Thai food sound?" Charlene asked.

"When I'm this hungry I'll eat just about anything."

After they sat down and ordered, Charlene stared at Cissy for a few uncomfortable seconds.

"What?" Cissy bobbed her head. "Do I have something on my face?"

"I was just hoping you'd tell me more about Tom, like more about what's going on that has you in such a dither. I feel like you just scratched the surface last time we talked."

"I'm getting all kinds of mixed signals, and I don't know what to do." She unfolded her napkin and put it in her lap to buy a moment to think. "My history with romantic relationships isn't good, ya know. I don't have the best judgment." She went into greater detail and explained why she felt so conflicted.

Charlene listened and nodded. "You do need to take some time to think and pray about this, but there is such a thing as overthinking."

"How do you know when you cross that line?"

"I sure wish I could tell you. I overthink everything." Charlene gave her a sympathetic look. "I do know that you can't expect perfection in any guy, or you'll wind up without one."

When their food arrived, Cissy led the prayer. As they ate, they changed the subject, something Cissy appreciated about Charlene. She instinctively knew when a subject had been beaten to death, and Cissy needed a break.

By the time they got back to their apartment building, it was almost dark. Once again Cissy was exhausted.

"I can't believe what this place is doing to me," Cissy said once they reached Charlene's apartment. "I get up with the chickens and go to bed before the old folks do back home."

"Ain't that the truth?" Charlene snickered. "I used to pay a fortune at the gym when I lived in Atlanta, but this place is too expensive to have a gym membership, and I still lost weight. Go figure."

"That's because you do so much walking." Cissy had noticed that too. She could eat almost anything she wanted, but her clothes had already started to get loose on her.

"Have you got plans with Tom this week?"

Cissy shook her head. "I've decided to back off a little bit. I don't want to go into a relationship so fast this time. I'm sure you understand after what happened."

"I do, and I think it's a good idea."

"I better go get my clothes ready for tomorrow. I hate having to steam my shirts in the mornings."

"I should probably get a steamer. I usually just iron the front of my blouse, but I can't take my jacket off all day, or my coworkers will see how wrinkled the rest of me is."

Cissy laughed as she headed toward her own apartment. An hour later she was curled up in bed, forcing her eyes to stay open to read another chapter of her book.

The next morning when she got to work she spotted

a note from Uncle Forest on her desk, telling her to go straight to his office. She knocked, and when he told her to come in, she did, closing the door behind her without his having to tell her to.

"Did I do something wrong?" she asked.

"No." He pulled a cooler out from beneath his desk. "I just wanted to make sure I gave you this. Bootsie was afraid you were sitting in your apartment all weekend starving to death."

She took the cooler. "Thank you, and tell Aunt Bootsie I'm fine, but I'll take anything she wants to send."

"What did you do this past weekend?"

Cissy shrugged. "I handed out sandwiches to some homeless and hungry people and went to church. Charlene and I walked around last night. How about you?"

His forehead crinkled momentarily, but finally he broke into a grin. "Sounds like you stayed pretty busy. How do you like being on your own so far?"

"It's okay, I guess."

His gaze held steady on her long enough to make her squirm before he turned back to his computer. She stood there and watched him for a few seconds and then he glanced back up at her. "That's all I wanted. Now get back to work. We have a bunch of sewing notions to sell."

After lunch Uncle Forest called everyone into the conference room for an impromptu meeting. He looked around at everyone and then broke into a grin. "I have some wonderful news. The Fabulous Threads account is about to undergo some changes, and that involves more sales opportunities for us." He turned to Dave and gestured for him to stand.

Dave spoke about prior sales to Fabulous Threads and explained how the changes would directly affect the account. "They plan to break things up into different departments, so more than one of us will benefit. In fact..." He glanced at Uncle Forest who nodded. "I think we'll be able to offer everyone here a piece of the pie."

Cissy took notes. As Dave spoke, she imagined making a name for herself with this great new opportunity.

The rest of the week seemed to drag. Tom let her know he was called away on a business trip, so she might not hear from him for a while. She texted him, and he sent a short response, letting her know how busy he was. Cissy thought about Tom off and on, but she resisted the urge to call him. And perhaps sensing her hesitance, he didn't call her either. This was probably what she needed in order to think clearly and evaluate her feelings.

Each evening she and Charlene took short strolls up and down the streets near their apartments looking for inexpensive wall hangings. "I so want that vase," Cissy said, pointing to one of the pieces in a local gallery. "But even if I could afford it, I wouldn't have any place to put it."

"One of these days you will," Charlene assured her. "Let's go see what else we can find."

Finally, the end of the week had arrived. Cissy still hadn't heard from Tom other than a few very brief text messages letting her know he was thinking of her and inviting her to a concert on Saturday. "Should I call him?" Cissy asked as she and Charlene walked to work together.

Charlene shrugged. "I don't see why not."

Cissy tried, but his phone went straight to voicemail. She didn't leave a message.

Tom finally called at seven that night. "Sorry it took me so long, but this has been a bear of a week."

She was slightly annoyed, but she wasn't about to let

him know. "That's okay. I've had some time to get a few things squared away. Where are you?"

"I just got back to the office. Do you still want to go to the concert with me tomorrow?"

"Yes."

"Good. How about I pick you up at nine in the morning? We can stop and get a few things from the deli on the way to the concert."

After she got off the phone with Tom, Cissy called Charlene. "Got a few minutes?"

"Sure. I was about to fix some mac 'n cheese. Want some?"

"Sounds good. I'll bring dessert."

On her way out the door Cissy pulled the last of the cookies from Dave's gift box from the freezer. Her diet had suffered since she'd been on her own, so she vowed to change that, starting on Monday. Even though she hadn't put on a pound she knew she needed better nutrition.

Charlene had opened her apartment door and left it open while she stood at the stove. Cissy walked in, closed the door behind her, and took a long look at her friend.

"What's the matter?" Cissy asked.

Charlene lifted one shoulder and let it drop. "I dunno. I've been feelin' a tad lonelier than usual lately."

Cissy could relate, but she didn't want to burden her friend with more of her own doubts. "I'm sorry I haven't been a very good friend. All I've done is talk about me, my work, my bare walls, and Tom."

"Oh no, it's not you. It's just that…" She contorted her mouth. "I want a date, but it seems like all the good guys are taken."

Cissy had thought that many times when she lived in Alabama. "Maybe you just need a change of scenery."

Charlene laughed. "Are you saying I won't find anyone inside these four walls?"

"Something like that. How about church? Aren't there any nice men there?"

"Most of the ones that are left are married or seeing someone."

"Since your church is about to close, why don't you go to Tom's church with me? I mean, you did say that you'll probably have to find a new church soon anyway."

Charlene tilted her head. "Are you saying I should use church as a dating service?"

"No, of course not. All I'm saying is that there isn't any reason you can't worship in a place where there are a few eligible bachelors in the congregation."

"Well…" Charlene bobbed her head. "You do have a point. Maybe I can try it out this Sunday."

They made plans over mac 'n cheese and cookies. Then Cissy told her about Tom's phone call and their date at a concert the following day.

"If it weren't for what he did to your uncle, he would seem perfect," Charlene sighed. "You really are in a pickle, aren't you? I've had my share of man problems in the past, but not a one of 'em is as interesting as what's happenin' to you."

"Maybe one of these days I'll write a memoir."

Charlene chuckled. "You'd have to sit still long enough to do it, and somehow I don't see that happenin'."

Cissy washed her dish, put it away, and gave Charlene a hug. "Have I told you lately how much I appreciate you?"

"I'm so glad you're here," Charlene said. "I have to admit

that I've been feeling mighty homesick lately. It's nice to hear a little back-home talk."

"I feel the same way."

"I know you have, sweetie. If it makes you feel any better, this feeling we both have will come and go. We just have to take advantage of the times we're not like this and have ourselves a little fun."

Cissy nodded. "You and I need to stick together, no matter what. There isn't any one place that's perfect."

Charlene snickered. "Ain't that the truth? If I'd stayed in Atlanta, I never would have had the opportunities I've had here."

"And you wouldn't have met me," Cissy reminded her.

"Yes," Charlene agreed with a smile. "There is that too."

That night as Cissy lay in bed, she thanked God for the gift of Charlene's friendship. Charlene had been so generous with her advice and comfort that she was grateful to have a chance to return the favor. She just hoped that Charlene would like Tom's church—and that she might find a good man there. What still baffled her was how Tom seemed to be one man at church and another man at his business. It was almost as though he could flip a switch and go from one person to another. How could she find out who the true Tom really was?

Slowly a plan began to form in her head. What if she blabbed just a tiny bit of a company secret, then watched to see how he handled it? He was fully aware of her propensity to chatter, so he wouldn't have any clue that she was setting him up.

The idea seemed dangerous and a bit devious, but she had no other idea of how to force Tom to show his true colors. And if she was going to stop herself from falling for him big time and getting hurt all over again, she needed to act fast.

Lord, she prayed, *I don't know what else to do. Help me!* She opened her eyes for a moment before squeezing them shut again. *And please forgive me if this isn't pleasing to You, but You must understand that I have to do something.*

Chapter 20

TOM SHOWED UP at her door precisely on time the next morning. In spite of nearly a week apart, as they walked to his car, she felt as though she'd seen him every day and known him all her life. She wanted to keep her distance, but when he reached for her hand or touched her cheek, the magnetic pull was too powerful for her to resist leaning into him.

The concert was a couple of hours away at a field owned by a farmer who hosted this annual event. He stood at the entrance of the makeshift parking lot and handed out flyers as people pulled in. There was no admission fee, but according to the flyer, a collection was being taken to provide safe drinking water for a village in Africa. As soon as they found a parking spot, Tom led her to the donation booth, where he discretely handed a check to the person collecting.

Tom turned to her. "Ready to find a good spot? I can't wait to hear the music."

Cissy loved seeing a different, lighter side of Tom. His love for the music was evident in the way he moved as the different bands played.

He nodded toward the stage. "I think you'll like this group."

She looked at the banner and saw the name Addison Road. "I've never heard of them."

"I like the messages in their songs." As he placed his arm around her, she couldn't imagine being anywhere else at that moment.

The concert was wonderful, but being with Tom would have been perfect even without the music. They'd started out the morning wrapped in the blanket he'd brought, but as the sun heated things up around noon, they shed the blanket. She unwrapped the sandwiches and poured the tea from the carton he'd brought.

"Want a grape?" he asked.

"Sure."

He reached over into the cooler, plucked a couple of grapes, and playfully popped one into her mouth. She leaned into him and sighed.

"This is the life."

"Enjoying the day?" he asked.

"Immensely."

Now it was her turn to feed him some grapes. As she held one in front of him, he grabbed her arm, pulled her closer, and tilted her face up to his. She knew he was about to go in for a kiss, so she held her breath and closed her eyes. As his lips touched hers, a shiver traveled down her spine.

"Now that was a nice kiss," he said. "I could easily fall in love with you, Cissy."

The impact of those words hit her like a thunderbolt. In the past Cissy would have responded by telling him she felt the same way. But now she knew she had to be much more cautious and wait until she was sure of his intentions. She pulled her bottom lip between her teeth as she allowed herself to gaze into his eyes.

"That's okay." He smiled. "You don't have to say a word. We have all the time in the world to see where this thing can go."

They kissed a couple more times, but Tom didn't let

them last very long. Cissy was glad he had self-restraint, a trait very few guys back home were willing to exercise.

"Why don't we talk?" He said as he put a few more inches between them.

"What do you want to talk about?"

"You. I'd like to know all about what you did in Alabama, your family, what you enjoy doing besides eating grapes."

She told him about college, her long string of jobs that didn't last long, her family, and how much she enjoyed shoe shopping. He listened without judging.

"What did you major in?"

"Retail merchandising." She shrugged. "I only went to college because that was what my parents expected me to do. I was more interested in life outside of class."

He laughed. "I'm sure you're not the only one."

"I was so naïve back then, but I'm finally starting to figure out life." She took a deep breath of the clean, country air and slowly exhaled. Now was the time to test him, before she fell too hard. "I love working for my uncle, even though it's pretty frustrating at times."

"Zippers Plus seems like a well-run company."

Cissy nodded as guilt washed over her. She swallowed hard and did her best to ignore the thought that what she was about to do might make things worse. "It is. And it's growing too. As a matter of fact, we have a new business plan that should make a huge difference. Oh, and there's this huge account...Fabulous Threads..." She gave her head a jaunty toss and flipped her hair over her shoulder so she wouldn't have to look him in the eye. This was much more difficult than she ever imagined it would be. "I'm sure you probably know all about them since you're in the business too." Her voice caught, so she cleared her throat. "Anyway, they're looking to make some major changes, which involves increasing their orders." After she made a show of rambling on, she stopped abruptly and put her hand over her mouth. "Oops. I just said way more than I should have." She let out a pretend nervous giggle. "This motor mouth is still a work in progress."

He glanced away for a moment before turning back to her with an odd look in his eyes. "We're all works in progress. Why don't we change the subject?"

"Sounds good to me." She grinned at him. "I have a few questions for you."

His smile faded momentarily, but he recovered and nodded. "Okay, ask away."

"Tell me more about how yourself. You already said it wasn't what you wanted, and you certainly don't seem like the type to get into the sewing notions business."

He shrugged. "You're right; I'm not, and it wasn't my first choice. However, I do have an eye for how to turn things around, so I couldn't very well sit back and do nothing. I did some research and figured out what the problem was."

"You must be very smart," she said.

"Business seems to be my strong suit. I have an MBA from Wharton."

Whoa. "You're kidding. Even I know about Wharton."

He smiled. "Anyway, back to how I wound up with my company. I walked into the Sewing Notions Inc. office, told the president of the company that I could help him turn his business around, and he basically told me he was done with it. If I wanted to turn it around, I was on my own."

"Wow."

He made a face. "Yeah, that's what I said. *Wow.* He literally walked out. It took several months, but I managed to buy it from him. He wound up with a little bit of cash, and I got stuck with a failing business that I never really wanted."

"Are you...I mean, how is your company doing now?"

He paused as he focused his gaze on hers. "The first few years were tough, really tough, but now it's doing much better than it ever did in the past. In fact, I actually heard from the previous owner's lawyer asking for more cash. Apparently he heard that the company was now on solid footing and well into the profit zone."

Cissy gasped. "You're kidding. That took some kind of nerve. What did you do?"

With a grin he tweaked her cheek. "He's gone, I'm still in business, and you're here with me. Let's talk about something else, okay?"

She swallowed hard and nodded. He'd told her way more than she ever expected. "I hope you don't mind that I invited Charlene to your church tomorrow."

"Of course I don't mind," he said. "Get there early, and I'll introduce her to some of my buddies."

"I'm sure Charlene would love that," Cissy said.

"No doubt."

Now that he'd said the *L* word and shared more about himself, she allowed herself to relax. Maybe his reasons for being such a shark were legitimate, and he had to be tough the early years of his business just to survive.

The rest of the afternoon was like a dream, now that the difficult conversation was behind them. Cissy couldn't ever remember having this much fun with a guy. What made it even more amazing was the fact that she'd given up waiting for something to ruin the day.

When they got back to her neighborhood, he parked behind the church because he needed to help set up. Tom held her hand as they strolled to the door of her apartment building. "Want me to walk you up to your apartment?"

"No, I'll be fine. You need to get back to the church."

He dropped a quick kiss on her lips and waved as she stepped into the building. Before the door closed behind her, she blew him an exaggerated kiss, and he laughed.

As soon as she was back in her apartment, Cissy called Charlene and let her know the details. "Don't bother dressing up. This is a come-as-you-are church."

"Can't wait. See you bright and early."

The next morning, as they got closer to the storefront church, Charlene's eyes widened. "Look at all those men, will you? It's like a regular smorgasbord."

Cissy laughed. "I thought you might like it."

Tom popped out of the building, glanced around, and when he spotted them, waved in their direction. "He looks so happy to see you," Charlene said. "That's what I want—a man who lights up the instant he lays eyes on me."

She patted Charlene on the arm. "That was what I always wanted too. I just hope I can find out who he really is—a sweet Christian man or a business shark who wouldn't let anything, including his faith, get in the way."

Charlene smiled. "It'll all be clear soon enough. In the meantime enjoy the journey. Let's find our seats."

Tom sat with them through the first half of the service, but he got up to help with the lights for the drama. Charlene's attention remained riveted on everything that happened. Afterward she blew out a breath. "Hoo boy, I can't get over how that moved me. I think I'll be coming here again."

"I know what you mean." She saw Tom heading toward her with a few of his friends. "Don't look now, but—"

Charlene spun around and then turned back to Cissy, her eyes about to bug out of her head. "Be still my heart."

Tom introduced everyone. "We normally go out for lunch after church, and we'd love to have you join us."

"Suits me just fine," Charlene said, but her shoulders sagged slightly.

Cissy knew that Charlene struggled financially. "Why don't you and I split something? I want to go, but I'm not all that hungry."

Tom looked back and forth at both women. "If you want to split something, that's fine, but it's my turn to treat. You can get whatever you want, and what you don't eat, you can bring back for leftovers."

A spark returned to Charlene's eyes. "In that case, I'm all in."

Lunch was fun, but it lacked the intimacy from the day before, when it was just Cissy and Tom. However, Cissy didn't mind. She had no doubt that she'd have plenty of time alone with the new man in her life if that was what God intended.

Afterward Tom pulled her to the side. "I'm finishing up a project this afternoon, but I'll call you tomorrow if that's okay."

"Of course."

He gave her a hug and kissed her on the cheek. "Thanks for bringing Charlene. She's quite a hit with the guys."

Cissy turned around and saw three men hovering around Charlene, hanging on every word she said. "I'm sure she's having a good time."

All the way home Cissy listened to Charlene yammer on and on about how wonderful Tom's church was. She lifted her take-home bag. "This is like edible gold. My body

won't know what hit it when I feed it something besides
mac 'n cheese and ramen two days in a row."

Cissy was glad to have a little bit of time alone that afternoon. The weekend had been full of fun but exhausting,
and she needed some rest and time to process everything
before starting her busy workweek. Tom had risen to the
occasion of being a hospitable host at church. The only
problem was that when she was away from him, thoughts
of his business dealings popped right back in to her mind.
She still wasn't sure if she'd ever be able to trust him. She
needed to be extremely cautious, but it sure was hard
when he looked at her the way he did.

Chapter 21

THE WEEK STARTED out slow, but it gained momentum as excitement grew over the Fabulous Threads account and all the new opportunities that popped up. Cissy was even given a small piece of it, and as Daddy would say, that made her happier than a butcher's dog.

She researched the new account, gathering information about suppliers that could fill the orders that she was certain would come pouring in, and compiled a priorities list. Uncle Forest would be so proud. She sighed as she imagined hearing from Mama about how he gushed over her ability to pick up on her new job so quickly.

Friday morning Cissy got to the office a few minutes early to prepare for the sales meeting about Fabulous Threads. When Dave gave her a questioning glance, she shrugged. "I don't want Uncle Forest to think you shirked your duties as a trainer."

Dave looked surprised but pleased. "You're making me look good."

Cissy smiled and relaxed. She liked making others happy, and for the first time in her life she thought she might be accomplishing that.

About an hour before the scheduled meeting, her uncle bellowed a sound she'd never heard before.

"What is going on?" Cissy asked.

"Uh oh." Dave's eyes widened as she stood. "That's the sound of a very unhappy Mr. Counts. He reserves that yell for a major mess-up."

"Like what?"

Dave pointed toward the conference room. "I think we're about to find out. Let's go get spots close to the door, just in case."

She jumped up and ran after Dave, following his lead. Mama had mentioned Uncle Forest's temper, and she'd seen it a time or two since being in New York, but never like this. He was downright scary.

As soon as everyone had a seat, Dave closed the door. Uncle Forest didn't utter a word in the beginning. Instead he picked up a foot-high stack of papers and dropped them with a thud on the table.

"See that?" he said as he pointed to the papers that had scattered across the table, some of them falling to the floor. "That is months of work wasted, because someone royally messed up."

Cissy let out a deep sigh. At least she couldn't be the guilty party. The only mess-up she'd made had been fixed with one phone call. But still she felt terrible for whomever he was talking about.

Uncle Forest's gaze skimmed the room and finally settled on her before he closed his eyes and clenched his teeth. A strange gurgling sound erupted from her stomach. Dave looked at her, shook his head, and turned back to face their boss.

"I should never have to tell anyone this, but when we are about to close on a deal that we've been working on for almost a year, all discussion ends at the door." He paused and continued glaring directly at her. "No one outside our office should have even an inkling of what we're doing. If no one has anything to add, this meeting is over."

"Uh oh." Dave leaned toward her. "Looks like you might be in trouble."

"I have no idea what you're talking about."

"Cissy," Uncle Forest said as he brushed past her. "In my office. Now."

With legs that felt like Gumby, she took off after her uncle. He didn't bother saying a word until he closed the door behind her.

He pointed to a chair. "Sit."

She gulped and did as she was told. "Did I do something?"

Uncle Forest narrowed his gaze and glared at her. "I don't know, did you?"

"What are you talking about?"

"Have you been seeing Tom Jenkins behind my back?"

She glanced down, took a deep breath, and exhaled before looking back up at her uncle. "Yes."

"I should have known."

"It had nothing to do with you, though." She paused and cleared her throat. "I just really like—"

His glare stopped her cold. "Did you mention anything to Tom Jenkins about the Fabulous Threads account?"

She felt as though someone had pulled the plug and drained all her blood. "Well…um…I might have said something…"

He took a couple of long strides toward her, widened his stance, and folded his arms as he glared down at her. "You have a big mouth, Cissy Hillwood." His nostrils flared, and his eyes got so big they looked like they might pop right out of his head. "Do you not see how your indiscretion has cost my business big time?" He paced for several minutes as he started on a tirade but stopped himself, spun around, and shook his head.

Cissy slowly shook her head. "I am so sorry. I would never do anything intentionally to hurt you or Zippers Plus."

He rubbed his neck and let out a deep sigh. "Cissy,

you're a very sweet young woman, but you don't seem to have any filters...in any situation."

"Are you gonna tell me what I did wrong?"

"Jenkins managed to take all the business we were supposed to get."

"I—" Cissy's eyes burned, and her throat constricted. She lowered her head. "I am so sorry. I didn't have any idea he'd do anything like that." *Or at least I hoped he wouldn't*, she thought.

"That's not enough."

Fear coursed through her. "Are you sending me back to Alabama?"

He blinked and pursed his lips. "I'm not sure what I'm going to do yet, but this just happens to be the final straw. Until I figure it out, you're only going to get assigned menial tasks. I can't have you spilling any more company secrets to that..." He shook his head. "Never mind. Go on, get outta here. I have some cleaning up to do."

As soon as she sat down at her desk, she pulled up her e-mail and sent Tom a message letting him know what she really thought of him. Without a moment's hesitation she clicked SEND. Then she glanced over at Dave, who quickly looked away.

She couldn't blame him. She'd just messed up, big time.

Tom sat at his desk staring at his computer screen, reflecting on the timing of acquiring the Fabulous Threads account. He knew Zippers Plus had been in the running, but he'd also gotten a verbal from their accounts manager that Sewing Notions Inc. had the edge, so he had flown out to the company a week ago to work on the deal. Soon after

Cissy's slip of the tongue he had secured the account, and he wondered how she'd take the news. Now he knew. Her scathing e-mail let him know exactly what she thought of him.

Marianne stood over Tom, grinning. "I can't believe you're upset about this. We've been trying to get the Fabulous Threads account for the past year."

"It's the timing." He buried his face in his hands as he thought about the flak Cissy would get.

"You don't have to tell me." Marianne took a step back and continued looking at him, only her joy transformed to understanding. "Mr. Counts will blame his niece for Zippers Plus losing the business."

"Yup." He hung his head. "I knew the instant she opened her mouth and started talking about it this might happen."

"Call him."

Tom shook his head. "I doubt that'll do much good."

"Doesn't matter. You have to do whatever you can to set this straight." She tilted her head forward and gave him a look only a practiced mother could do. "With your history he'll naturally assume you were using her. And you might as well forget about any hope of a relationship with her if that happens." She gave him a sympathetic smile. "This is what I was talking about when I said you need to wear your faith all the time—even when you're conducting business."

She was right, but now he knew his ego and pride were bigger than he'd realized. "I'll think about it."

"Okay, you do that." Marianne backed toward the door. "In the meantime I'm going to make reservations for the team to celebrate."

Tom knew that was exactly what they should do, but it didn't change the fact that he didn't feel like celebrating.

He stared at the phone for a long moment before picking up the receiver. He held his breath and put it back down. He didn't know if he should call Cissy or her uncle.

He lowered his head and prayed for guidance. When he opened his eyes, he knew what to do. He didn't owe Mr. Counts an explanation; after all, this was what happened in business. You win some; you lose some. However, he was on a whole different playing field now that he was involved with Cissy.

She didn't hesitate to answer the phone. After one ring she clicked in and said, "I don't want to talk to you, Tom Jenkins. You're no better than Spencer."

"Let me explain." He'd half hoped she didn't know about the Fabulous Threads account, but that was rather naïve thinking on his part.

"There's nothing to explain. I get what happened. You saw an opportunity to exploit this country girl to build up your company's bottom line, and that's exactly what you did. Maybe I would have done the exact same thing if I'd been in your shoes."

"No, you wouldn't have," he said softly.

"You're right. I have integrity. I don't use people."

He had to take a deep breath. "That's not what I did."

She let out one of her strange laughs that ended in a snort. "Don't bother calling me again, Tom. I might be a small-town girl new to the big city, but I'm a fast learner."

"Cissy, wait—"

The click of the phone let him know she wouldn't hear him out. He dropped the phone back into the cradle and let the sadness wash over him. He should have known something like this would happen, but he'd allowed his feelings for Cissy to explode before he had a chance to really sort through how their relationship could be affected by his business, and vice versa.

Tom leaned back in his office chair and closed his eyes. He'd dealt with some gigantic blows in his career, but this is the only one that hurt personally. Ever since meeting Cissy Hillwood, she'd occupied his thoughts morning, noon, and night. Even when he was in the middle of a business deal or working at the church, an image of her would pop into his mind, making him smile. Now all he wanted to do was punch something.

"Tom."

He opened his eyes at the sound of his name. "Hey, Marianne. Did you book the restaurant for the team?"

She nodded, but the sympathetic look in her eyes let him know she felt his pain. "Did you call Mr. Counts?"

Tom shook his head. "No, I did one better. I called Cissy." He pursed his lips and raised his eyebrows.

"So how did that go?"

"I got an earful. She doesn't think much of me now."

"Of course she doesn't. You stole something precious to her."

"You know good and well I didn't steal a thing from her or her uncle."

"I'm talking about trust." Marianne took a step toward him. "I know you didn't steal anything, but you have to admit that from her perspective it looks like you were using her. I'm sure you would feel the same way if the tables were turned. And don't forget about your reputation as a shark in business."

He frowned and thought about it. "Yeah, you're right. It does appear that I used her for business." The fact that he might have done that in the past bothered him even more. "But you know this deal was already in the works, right?"

"Yes, of course I knew." She narrowed her gaze. "So what are you going to do about it? You certainly can't turn down the business."

"You're right—at least not at this point I can't. It wouldn't be fair to the sales team."

Marianne shook her head. "Balancing your business with a romantic relationship with your competitor's niece is obviously a precarious situation."

He nodded. "A high wire with electricity running through it."

"Great analogy." She gestured toward the door. "The meeting room is starting to fill up. Want me to let everyone know you'll be a few minutes late?"

"No." He stood. "I can't let this affect everyone else. They all have families to feed, and I don't want to let them down."

"Deep down you're a good man, Tom." Marianne gave him a sisterly pat on the arm. "We're fortunate you're at the helm now." She held his gaze. "But remember that you can't neglect your personal life. I've been concerned that all you do is work here and at your church. Cissy has been good for you. I can see behind your businesslike façade that you're happier and more relaxed. Now you just need to figure out how to balance your business persona with your personal life." She started to turn and walk away, but stopped to face him again. "By the way, this is a lesson you'll be working on for the rest of your life."

He grunted. She went on ahead into the meeting room.

A few people had warned him in the past that his business practices would eventually catch up with him, and he'd suffer the pain he'd caused others. He never thought that would happen because he was so good at what he did. Now look where that got him. While trying not to make the same mistakes his own father had made, he'd done something worse. He'd stomped on anyone who got in his way. The suffering was more than he could handle alone.

Tom squeezed his eyes shut. *Lord, I now see how separating work from faith is wrong. First of all, please forgive me for not keeping You in the forefront of my mind and heart at all times. Second, I pray that You will show me a way to make this up to Cissy, her uncle, and all the people at Zippers Plus. I see that it's not enough to only look after my personal interests. I should care for everyone.* He opened his eyes and looked back up at the screen with the big fat numbers from Fabulous Threads. *Thank you, Lord, for allowing me to feel guilty. Without that I might never have learned humility.*

Chapter 22

Cissy went to her apartment that night wishing she'd stayed behind in Hartselle. At least there she had Mama who understood her and Daddy who loved her in spite of her mistakes. The physical pain Spencer threatened couldn't possibly hurt more than the emotional pain of what Tom had done and the disappointment she'd seen on Uncle Forest's face.

Here in New York she felt more alone than ever. Not only had she upset her uncle, who just happened to control her income, but the guy who'd duped her into making her think he might be "the one" had turned out to be a traitor. His true colors had been exposed, and she had no choice but to sever all ties with him as she figured out a way to make it up to her uncle. How could she have been so blind?

She'd been inside her apartment for five minutes when the knock came at the door. It had to be Charlene. For a moment she teetered between pretending she wasn't in and answering it. Since the one person who hadn't let her down yet was Charlene, she decided to open the door.

Instead of Charlene, she found herself face-to-face with Tom.

Anger boiled inside her. "Did you sneak in behind some unsuspecting tenant again?"

He shook his head. "No, I watched someone else punching in the code, so I let myself in."

She snickered. "I shouldn't be surprised. You don't miss a trick, do you, Tom?"

"Cissy, I—" He reached for her.

She stiffened. "Go away. I don't want to talk to you."

"But I want to talk to you. Please give me ten minutes to explain."

"Why should I?" She tried to will herself to slam the door in his face, but she couldn't bring herself to do it.

"Because you're a sensible woman who wants to know the truth."

She let out a sardonic laugh. "Yeah, but whose truth?"

"There is only one truth, Cissy. You and I both know that. Sometimes things aren't as they seem."

"Boy howdy, don't I know that." She remembered walking hand in hand with Tom, feeding each other grapes, and stealing kisses, feeling as though nothing could go wrong. She also remembered telling him way more than she should have, which now that she thought about it was probably the reason he wanted to be with her in the first place. She obviously still had a lot to learn about relationships and big business.

"Please let me explain."

The tug at her heart when she looked at his pleading expression was powerful. Cissy was tempted to invite him in, but the memory of Spencer coming after her made her pause. She narrowed her eyes and tried to picture Tom backhanding her, but even after what he'd done, she couldn't. She might be a bad judge of motives, but she knew for certain Tom Jenkins wasn't a physically violent man.

"Okay, come in, but only for ten minutes…" She glanced at her watch. "Starting now."

Tom's lips started to twitch, but he didn't give her a full-blown smile. Instead, he started talking right away. "The business deal was already in the works. One of our

215

salesmen had been working on getting that account for quite a while, and in fact, that last-minute business trip I took over a week ago was my final attempt to seal the deal. Our securing the Fabulous Threads account had nothing to do with you or anything you told me."

"But you have to admit I told you way more than I should have." She leveled him with what she hoped was a firm look.

"Probably…at least for most people. But you must know that I care about you too much to use you like that."

She folded her arms and shook her head. "I don't know that. In fact, come to think of it, I hardly know you at all, except what I've heard, and it isn't all that great."

"Come on, Cissy. You know that I love the Lord with all my heart. My desire is to live my life for Him, and it's obvious that He wouldn't be happy if I took advantage of you in business…or otherwise."

"What I know about your relationship with the Lord, Tom, is that you attend a church around the corner from my apartment, you hand out sandwiches in the subway, and you make friends with teenage gang members. That's all. It says nothing about how you conduct your business."

"Yes, I do attend church…and all that other stuff. And I now see that I haven't always remembered to follow Christ in my business dealings."

She bobbed her head. "Ya think?"

"I suppose I deserve that." He lowered his head. "Those first few years when I was struggling to save the business, I admit that I did some things that shouldn't have done, including hurting your uncle. I know that what I did when I first started with Sewing Notions Inc. negatively impacted your uncle's business, and I'm truly sorry about that. I have to admit that I still have a lot to learn about what it means to be a Christian in the business world." He ran his fingers through his hair in obvious frustration. "My motives for wanting to be with you have nothing to do with business. You have to see that." He paused. "You do, don't you?"

"Do I know your motives?" She shook her head. "I thought I did, but maybe not. I also know that you're my uncle's biggest domestic competitor, and you stole one of his accounts... right after you got me to talking about business."

"I didn't get you... to talking. Whatever you said was of your own volition."

"But you didn't try to stop me."

A sound of exasperation escaped his lips. "That's because nothing you said wasn't something I already knew!"

"So you just let me chatter on, amusing you with what you call my cute accent." She continued, gathering steam, expressing what she'd feared. "I don't belong here. I don't belong in New York City, I don't belong at Zippers Plus, and I certainly don't belong with you."

He shook his head in genuine disbelief. "You can't possibly mean that."

Tears came to her eyes, threatening to spill over, but she bit her bottom lip and tried to redirect the pain.

"Cissy, I really had a good feeling about you... about us. There is something special between us that I don't think you can deny."

"Please stop." Turning her head, she pointed to the door. "You need to leave now. Your ten minutes are up."

"I understand why you're doing this." He stepped out into the hallway and turned back around with the same intensity in his eyes. "I really do, and I can't say I wouldn't do the same thing. But I would like to ask...no, beg...for you to give this more thought."

Cissy didn't dare to look at him. "I think it's best if you don't call me or come by again."

The old Cissy would have listened to everything he said and buckled. But that was before Spencer. That was before...she really knew Tom. She still had no idea how she would handle this, how she would make things up to her uncle. She might even be out of a job, and then what? Oh, the whole thing was so confusing, and having him here, begging and tugging at her heart, made it worse.

"Please leave," Cissy repeated.

With one long, last sorrowful look, he did just that.

After he left, she let out a heavy breath and slumped against the door. Maybe she could believe that he had secured the account before she leaked anything, but that didn't change the fact that she worked for his competition. She now saw that getting an apartment hadn't been enough to make herself happy. As long as she worked for Zippers Plus, she'd be forced to choose over and over again between loyalty to her uncle and love for Tom. How could she afford her apartment, stay in town, and be in a relationship with Tom if she didn't have her job at Zippers Plus? But how could she in good conscience work for her uncle after he'd found out that she was dating his competition? What a mess she'd made—again.

Tom appeared to have all the traits she was looking for in a man—committed to the Lord, hardworking, kind to others, self-disciplined, considerate, and intelligent. Add all that to the fact that he was amazingly handsome and made her knees go all wobbly, and it was no wonder she had gone against her uncle's wishes and continued seeing Tom even when he expressly forbid it.

Suddenly the irony of the situation slammed her hard. Here she had accused Tom of deceiving her, when it really was she who had deceived him—*and* her uncle. Even though she hadn't blatantly lied, keeping her relationship with Tom a secret was just as bad.

Cissy barely had time to absorb the knowledge of her own guilt when Charlene came knocking. "Hey, girl, I thought you might need a listening ear." She made a funny face. "I ran into Tom in the street a few minutes ago, and he looked pretty miserable."

"I don't think anyone's happy right now—Tom, me, my uncle, or anyone at Zippers Plus." Cissy stepped back. "Come on in. I'll tell you what happened."

"Are you sure?" Charlene walked into the apartment. "I don't want to pry, but I do want to help if I can."

"Tea?"

Charlene nodded. "Sounds good."

After pouring two glasses of sweet tea, Cissy sat in the folding chair across the TV tray from Charlene. "Boy, did I get myself in a pickle." She started from the beginning, when she'd decided to test Tom's integrity in his business by letting a few business details slip out. Then she told of how Uncle Forest had raked her over the coals for divulging business secrets that enabled Tom's company to steal an account right out from under their noses.

Charlene frowned. "I can see how your uncle would be upset, but when someone signs a contract for a new account, especially with a company of any size—and you said this is a big one—they probably have a process that takes many days, weeks, or maybe even months. Tom probably had a deal in the works long before you ever mentioned the account."

Cissy nodded miserably. "That's what Tom said. He

said he was on a business trip to finalize the deal. But that doesn't change the fact that I used some business information to try to test Tom and that I now have to choose between working for my uncle or a relationship with Tom. But I can't even see Tom if I don't have a job with my uncle!"

"Oh, wow." Charlene went silent as she pondered Cissy's dilemma. "You really *have* gotten yourself in a bind."

After several more minutes of silence, Charlene finally said, "Seems like your first step is to talk to your uncle, admit your mistakes, and apologize. Tell him when you mentioned the new account and ask how long it takes to finalize the deal. Then really listen to him and hear what he says."

Cissy nodded slowly. "I dread the thought, but I think you're right."

Charlene gave her a sympathetic glance before lifting her tea glass. She barely wet her lips, so Cissy suspected she was using it as a prop to keep from saying something she was thinking.

"What?" Cissy said.

Charlene squinted. "What what?"

"What are you thinking that you don't want to say?"

"Oh, you're good." Charlene put down her tea glass and folded her hands in her lap. "I was just thinking, where are we going to church tomorrow?"

Cissy leaned back. "I hadn't thought of that. I suppose I should go with Aunt Bootsie. That way I'll have a chance to talk with Uncle Forest before Monday. If he wants to fire me, he can do it without everyone in the office listening."

Charlene scoffed. "Maybe he won't fire you."

"You don't know that."

"Maybe not, but you've got to admit, he's probably feeling

torn about all of this too. He can't let your mama down by firing you, but I'm sure he doesn't want you to keep seeing Tom if it has a chance of hurting his business."

"See!" Cissy moaned. "This is the kind of thing I can't seem to stop doing, even when I try!" She sighed. "I make things impossible for everyone."

Suddenly Charlene grinned. "Not everyone. I know Someone who does an excellent job with anything we think is impossible." She took Cissy's hand and squeezed it. "Let's say a prayer and ask Him for guidance."

Charlene started the prayer, and Cissy followed with her own plea for forgiveness. When they opened their eyes, warmth flowed over Cissy as Charlene smiled back at her.

"Already feels better, doesn't it?"

Cissy nodded. "Yes. It's amazing how knowing that I can rely on the Lord, no matter what, makes everything seem not so impossible." She cleared her throat. "Will you please go with me to Aunt Bootsie's church?"

Charlene's grin remained as she crinkled her nose. "I'm not so sure that's such a good idea. This might be something you need to work through without a stranger in the house."

"Uncle Forest knows you, so you're not a stranger. I really need you for support."

"Well, since you put it that way, of course I'll go."

Chapter 23

SUNDAY MORNING TOM took an extra glance in the mirror on his way out the door and noticed the strain on his face. The realization of how he'd hurt so many people affected him more than any work stress ever had. He needed to focus more on keeping his faith at the forefront of everything in his life. All day Saturday and late into the night he'd prayed that the Lord would somehow guide him in what to do about Cissy, but so far he didn't have an obvious answer. It was probably wishful thinking, but he hoped he might see her in church this morning.

He stood at the door greeting visitors. Every now and then he glanced in the direction of her apartment. By the time the worship team started playing, he knew it was highly unlikely she'd be there.

It took every ounce of brainpower to focus on the sermon. When the service was over, he closed his eyes, inhaled deeply, and slowly let it out.

"Rough week?"

As soon as he heard Lester's voice, Tom opened his eyes. "Yeah."

"Work or girl problems?"

Tom laughed. "Maybe a little of both?"

"I would tell you to pray about it, but I'm sure you've done that already. Anything you want to talk about?"

Tom's first inclination was to say no, but maybe he did need to talk. "Sounds good. How about grabbing a burger? My treat."

"Let me go put my guitar away. I'll be right back."

Tom stood at the door and waited. Every now and then he cast a glance in the direction of Cissy's apartment, but he didn't expect to see her, until he spotted the bright red flash of what looked like her handbag a block away. His pulse quickened, but when it became obvious that it wasn't her, a sense of regret flooded his body.

"Oh man, if I didn't know better I'd think you'd just lost your best friend." Lester walked up to him and clapped him on the shoulder. "Looks like lunch might be a long, sad one today."

"I'll try not to bore you with too many details."

Lester slapped Tom on the back. "No worries. I've dumped enough of my problems on you, it's the least I can do."

Once seated, Tom started with prayer. Lester echoed his amen before he began talking.

"Everything seemed to be just fine—maybe too fine, now that I look back on it. My company is doing great, and then Cissy came along. I was so happy to find a girl I clicked with and who loves the Lord. I was thinking she just might be the one. But now..." Tom shook his head. "She pretty much told me to get lost."

"Is that what she said?" Lester folded the menu and put it down on the table. "Maybe you're reading into things."

"Nah, she let me have it. Her uncle's company considers Sewing Notions Inc. to be his biggest competitor, but in all honesty we don't even come close. I've been wanting to take it in a different direction, get into manufacturing instead, so I'm thinking this might be a good time to do it. It's been on my mind quite a bit lately. In fact, I'd thought that I might even meet with Mr. Counts and work some sort of business deal so he could take over our wholesale accounts once we make the transition."

"Have you told Cissy any of this?"

Tom shook his head. "I don't like talking business when I'm with her. She did say a few things that in the wrong hands could be bad for her uncle, but I didn't do what she accused me of."

Lester gave him a dubious look.

"You believe me, don't you?"

"I have seen the changes, and I don't think you're quite so cutthroat as you used to be in the past, but you have to admit it could look bad." Lester frowned. "She knows where you stand in your faith, right?"

"I thought she did, but obviously she doesn't take me at my word." He cleared his throat. "Can't say I blame her."

"Want me to talk to her?" Lester offered.

"Yeah, and while you're at it, would you mind having a chat with her uncle?"

"You know I would if it would help, but it sounds like that's what you need to do."

Tom nodded soberly. "Yes, I think you're right."

But man, he dreaded having that conversation.

Cissy, Charlene, and Aunt Bootsie walked out of the church, still smiling after the joke the pastor closed with. "Is he always this funny?" Charlene asked.

Aunt Bootsie cackled. "He tries to be, but some of his jokes don't come out the way he wants."

"At least he tries. It's a whole lot better to see people leaving church with smiles on their faces than looking all glum," Charlene said.

"I know." Aunt Bootsie led the way to her car. "Speaking of smiles, I sure hope Forest is in a good mood. He's been mighty upset lately."

"Has he told you why?" Cissy asked, although she suspected she knew the answer. Because her aunt hadn't brought it up, Cissy wondered if she knew anything about the situation with Tom, but she needed to be sure.

Her aunt shook her head. "Something to do with his business. I keep trying to get him to talk about it, but so far he's refused."

If Cissy had any doubt before about the depth of Uncle Forest's anger and pain, the fact that he'd kept it from Aunt Bootsie confirmed it. He typically chatted about his normal workdays, even the moderately stressful ones, but she'd seen him clam up about the real problems.

Aunt Bootsie tipped her head and held her gaze. "Cissy, have you noticed anything unusual happening at work that would upset him?"

Cissy opened her mouth, but Charlene gave her a quick jab in the ribs. Cissy shot her a puzzled look, and Charlene continued to frown. In spite of Charlene's painful warning, Cissy decided to get it out in the open. "We just lost a big account that he'd been hoping for."

Aunt Bootsie gave her a knowing smile. "I do know about that, but there's something else I can't put my finger on."

"Maybe it's that I've been going out with his biggest competitor, and I haven't exactly been straight with him about that." Cissy paused and cleared her throat. "It's not that I came right out and lied or anything, but I guess you can say I was dishonest by not saying anything. You do know I've been seeing Tom Jenkins, don't you?"

Aunt Bootsie nodded. "Yes, of course I do." She patted

Cissy on the hand. "It's not the worst thing you could have done, but it does make things awkward."

But all the way to her aunt and uncle's house, Cissy's stomach churned. She knew she'd have to face Uncle Forest on personal ground sooner or later, but that didn't make it any easier. At least she had Charlene with her. She didn't think he'd totally blow his cool with someone else there.

As they entered the kitchen, the aroma of baked chicken filled their nostrils. Charlene looked like she'd melt right into the hardwood floor. "Now that Cissy has moved out, have you thought about adopting a new niece?"

Aunt Bootsie smiled at her and winked at Cissy. "We're keeping her room open just in case she has a change of heart and decides to move back in, but there is another guest room that I keep thinking we can turn into a sewing room. Problem is, I need Forest's help with that, and when he gets home he's so sick of sewing notions he doesn't want to see another one."

"Where is he?" Charlene asked.

"He has to be in the house somewhere. Forest would never leave with the oven on."

Cissy decided this was as good a time as any to talk to him. "Why don't I go find him? Y'all wait right here."

Aunt Bootsie started to argue with her, but Charlene interrupted her with a question. "So tell me more about your church and how you found it."

Cissy used the opportunity to dash out of the kitchen and up the stairs. When she got to the master bedroom, she saw that the door was partly open, and the bedside lamp was on. She glanced in there and saw Uncle Forest perched on the edge of his bed, a Bible in his lap, bent over with his reading glasses about to fall off his nose.

She knocked lightly. "Uncle Forest, mind if I come in?"

He quickly shut the Bible and placed it on the night-stand. "What do you want, Cissy?" His expression went blank, as though he wanted to hide his feelings. She'd seen him in a variety of moods, but she'd never seen him so...so...closed—much worse than his grouchy grumbling or sudden outbursts.

"Are you reading your Bible?"

He glanced at the book and then turned back to her. "What does it look like I'm doing?"

This was going to be even harder than she thought. "We really need to talk."

"That's the problem, Cissy," he said in a monotone. "You talk entirely too much. I don't understand how you can blab everything and expect people to tell you anything." His tone was flat, and his voice was scratchy, indicating exhaustion.

"Would it help if I said I'm working on that?"

He folded his hands and gave her a blank stare. "I don't know."

"I love and appreciate you and Aunt Bootsie so much, it just kills me to see you so upset." Her chin quivered, so she stopped talking and pulled her lips between her teeth.

Cissy's chest tightened as she saw a look of anguish flash across his face before he quickly extinguished it. She took a few steps closer but stopped a few feet away from him. "I'm really sorry if I really caused you to lose business, Uncle Forest. Will you ever be able to accept my apology?"

He shot her a dubious look. "Maybe, but it'll take some time and some major changes."

She wanted to be a little girl again and throw herself into his arms. But as she watched his demeanor, she realized he was tired and unsure of what to do himself, let alone how to react to her.

It would have been so easy to turn around and leave him sitting there, but she was an adult now. She couldn't always take the easy way out. It was high time she pulled on her big girl pants and accepted responsibility.

She lifted her chin, took a step toward him, and waited for a reaction before proceeding. When he didn't budge, she closed the distance, plopped down on the bed beside him, and put her arm around his rigid shoulders.

"Uncle Forest, Tom came and talked to me Friday night."

He stiffened even more as he pulled away. "Why are you telling me this?"

"He said he had been working on the Fabulous Threads account for weeks, and that what I told him had nothing to do with your losing the sale."

Uncle Forest grunted. "You expect me to believe him?"

"He also said he was sorry about what he did to you when he first started with Sewing Notions Inc. and that he'd never use me to steal your business."

Uncle Forest snorted. "He would say anything to get the girl, just like he would say anything to advance his business."

Cissy shook her head. "I thought so for a while, but now I'm not so sure. I think he's a better person than you give him credit for, and..."

She took a huge breath, then forced herself to continue. "And I think I'm a worse person than you realize."

"Oh yeah? How's that?"

It was difficult for Cissy to put her wrongdoing into words, but she knew she had to do it. "Well, I dated Tom after you told me not to, and I hid it from you. And then I told him a company secret just to find out if I could trust him."

Uncle Forest's jaw dropped. "You're saying you deliberately told him? You weren't doing your normal chatterbox thing?"

Cissy nodded solemnly, waiting for the ax to fall.

But to her surprise, he began to chuckle. And then to laugh. And then howl uproariously. "Ya know, Cissy, you're smarter than I give you credit for. I may not like Tom Jenkins, but it's not my place to stop you from seeing him if that's what you really wanted. I wish you'd been more honest with me."

She lifted her eyebrows. "What would you have done if I'd come right out and told you?"

"At first, I probably would have gotten mad, but after I got over it, I would have cautioned you about what to say and what not to say. You learn soon enough in the business world that you'll be rubbing shoulders with the competition all the time—at trade shows, out on the street, in restaurants. Most people understand the importance of discretion but—"

She interrupted. "You might not believe this, but deep down I understood. And I started to watch what I said around Tom. That's why I feel even worse for using my reputation as a motor mouth so I could test him with a company secret."

Uncle Forest softly chuckled. "If that's what it took to ferret out his character and see if you could really trust him, I see why you did it, especially after what you went through with Spencer."

Cissy mentally scrambled to keep up with the unexpected change in her uncle's response and demeanor. "I will do anything it takes to make things right again, Uncle

Forest. You can take whatever money you lost out of my paycheck until it's all paid back."

"There you go again, speaking before you think." He looked at her with a deep wisdom in his eyes. "You know that's not the answer. It's not just about money or about your mouth or who you see on your own time. It's much more complicated than that."

"I'm really working hard at holding back, but it's not easy for me."

Uncle Forest broke into a smile, and he patted her shoulder. "I know. I remember when you were little and people used to laugh at everything you said, including the most inappropriate things. I told your mama she needed to nip that in the bud, but you were so darn cute."

"Well, I know it's not cute anymore. I'm a grown woman now, and I need to take responsibility for the problems I cause."

He looked her in the eye, and in the course of less than a minute his gaze softened. "Seems to me the biggest problem you have is how to straighten things out with a certain Tom Jenkins."

The conversation had taken so many unexpected turns that she was still struggling to catch up to her uncle's reaction to what she'd done. "So are you going to let me keep working at Zippers Plus?"

"Yes, and I'm not going to forbid you from seeing Tom." He laughed when she gasped. "You've already apologized, and I see some of your points. In fact, you've even given me the desire to talk to the man so I can see—and hear—a few things for myself." He stood and extended a hand to help her up. "Lunch should be ready right about now. What do you say we go on down and enjoy it?"

"I'm starving." The knot in her stomach had loosened,

---

and she was eager to dig in to her aunt's cooking. Cissy led the way to the stairs. "Charlene and I enjoyed church with Aunt Bootsie this morning. I wish you'd gone with us."

"I was thinking the same thing this morning after you left."

Cissy blinked and stopped at the head of the stairs. "Maybe we can come back next week and all go together."

"How about you and your friend find a church closer to your apartment, and Bootsie and I go to our church, just the two of us."

"Are you saying you don't want us here next Sunday?"

He hesitated then nodded. "That's exactly what I'm saying. You and Charlene are grown women, and you live a long way from here. There are plenty of excellent churches that will be much easier for you to get involved with. I just happen to know about one that's walking distance from your place."

"You do?"

He nodded. "It's called Inner City Outreach Church. In fact, I was curious about it, so I visited there a few weeks ago."

Cissy's heart stopped for a couple of seconds. "Um...I'll talk to Charlene about that. I'm sure we'll find a good church...somewhere close."

She practically fell over her own feet as she made her way to the kitchen. Uncle Forest probably had no idea what he'd just suggested, and she wasn't about to tell him right now. There was no way she'd go back to Inner City Outreach Church knowing Tom would be there, at least not until she did some serious thinking and praying about what to do.

Charlene grinned at her as she entered the kitchen. "Your aunt is teaching me how to make flaky biscuits."

"Are you kidding?" Cissy made a face. "I would have thought you knew how."

Charlene shrugged and made a goofy face. "I never really cared how to make 'em as long as there were plenty on the table. Now that's one of the things I miss most from back home."

"Just remember," Aunt Bootsie said, "work the shortening into the flour real good before you add the buttermilk."

Charlene turned back around and beamed. "Mama will be so proud when I tell her I can do this now. She used to try to teach me, but I never listened."

Aunt Bootsie winked at Cissy. "Sometimes young'uns listen to everyone but their parents. I know my own did…that is, until they got old enough to think I had brains."

All four of them, including Uncle Forest, finished preparing lunch. Cissy expected Aunt Bootsie to offer the blessing, but her uncle surprised her as he cleared his throat and instructed them to bow their heads. As he prayed, she heard the conviction in his voice. Something had happened to him, and she knew it was a big deal for him.

When she opened her eyes, she looked around, first at Charlene, who seemed happy as a lark. Then she glanced at Uncle Forest, who did everything he could to avoid her gaze. Aunt Bootsie's eyes were misty, and her chin quivered. Time to lighten things up. This was when she needed to let loose with her motor mouth.

"So Charlene has been showing me around the neighborhood. Now I know where to buy canned food for the best price, and there's a produce stand less than a block away."

Charlene nodded. "The thing I had to get used to was

only buying enough food for a day or two and not try to do a week's worth of grocery shopping. There's not enough room in the itty-bitty kitchen to store more than that."

"What all do you need for your apartment?" Aunt Bootsie asked Cissy. "I have more towels and dishes if you have room for them."

"I'm fine for now. Maybe later I'll look for a small table and chairs, but the TV trays you gave me will work for the time being."

"We can keep our eyes open for some curbside deals," Charlene said.

"Curbside deals?" Aunt Bootsie asked.

Charlene nodded. "Sometimes people put stuff they don't want by the curb. You'll be surprised at the things I've gotten."

Uncle Forest practically choked on his food. "Are you serious? Do you think my niece would actually pick up someone's castoffs from the curb and take them home with her?"

Cissy frowned. Before moving to New York, she never would have dreamed of doing that, but she'd changed. "I might."

They spent the rest of the afternoon talking about how to make the tiny apartment more like home. Aunt Bootsie had some suggestions for the bathroom.

Midafternoon Cissy and Charlene decided to head on back to the city. Uncle Forest offered to drive them, but they wanted to do it on their own.

"It's not like we have to be anywhere on time," Charlene said. "I thought it might be fun to do a little sightseeing on our way home."

Chapter 24

ONCE THEY WERE seated on the bus, Charlene turned to Cissy and grinned. There was no doubt in Cissy's mind that Charlene was about to give her the third degree, and it was coming very soon.

"You looked like you'd just seen a ghost when you and your uncle came into the kitchen," Charlene said. "What did y'all talk about that had you in such a dither?"

"I knew you'd ask me that." Cissy sighed and gave Charlene a sideways glance. "He made a church recommendation."

"Don't tell me; let me guess. Inner City Outreach Church?"

Cissy nodded. "He said he went there a few weeks ago. I have to admit I'm puzzled by that."

"Does he have any idea that's where Tom goes?"

"I have no idea about anything anymore. As soon as I have something figured out, either it changes or I discover a new wrinkle." She didn't want to go into detail about her conversation with her uncle until she had time to absorb it for herself.

"Oh, don't I know it." Charlene grinned. "Life is full of wrinkles, isn't it?"

"Way more than I ever imagined. So let's talk about what church to try next. It'll be fun to research and visit a few places together."

"That's what I'm thinkin'. I hate church shopping all by myself."

Cissy crinkled her nose. "I've always hated that expression. 'Church shopping' makes it seem so trite."

"True. And we don't want the Lord to think we're anything but serious about finding a place to worship."

"I think He knows what's in our hearts." Cissy giggled. "If we're supposed to meet men in church, I have no doubt He'll make it happen."

"Do yourself a favor before you start looking for a new guy," Charlene said, her voice dropping to a more serious tone.

"What's that?"

"Give Tom another chance. Did you talk about him with your uncle?"

"Yes. He gave me a lot to think about." She hoped her clipped answer would let Charlene know she wasn't ready to discuss it yet, and she didn't want to hurt her friend's feelings by coming right out and saying it.

To her relief, Charlene caught on. "Well, I'm sure you have a lot to sort through. Anyway, how about trying New Life Church? They're not too far from the apartment. Only trouble is, they have extremely early services because they use a real estate office that's open on Sundays."

"Okay, we can try that one next," Cissy agreed. "I used to be able to sleep in, but that seems impossible these days anyway."

"Maybe it's the sirens blaring outside your window."

"Could be."

Charlene shrugged. "It may take a while, but you'll eventually get used to it. When I first moved here, I jumped every time I heard a siren. And then I prayed for the person who needed the service. Now I don't even hear it anymore." She frowned. "And now that I think about it, that's pretty sad. I should still pray for the people."

"Maybe we can start a siren ministry," Cissy said.

"Great idea! Every time we hear one, we'll stop what we're doing and pray."

The sound of a siren echoed through the streets as the bus pulled to a stop. Another one several streets over shrieked through the air.

Cissy sighed and shook her head. "With all the sirens around here we'll be praying constantly. Maybe we can have periodic prayers for anyone who needs a paramedic, fireman, or police officer."

"Yeah, like twice a day."

Another siren sounded, making Cissy shiver. "Maybe three times a day would be better."

They got off the bus and started walking toward the subway station. Most of the stores were open, but Cissy had no money to shop, and she wasn't in the mood to just browse. Back before coming to New York, she had plenty of money to buy whatever she wanted. But now that she lived in the midst of some of the best shopping in the world, she couldn't afford it. To make matters worse, homesickness washed over her at the least convenient times throughout the day.

"Why are you suddenly so quiet?" Charlene asked.

"I miss home."

"Yeah, me too. New York is cool and all, but it's different living here. All the stuff I used to do when I visited is out of my price range now."

"You used to visit here?"

Charlene nodded. "Every chance I got. The first time I was in high school. Mama brought me and my sisters for a little back-to-school shopping. We'd been complaining that we were tired of wearing the same thing everyone else wore, so she and Daddy saved up their money for that very special trip." She sighed. "That was my first taste of the Big Apple, and it sure was delicious. And then there was the time when Daddy sprang for what he called a family Broadway vacation, and we stayed at the Marriott Marquis on Times Square. It got me thinkin' about moving here. How about you?"

"This was my first time."

"You didn't even come to visit your aunt and uncle?"

"No, they came down to Alabama to visit us a couple times a year. But I'd seen enough TV shows and movies to have a pretty good idea what it looked like."

"Too bad that what it looks like and how it is to actually live here are two different things."

"Have you ever thought about going back home?" Cissy cast a quick glance at her friend.

Charlene let out a deep sigh. "Unfortunately I don't think I can return to my old life. Now when I go back home, I feel like a stranger." She shrugged. "But maybe. Stranger things have happened."

A pang struck Cissy hard. "If it weren't for what happened with Spencer, I might actually consider moving home. According to Mama, folks are still talking about it, so moving back isn't an option for me yet. And by the time they move on to something else, I'm afraid I'll wind up just like you." The instant those words escaped Cissy's lips, she gasped and covered her mouth with her hand. "I am so sorry. That didn't come out at all like I'd intended."

Charlene laughed so hard she snorted. "I know what you meant."

"Will I ever learn to keep my trap shut?"

"I think so." Charlene put her arm around Cissy and squeezed. "But don't stop completely. That's part of your charm. A few extra filters will be good, but I still enjoy some of your spontaneous comments."

"I'm getting hungry," Cissy said.

"Are you kidding me? After all that food your aunt fed us?"

Cissy glanced at the time on her phone. "It's been a few hours, and I've worked up an appetite."

"Okay, let's stop at that deli."

As they stood in the long line, Cissy listened to the noise, wishing she could be back home, either with Mama and Daddy or in one of the apartments she'd shared with friends over the past couple of years. She actually missed the sound of birds and the occasional, "Hey, how are you?" from people she didn't know.

Almost as though she'd dreamed it, she heard a soft Southern accent at the head of the line. "I'd like a pastrami on rye please. Hold the mayo." There was a slight pause. "And a bottle of spring water please."

Cissy leaned over to see who was talking, but Charlene yanked her back. "Did you hear that? There's another one of us."

"We gotta see who it is and find out where she's from." Cissy stepped to the side and spotted the woman handing her money to the guy behind the counter. "I bet she leaves as soon as she gets her sandwich."

"Tell me what you want, and I'll get it while you go talk to her."

Two minutes later Cissy chased the woman out the door. "Hey, wait up."

The woman glanced over her shoulder as she quickened her step.

"I couldn't help but overhear your accent," Cissy hollered. "I'm from Alabama."

The woman stopped in her tracks, spun around, and a slow grin spread across her face. "I'm from Mississippi."

Cissy caught her breath as she approached the woman. "My name is Cissy, and I've only been here a few weeks. My friend Charlene is from Atlanta."

"I'm Bethann." The woman shifted from one foot to the other. "Do y'all live here?"

Cissy nodded. "Yes, how about you?"

Bethann's smile faded. "No, I'm just here stayin' with my aunt. She took sick, and my parents are worried about her, so they sent me to check on how she's doing."

"I'm sorry to hear that."

Charlene scurried toward them, holding out a bag. "I didn't know if you wanted pickles, so I told them to put them on the side."

Cissy took the bag and gestured toward Bethann. "This is Bethann from Mississippi." She relayed the information about the woman's sick aunt.

"I am so sorry about your aunt. If there is anything you need—"

Bethann shook her head. "I'm just here for a few days. She's actually my mother's aunt, and she's gettin' up there in years. She refuses to go to a nursin' home, so I think I'll have to find someone to come by to help with some of the...you know, normal things like bathin' and eatin' and all that. Mama wants me to think about movin' in with her, but I'm not sure I'll fit in." She gestured around. "This is so different from back home."

"You can say that again." Charlene shook her head. "I'm so sorry to hear about your aunt."

Bethann sighed. "I just wish I knew someone who could check on her every once in a while."

Cissy took a step back. She wanted to help, but she

wasn't into caring for the sick. Charlene, on the other hand, seized the opportunity to show her hospitality.

"I'm not too far away. I can—"

"Oh, no, that's awfully sweet of you, but I'm talkin' about a home health care agency...at least for the time bein' until I can give notice on my job and find someone to move in with my roommates...that is, if I decide to do what Mama wants me to do."

Cissy let out a sigh of relief. "So you're actually thinking about moving up here?"

Bethann nodded. "Yes, but I reckon I don't have to tell y'all how scared I am. I've never lived in a big city like this, and it's overwhelming." She shrugged. "I was hoping that I could go back to Mississippi with the news that everything was just hunky dory here." She lowered her head as a look of consternation came over her. "But it's not. I hadn't seen her in about three years, and during that time she's really gone downhill. It's just so worrisome."

"We'll pray for her," Charlene said.

Bethann's eyes lit up. "That is so sweet! Do y'all have a church here?"

"Not exactly." Charlene cast a glance at Cissy. "I used to, but my church hasn't fared very well, so we're going to start looking next week."

"Maybe if I move here, I can go with y'all." She took a step back. "I really need to run now. I don't want my aunt worryin' about me. Thank y'all so much for stoppin' me and introducin' yourselves. Y'all were a gift from God!"

Charlene hugged Bethann. "Our pleasure. Before you leave, why don't I give you my phone number in case you have questions or need something?"

"Y'all are the sweetest two people I've met since I've been here!"

The three of them exchanged phone numbers before Bethann disappeared down the street. "We definitely need to pray for her and her aunt," Charlene declared.

"Yes, of course."

Cissy's feet ached but not as much as her heart. The homesickness that had been tugging on her lately was compounded by meeting Bethann. They finally got back to their apartment building right as it was getting dark.

"I can't believe I'm so tired, and it's not even eight o'clock yet," Cissy said as she took her shoes off in the elevator.

"You're getting old," Charlene teased. "I think I'll go in and watch something on TV. Wanna join me?"

Cissy shook her head. "I think I'll read for a little while."

"I can't believe you still don't have a TV."

"I know. I used to watch it a lot, but now I prefer to read when I get home."

"Must be a good book."

"It is." Cissy smiled. "I'll let you borrow it when I'm finished."

She trudged toward her apartment and hesitated at the door. The apartment seemed to shrink each time she entered it, and it still didn't feel like home. A deeper wave of homesickness washed over her. Maybe she could go back home soon. She didn't think Uncle Forest would put up much of an argument after all the things she'd done to mess up his business. It seemed as though everywhere she went, she left a trail of destruction. And now she wasn't sure if it was even possible to recover from her biggest disaster—her relationship with Tom Jenkins.

Chapter 25

MONDAY MORNING TOM sat at his desk and tried hard to concentrate on the numbers on the spreadsheet in front of him, but Cissy's image kept popping into his head. He had tried to call her several times yesterday, but she never answered. He left one message, asking her to call. Other than that he had no idea what to do next.

He picked up his cell phone again, pulled Cissy's number up on the screen, and stared at it. As much as he wanted to call her, he knew she'd probably spit fire at him, or worse, continue to ignore his calls. And he didn't think it was appropriate to try to straighten out this mess during the workday. He thought about calling Charlene, but that didn't seem like a good idea either. Then he thought about Dave. Even though Dave worked for Zippers Plus, he still seemed open to talking with him when they passed on the street. Tom didn't know Dave very well, but he wondered if perhaps the guy was keeping his options open in case things didn't work out at his current employer.

After more than an hour of not being able to concentrate, Tom decided to go for a walk. He had to get out of the office and burn off some of his frustration, so he picked up his gym bag, ducked into the men's room, and changed into his workout clothes. Marianne waved and smiled as he walked past her on his way out.

"I'll be back after lunch," he said.

"Take your time. The work will be here when you get back."

Once Tom got to the gym, he hopped right on the elliptical and went full throttle. One of the trainers walked up, leaned on the equipment, and blew out a low whistle. "The only time I ever see someone pushing that hard, it's woman problems."

Tom slowed down a bit and laughed. "Woman, business, life…everything."

"If you get the woman issue settled, the rest of it will all fall into place."

Tom thought about that comment as he did his best to maintain a steady pace without pushing so hard. The trainer's advice was close, but Tom knew that one element—God—took priority over everything. He'd prayed about what to do about Cissy and his work, but he wasn't so sure he'd listened to God's answers.

As Tom continued his workout, he prayed silently and then stopped, hoping for some divine advice. His mind became silent, and his heart grew heavier by the minute. Then he remembered something the pastor had told him years ago when he'd lost the desire to work for Wall Street. *Sometimes silence is the answer we need for the moment.*

It was time for a change of scenery. He stopped off at a deli he'd wanted to try and brought his bagged lunch to a park where he'd never been. As he ate, he thought about his predicament and wondered why the answer hadn't come to him sooner. The only solution he could think of was to act more quickly on his plan to transition to manufacturing instead, and it actually made business sense to move forward since he struggled to meet the expectations of some of his high-end designer clients.

By the time he returned to work after lunch, he was exhausted. Marianne took one look at him and laughed.

"I've never seen you like this. The love bug must have bitten harder than I realized."

"I don't know what you're talking about."

With that he went into his office, closed the door, and prayed for guidance for what he knew he needed to do next. He had all his ducks in a row to start manufacturing by the next quarter. He'd have to operate in the red for a while, but he'd already counted on that. Besides starting early, the biggest difference between his current plan and what he'd originally wanted to do was that there would be less overlapping of the two businesses. It would also mean working longer hours for a month or two, but that never bothered him before. Maybe once he got the ball rolling on the new business, everything else would work itself out.

He punched in Marianne's number. "Can you come to my office?"

"Is it urgent?"

He hesitated. "Yes, it's very urgent."

"I'll be right there."

As soon as Marianne showed up at the door, she paused, took a long look at him, and then walked into his office, closing the door behind her. "Looks like you have something big up your sleeve."

"I've decided to start manufacturing right away."

Marianne tipped her head forward. "Does this have anything to do with a cute Southern gal?"

"Maybe." He leaned back and steepled his fingers.

"That's as good of a reason as any, as long as you've prayed about this decision."

He nodded. "I have, and there's no doubt in my mind that it's the right thing to do. Here's what I need from you."

They spent the next hour chatting about all the things they needed to do first and how he'd share his plans with the rest of the employees. Marianne offered a few words of advice, and he fully planned to use them.

All day Monday Uncle Forest acted strange. Cissy expected him to snap out of it by Tuesday, but when she arrived in the office at her normal time and he wasn't there, she knew something was different.

Dave gave her a brief nod as she sat down at her desk and booted up her computer. "Good morning."

"Hey." Cissy dropped her handbag into the bottom file drawer. "Have you seen my uncle?"

"No." Dave propped his elbows on his desk, and she saw his puzzled expression.

"That's odd."

"Yeah, I know. This is the first time since I've worked here that he hasn't gotten to the office before me."

"I hope I didn't mess up something else." Cissy contorted her face. "He probably dreads seeing my face in the office."

Dave did a cocky head bob. "I hate to break it to ya, darlin', but it ain't always about you."

She leaned back and laughed. "That's the worst imitation of a Southern accent I've ever heard."

"Aw shucks," he said, continuing with the accent. "I spent half the evenin' last night practicin', and you mean ta tell me I still ain't got it right?"

"Drop the *ain't*. Not all Southerners use that word."

"What word do they use?"

Cissy shook her head, still laughing. "Don't assume we have bad grammar just because we have a drawl. And we all use different words, but most of us say *y'all*."

"I'm never sure how to use that word."

"Give it a shot."

"So where are y'all goin' to lunch today?"

"All depends on who you are talking to. If it's just me, you don't say *y'all*...at least I don't."

"What would you say?"

She bugged her eyes. "You."

"This is much more complicated than I ever would have thought." He scratched his head. "I thought plural was *all y'all*?"

"*Y'all* is plural. *All y'all* is more inclusive and extends beyond the people standing right there with you."

"Well, slap my granny. It's all so confusin'."

Cissy almost fell out of her chair laughing so hard. "Where on earth did you hear that?"

"Sounds like I got it wrong again." He made a face. "I guess it's back to the drawing board. I found some old clips of *Hee Haw* on YouTube and replayed them a few times."

"If you're gonna watch video clips, maybe you should watch something a little more accurate, like *Designing Women*."

Dave scrunched his nose. "Not in this lifetime. My mother—or should I say, my mama—used to torture me with it every Monday night."

"Well, I like it."

He flipped his hand. "Must be a chick thing. Anyway, the point is, I don't think you have anything to do with your uncle's mood."

The elevator dinged, and out stepped Uncle Forest. He looked directly at Cissy and pointed to his office door. "My office. Now."

On her way past Dave's desk, she whispered, "What were you saying?"

He grimaced. "Never mind."

Cissy's knees wobbled as she approached Uncle Forest's office. He didn't look up at her, but she still had the feeling he was watching out of the corner of his eye.

"Close the door and have a seat," he instructed.

She quickly did as she was told. "D-did I do something wrong... again?"

He slowly looked up and met her gaze, an odd expression covering his face. "Now what makes you think that?"

She blinked. "Um, you sound mad... and since I... well..."

He faked a smile. "Maybe I am." His jaw tightened. "I got a call early this morning from your friend."

"My friend?"

"*Mm-hmm.* Now why do you think Tom Jenkins would call me?"

"Oh, that friend." She'd automatically assumed he'd meant Charlene. "I have no idea. What did he say?"

"I don't know. I didn't talk to him. He left a message saying he wanted to see me as soon as possible."

Cissy frowned. "So are you going to meet with him?"

"All depends on what he wants." He leaned back in his chair, propped his elbows on the arms, and steepled his fingers as he held her gaze. "I assume it has something to do with you."

"Why would you assume that? Maybe he wants to apologize for stealing your account."

Uncle Forest's eyes practically bugged out of his head. "You're kidding, right? I know you're naïve, but you have to know better than that."

Cissy shrugged. "It was just a thought. Why do you think he would call you to talk about me? He knows my number."

He pulled his head back. "Are you taking his calls?"

"Um…" She'd ignored the first several of his calls and eventually blocked his number. "No."

"There ya go."

"So what do you want me to do about this?" Cissy asked. She knew she sounded sarcastic, but so much had happened over the past couple of months she didn't care. So what if she went back to Alabama? What was the worst thing that could happen? No one would talk to her, or Spencer would come after her when he got out of jail? She could deal with no one talking to her, and she'd make sure she only went places where there were lots of people. Even Spencer wasn't stupid enough to take action when his adoring fans were around.

Uncle Forest leaned forward and held her gaze. "I want you to call your friend and ask him what he wants."

"No, I'm not doing that."

He pointed his finger toward the door. "Oh, yes, you will. You're on my dime now. Do it and then come back and tell me what he said."

"But Uncle Forest…" She cleared her throat to try to get rid of the whininess even she could hear.

"Just do it." His tone left no room for argument. He punched a button on his computer keyboard and gave all his attention to the monitor, letting her know he was done with her.

As she passed Dave's desk, he let out a low whistle. "Judging by your expression, that must have been bad."

"The worst." She swallowed hard.

"Care to give me a hint?"

She looked directly at Dave. "He wants me to call Tom."

Dave shoved his chair back and gave her a look of incredulity. "You're kidding."

"Nope." She pulled out her cell phone and stared at it.

"So are you going to do it?"

"I don't want to, but I don't see that I have a choice."

"This is one of those times I don't envy you being related to the boss."

"Do you ever envy me?" She asked.

He shrugged. "Sometimes. You can mess up in a big way, and he won't fire you."

Cissy chewed on her bottom lip. "But I know he probably wants to, which is what makes it even more complicated. If I could go home now, I would."

"Wouldn't that be running from your problems?" He folded his arms as she took in that question. "Want to know what I'd do if I were you?"

"Not really, but go ahead and tell me since I know you're dyin' to."

He smiled. "Take advantage of the situation. Do what your uncle says. Call Tom and try to make things right."

"Are you talking about making things right with Tom or my uncle?"

"Your uncle for sure. Tom is up to you. Just keep your head straight and learn what you can. After a few months maybe things will have died down in Alabama, and then you can go back home to start over there, and you'll have some decent business experience to add to your résumé."

That made sense. Cissy smiled. "Ya know, Dave, you keep getting a whole lot smarter by the day."

"Maybe you can tell your uncle how brilliant I am. I like my job, and I want to keep on moving up in the company."

She knew he was aware that she didn't have that kind of clout, but she played along. "I'll make sure to do whatever I can to help make that happen."

"Now call Tom and find out what he wants." He pointed

to her phone. "Why don't you take it to the conference room?"

Without another word Cissy walked into the conference room and closed the door behind her. She sank down into the chair and lowered her head. *Lord, I have no idea what to say, and I pray that I won't be put on the spot. Please stand beside me during this conversation with the guy I thought I could fall in love with.* She opened her eyes then slammed them shut again. *And don't let me say anything I shouldn't.*

Tom answered before the first ring ended. "Cissy? I've been wanting to talk to you. Why haven't you taken my calls?"

In spite of her nervousness the sound of his voice made her tingle all over. "Hey, this is my call, so let me ask the questions."

"Okay."

"My uncle said you left a message for him to call you back. What do you want?"

"It's strictly business." His tone changed and sounded much colder.

"So it has nothing to do with me?"

A long silence fell between them.

"Well?" she asked. "Are you gonna answer my question?"

"I would like to talk about us, but that's between you and me. The call I made to your uncle is business related. It's something only he and I can discuss."

"Oh." She tried to disguise her disappointment, but she wasn't sure she was successful.

"Let him know that I'd like to meet with him soon. I'll be available most of today and at various times throughout the rest of the week."

"Is that all?" Cissy said. "You can't even give me a hint of what this is all about?"

"It's a rather complex issue, so it's probably best if I just wait and discuss it with him. Let him know that this is not an adversarial request. I think he'll like what I have to say."

"Okay. I'll tell him."

"Cissy?"

The softness in the way he said her name sent her senses on alert. "What?"

"I'm sorry about what happened. If there's anything I can do or say, I would—"

Cissy interrupted. "This call was strictly business at Uncle Forest's request. I'm on company time, so I can't discuss my personal life with you right now. I'll give my uncle your message as soon as I get off the phone." She knew her tone sounded clipped, but she didn't want to let her personal feelings interfere with what she needed to do for Uncle Forest. Right now his business needs came before what she wanted.

She heard the *whoosh* of his breath as he sighed. "Okay, if that's the way it has to be, I'll accept it for now. We can talk later."

Numb from head to toe Cissy ended the connection without even a good-bye. Her one chance to clear the air with Tom had been handed to her on a silver platter, but the timing had been off. *Lord, please give me this chance again, only I'd appreciate it if it's when I'm not working!*

Chapter 26

A**FTER THE FINAL** click Tom pressed the off button on his phone and leaned back in his chair, staring at the wall. He'd had to exercise patience in business in the past, and that was one of the things that had given him an edge in negotiations. However, this was different. His heart was involved.

Lord, guide me through these turbulent times. I have no idea what lies ahead, but whatever You've chosen for me to face, give me the strength to deal with it.

He didn't know when to expect Mr. Counts's call, or if he'd even hear from him, so he got up and walked out to see what Marianne had on her agenda. He needed her to go to the Chamber of Commerce meeting later if she had time.

"Sure, I'll go," she said. "I just had an appointment cancel, so my whole afternoon is free."

The office phone lit up right before it rang. Marianne leaned over to make sure the receptionist would catch it before settling back to talk to Tom.

"I've been working on the information you want to present to the salesmen," she said. "One thing I don't have is the list of job descriptions you'll need for the new company."

"Excuse me, Tom."

He glanced over and saw Stella smiling apologetically. "What do you need?"

"Mr. Counts is on the phone. I knew you would want to talk to him, or I wouldn't have interrupted you."

"Okay, I'll go to my office and take the call. Tell him I'll be right there."

Marianne smiled but didn't say a word as she turned her chair back to face her desk. He appreciated her ability to read him well enough to know when to talk and when to remain silent.

He picked up the phone in his office with a shaky hand. "Tom Jenkins here."

"What do you want that's so urgent?" The gruffness of Mr. Counts's tone cracked, allowing his weariness to come through.

Tom licked his lips, which had suddenly gone dry. "I've had a business plan in the works for some time now, and I would like to discuss it with you."

"Business plan? I hardly think that anything Sewing Notions Inc. does would interest me." Mr. Counts didn't even bother trying to hide his distrust.

"This is different, and it just might interest you."

"I don't think—"

"At least hear me out. Please let me buy you lunch. I can present what I have, and if you aren't interested, we can shake hands and part ways."

There was a long enough pause to let Tom know there might be a possibility. "When?"

"Today?"

Mr. Counts snorted. "You don't believe in wasting time, do you? My niece must have really gotten under your skin."

"This isn't about your niece. It's about Sewing Notions Inc. and Zippers Plus."

"Oh, I'm sure it has something to do with my niece. You can't convince me otherwise."

Tom didn't bother trying to argue with Mr. Counts,

particularly since he was partially right. "Can you meet me at Mario's Bistro around one o'clock?"

"I generally like to eat lunch earlier than that."

Okay, so Mr. Counts was testing him. Tom could certainly understand. "What time sounds good to you?"

Mr. Counts made a few sputtering sounds before blurting, "Let's beat the lunch crowd and meet at eleven thirty."

"Perfect." After hanging up, Tom glanced up at the clock and headed out the door of his office. "Stella, would you mind making some copies of the file on my desk? I have to run a quick errand, and I'll need that when I get back."

"Sure thing," Stella said as she stood and headed for Tom's office.

He glanced over his shoulder as he brushed past her and saw Marianne standing in the doorway of her newly decorated office, arms folded, one eyebrow lifted, and a silly grin on her face. Before she had a chance to tease him, he left.

Fortunately his buddy Anthony, the owner of Massaro's Office Supplies, was in today. "Any way you can do a rush order on a nameplate for me?" Tom asked.

"You're in luck. My engraver is in today."

Tom gave him clear instructions on what he wanted. "I'll wait."

Anthony gave him a nod. "With all the business you've brought to me over the past couple of years, I owe you, so I won't charge you the rush fee."

"You know I don't mind paying it," Tom said.

"I know, and that makes it all the better to not charge you."

A half hour later Tom was on his way back to his office with the nameplate in hand. He'd decided not to have it wrapped. Instead he folded the paper bag over it several times and secured it with tape.

Stella grinned. "Copies are made and on your desk."

"Thanks!" Tom closed his office door and spent the rest of the morning going over what he planned to talk to Mr. Counts about. Then he remembered that part of his new plan included involving the Lord in all his business dealings, so he said a prayer asking for guidance and blessings.

At eleven fifteen he left the office and walked toward the restaurant. Mario's Bistro was moderately priced, so he wouldn't appear too pretentious, but it was a nice enough place to conduct a business lunch. Tom had enough experience from Wall Street and Sewing Notions Inc. to know how critical it was to walk that fine line.

To his surprise Mr. Counts was waiting by the hostess desk when he entered the restaurant. "I'm glad you were able to do this on such short notice."

"Yeah, well, I'm pretty busy, so I can't stay long." Mr. Counts turned toward the hostess. "You can seat us now."

"Right this way, gentlemen."

Tom followed behind Mr. Counts, continuing to pray for the right words. As soon as they were seated, Mr. Counts pointed to the paper bag sticking out of Tom's shirt pocket.

"Nice accessory you got there. I would think after using my niece to steal a huge chunk of my business, you'd be able to afford a pocket square and a nicer briefcase."

Ouch. Tom momentarily pondered not following through with his plan, but he knew what he had to do. He pulled out the bag and laid it on the table.

"So what is it?" Mr. Counts asked.

"Before I tell you, I would like to let you know that it was never my intention to use your niece to steal your business or do anything unethical."

"*Humph.* That's what she told me, but I'm not sure I believe that." Mr. Counts lifted the glass of ice water but put it back down on the table without taking a sip. He leaned forward and placed his face much closer to Tom's than was comfortable. "Listen to me, young man. The bad business deals you make today will come back to haunt you…maybe tomorrow or maybe even years later."

Tom shook his head. "I can certainly understand what you're saying, which is why I've decided to move forward with something I've been thinking about for quite some time."

"What's that? Taking over all the sewing notions businesses in the US?" Mr. Counts shook his head. "Not gonna happen…not as long as I have a breath left in my body."

Losing the account must have affected Zippers Plus much worse than he realized. Tom inhaled deeply as he held Mr. Counts's gaze. "I'm not going to take over any sewing notions business…at least not wholesale. I'm changing the direction of Sewing Notions Inc. and I would like to work a deal with Zippers Plus."

"No way."

Tom reached for the folded brown bag, slowly unfolded it, pulled out the nameplate, and placed it on the table. Mr. Counts squinted at it, glanced up at Tom with a puzzled expression, and then back down at the nameplate. Tom had engraved *Forest Counts, CEO*, above the names of two businesses: his and his competitor's.

"What's this all about?" Mr. Counts demanded. "Have you gone and lost your mind or something?"

Tom shook his head. "Nope. I had this made in good faith so you would at least listen and consider a deal I'm offering."

Mr. Counts lifted his hands and shook his head. "I'm

not buying your business from you, if that's what you're asking. You can't steal my accounts and then try to sell them back to me."

"That's not what I'm asking." Tom leaned forward on his elbows. "I would like to gradually shift from wholesaling and distribution to manufacturing."

"Manufacturing? Why would you go and do something like that?"

"As you know, it's getting increasingly expensive to import some of the products we sell, especially the higher quality ones. With the trend of some of our more exclusive accounts wanting to buy as much American-made as possible, I'd like to give them what they're asking for. There is also a need for products we can't find."

Tom paused to see if Mr. Counts wanted to comment, but he didn't say a word. He just stared back, in apparent shock. Tom continued. "I've managed to secure the facility, and I'm having some older machines retooled to make the notions I'd like to offer."

"So what is it you want me to do with your business?" Forest asked.

"I thought we could work a deal that is mutually agreeable."

"I don't know if any such deal exists."

"I think it does. In fact, I have some thoughts sketched out here." Tom lifted his briefcase and pulled out some papers. "Why don't I give you an overview while we're waiting for our food? This is your copy, so you can take it back to your office and look over it at your leisure. Just remember that this is open for adjustment and negotiation."

To Tom's relief, Mr. Counts took the papers, although somewhat reluctantly. "Let's see what you got...not that

I'm interested or anything. I just wonder how a mind like yours thinks."

Tom allowed a twitch of a grin, but it didn't last long. "This is the schedule of the transition and how we can handle the merger financially," he continued.

"Merger? You didn't say anything about a merger. Why would I want to merge with someone who starts rumors about my company and then turns around and steals my hard-earned business?"

Tom's face tightened. "Okay, let's get this straight, once and for all. I never started a single rumor about your business. All that happened before I ever took over Sewing Notions Inc. I'll tell you what I did do, and what I'm sorry for." And then Tom apologized for offering larger accounts the loss leaders that he knew Mr. Counts couldn't match and still make a profit. He also asked forgiveness for implying that Mr. Counts was having a mental breakdown during an extended vacation a couple of years earlier. "I never came right out and said as much, but when one of the account managers mentioned the rumor, I didn't say anything. Even though I didn't say it, I know it was still wrong to let anyone believe that."

"Yeah, that was a low blow," Mr. Counts said. "I've worked hard to get where I am, and to have someone like you..." Tom could see the pain on the older man's face as he tightened his jaw.

"I'm very sorry, and that will never happen again. When I bought this business, I had just left Wall Street, and I had no idea what I was doing. All I knew was that it was in a heap of trouble."

"That's no excuse. What you did—"

"Yes, I was a shark, and I'm sorry about that. You may not understand this, but I was acting out of desperation.

It was wrong for me as a Christian to leave my faith at the office door. Now that it's been pointed out to me, I'm working on changing my business tactics." Tom held Mr. Counts's gaze, knowing the older man was measuring him—not just for his business integrity, but also for whether he was worthy of his niece.

"Well…" The older man paused, appearing to collect his thoughts. "I'm willing to forgive your questionable business deals, but there is still that issue of dating my niece behind my back."

Tom's breath caught in his throat. "You mean Cissy never told you she was seeing me?"

Mr. Counts slowly shook his head.

Tom frowned. "I should have realized that, but I'll take responsibility for her secrecy. After all, she's a very sweet woman who didn't want to fan the flames of anger, and she was fully aware of the bad blood between our companies."

For the first time Tom fully realized the awful position he'd put Cissy in. Here he'd been so taken by her that he'd never given full thought to how being with her affected the other relationships in Cissy's life—not to mention her professional life. He'd very nearly destroyed both!

Tom apologized again. "Sir, I am so very sorry. I was blinded to the implications because of my feelings for her. It's rare to find someone who loves God as much as I do. She's such a breath of fresh air and so much fun to be around…"

"That you didn't think."

Tom nodded as he fell into a glum silence, sure he had ruined things forever.

Mr. Counts began to chuckle. Surprised, Tom looked up.

"My niece does have that effect on men," Mr. Counts

said. "Trying to grasp Cissy is like...trying to catch a butterfly. Every time you think you've got her...she flitters away."

Tom leaned back and nodded ruefully. "That is exactly how it is."

"Now that I think about it, I understand something else she did that made no sense at the time."

"What?"

Mr. Counts smiled. "Why she left my perfectly fine house and moved into that horrible apartment." He gave Tom a knowing look.

Tom was aghast. "She did that for me?" "That's what I'm thinkin'."

Light bulbs were going off all over the place. "So without knowing it I put her in an even more precarious situation, professionally and financially." He gestured toward the papers in front of them. "No doubt you see my attempt at solving this...issue as ridiculous and unworkable."

Mr. Counts leaned back, folded his arms, and gave Tom a long, assessing look. "Not really. Actually I'm happy to see your humanness." He paused as he leaned forward and propped his forearms on the table. "In fact, I see that there just might be something to your business proposition, but I do have a few questions."

"That's what we're here for," Tom said. "I'll be happy to answer any questions you have."

"In a nutshell, how do you propose we handle the accounts your salesmen have taken on? Don't tell me you're ethical in one breath and in another you'd hand everything over to me, leaving them stranded."

"No, that's not what I'd do. This is where it could get somewhat complicated. You'd have to be in a position to take on at least four new salespeople."

Mr. Counts frowned. "Four? I just happen to know that you have at least twice that many working on national accounts."

"I do, but some of them would go with me. I'll need a sales force for the new company."

Mr. Counts lifted the papers and started to shuffle through them. His expression slowly changed as he went from one to the next, carefully studying those with numbers on them.

The server arrived with their plates, so Tom shoved some more papers into an envelope that he handed to Mr. Counts. "You don't have to give me an answer now. Take a little time to go over this."

"How much time?" Mr. Counts asked.

"I can give you at least a week before we get together again to iron out some of the details."

"A week isn't very long for a business decision of this magnitude."

"I'm aware of that, so if you need longer, let me know. But first please read what I put together. You can have your accountant and attorney take a look at it as well. I want to make sure everything is done to the satisfaction of both parties."

"I could give you an answer now," Mr. Counts said. "It isn't likely—"

"Please at least look at it." Tom gestured toward the food. "How's your pasta?"

"Good." Mr. Counts lifted his fork and ate a few more bites before shoving away from the table. "I need to get back to the office. There's work waiting for me, and unlike some business owners I don't leave everything in the hands of my employees."

Tom smiled as he started to reach for the check. "Understood."

"I'll get lunch," Mr. Counts said as he made a grab for the check.

Before he could get his hands on it, Tom picked it up. "No, I called this meeting, so I'm the one who should pay."

After the server took the money, Mr. Counts held up the envelope. "I'm not sure when I'll have time to look at this...maybe not even before your deadline, but it is an interesting proposition. Does anyone else know about it?"

"Just a few trusted employees, my accountant, and my lawyer." Tom nodded toward the envelope. "If you decide you're interested, I'm willing to answer any questions that you, your accountant, or attorney has, and I'll meet with them if you'd like."

"That goes without saying."

"I can call you in a few days to set up another meeting."

"Oh, about calling me..." Mr. Counts reached into his pocket, pulled out one of his business cards, and jotted down his cell phone number. "Don't call the office. Use this number. I don't want folks in the office to speculate."

Tom took the card and stuck it in his own pocket. "I understand."

"I don't want you telling Cissy about this either," Mr. Counts added.

"You don't have to worry about that. She's not speaking to me."

The server returned with the receipt, so both men stood. Tom led the way out of the restaurant and turned to face the older man when they reached the sidewalk. "I enjoyed lunch, Mr. Counts. I hope to have the opportunity to do business with you in the future." He extended his hand.

Mr. Counts stared at Tom's hand for a split second

before grasping it. Tom suspected the man's pride made it difficult, but he clearly was a Southern gentleman at heart. As they parted ways, Tom silently prayed for the Lord's will to be done.

As soon as Tom walked into his office, he started working out the details of the merger, just in case Mr. Counts went along with his plan. Even if he didn't, some changes needed to be made to transfer some people over to the manufacturing side of the business. He placed a quick call to a couple of the accounts he personally handled, letting them know that he was downsizing his wholesale business. He recommended they go with Zippers Plus.

By late afternoon he had the basic skeleton of the ideal plan and an alternate one laid out. He called Marianne to his office and went over everything with her. She had a few suggestions that he added. When they were finished, she stood and grinned down at him.

"Why are you smiling at me like that?"

Her smile widened. "I'm happy that you've finally allowed the Lord into the office."

"Oh, He was here. The problem was me and the fact that I ignored Him. That's all going to change."

Chapter 27

WEDNESDAY MORNING CISSY stood at her uncle's office door, fear welling in her throat. Finally she forced herself to knock.

"Come in."

She turned the knob and entered. "How was your lunch meeting yesterday?"

"Good." He leaned back, clasped his hands behind his head, and stared at her. "I'm busy. What do you need?"

"I've been thinking that maybe you made a mistake by asking me to come work for you."

"Huh?" He straightened up and pulled his chair closer to his desk. "Sit down and let's discuss this."

Her insides churned, as she knew what she had to say. She was tired of always feeling like nothing she did was the right thing, and it was time to make things right. "Uncle Forest, if you want me to go back to Alabama, I will. Just say so. If you're worried about what Mama will say, I'll just tell her I was homesick. I don't want to keep messing things up for you. I know how important your business is, and—"

"That's just it, Cissy." Uncle Forest rubbed the back of his neck.

"What's just it?"

"My business. It is important to me. Perhaps too important."

"Wha—?"

"I've been doing quite a bit of thinking lately, and last night Bootsie and I had a long talk."

"Is everything okay between you two?"

"On a personal level, yes, but business is altogether different. I've let it cloud my judgment on personal matters." He leaned back in his chair and tilted his head as he studied her. "You, on the other hand, know how to live life. You're carefree and find joy in the moment."

"I do?" Cissy hadn't expected the conversation to go in this direction. "So why are you so mad at me all the time?"

"Mad at you?" He let out a low chuckle and cleared his throat. "I'm not mad at you." He pursed his lips.

"Who are you mad at?"

He shrugged and leaned forward. "Myself. You really like that Tom Jenkins guy, don't you?"

She slowly nodded. "Yes, I do... or at least I did like him. A lot." She sniffled. "But I don't appreciate him using me to steal your business."

He squirmed around in his seat as he glanced around his office. "Do you realize how many hours I've put into this business to make it what it is today?"

She nodded. "Yes... at least I think I do." *Uh oh, here it comes. The lecture.*

"I'm afraid I've been wrong all these years."

Whoa. She didn't expect that comment. "Wrong?"

"Yeah. I spent so much time making sales, doing what I thought I needed to do to make this business successful, but I left out one key ingredient." He licked his lips, closed his eyes for a few seconds, and then opened them with his gaze directly on her. "Faith."

"Huh?" His timing was odd, but everything around her seemed that way lately, so she shouldn't have been surprised.

Uncle Forest stood and started pacing. "I think you heard me. Before coming to New York, I never missed church, and after we got here, I followed Bootsie to the church she found. I was doing church every Sunday but only with actions. Sometimes she'd rope me into something else, like a potluck or a midweek prayer meeting."

"What's wrong with that?"

He stopped by the window and pointed. "There are all kinds of hurting people out there, but I never bothered to stop and see what I could do to help them."

"What on earth are you talking about, Uncle Forest? I am so confused."

His eyes glistened as he turned back around toward her. "You're confused? No, I'm afraid I'm the one who's been confused. Cissy, since you've been here, you've cast a different light on everything for me. I've been forced to stop and think about things I'd shoved to the back of my mind."

"You have?"

He nodded. "I now realize that I'm wrong about so many things that I thought I knew. For starters, all the long hours and hard work in the world won't make my business truly successful."

"But your business is very successful." Cissy thought for a moment. "It is successful, isn't it? I mean, you're not hiding something bad, are you?"

"The only thing I'm hiding is myself." He sat back down. "I've been hiding from the Lord."

Cissy sure did want to know what brought all this on, but she wasn't about to come right out and ask—at least not now. "So what can I do?"

"For starters, you can continue doing what you've been doing, except one thing." He leveled her with one of his squinty-eyed gazes. "Talk to Tom Jenkins."

"But I thought—"

He held up a hand to stop her. "I thought a lot of things,

but that's another thing I was wrong about. My problems actually started before Tom bought Sewing Notions Inc. although he didn't do a thing to improve them." He paused. "He and I have already discussed the whole Sunday-only Christian thing that I'm afraid we're both guilty of. I think we're on the same page now."

"I thought…" Her voice trailed off as she realized she was making another assumption.

"What did you think?"

She shook her head. "So what do you want me to talk to Tom about?"

Uncle Forest lifted his hands. "Whatever you were talking to him about before."

"Didn't he just steal some business away from you…us?"

"One of his salesmen had been working on that account. We'd barely managed to hang on to it. When they contacted their suppliers and said they were increasing their business, I thought that meant we were in. Even though I knew Jenkins had been talking to them, I didn't think they'd actually turn everything over to Sewing Notions Inc." His contrite expression tugged at her heart.

"I thought you were upset about that."

Uncle Forest slowly shook his head. "I was upset, but it was more about my own life than anything else."

"Does Aunt Bootsie know about this?" Cissy fluttered her hand in the air. "I know you said you discussed some things with her, but I'm talking about all this *thinking* you've been doing."

He roared with laughter. "She knows I've been acting like a crazy man lately, going back and forth between blaming God and punishing myself. In fact, last night she told me it was time for me to get a grip." He snorted. "Can you believe that? My wife who promised to love me for better or for worse came right out and told me to get a grip."

Cissy could imagine Aunt Bootsie saying just that. The woman didn't like nonsense.

"So I'm supposed to go out there and call Tom? Tell him never mind the fact that I was upset that he used what I said against Zippers Plus to get the business?"

"No, that's not what you're supposed to say. He didn't use anything you said against this company. Granted, you do talk too much, but this has nothing to do with you. Just give him a chance to explain."

"That'll be hard," Cissy admitted. "I was pretty rough on him."

"I know you were, but you can talk to him and apologize." He motioned toward the door. "You can go on back to your desk now."

"Not yet. I have some questions for you now."

Uncle Forest's eyebrows shot up. "Questions for me? Like what?"

"I want to know how I'm doing here, because if you don't want me to stay, I don't want to make you miserable."

"Granted you're probably not cut out for this business, but you're not making me miserable." He paused and smiled. "Uncomfortable maybe, but not miserable. As I already said, since you've been here, I've been forced to think about some things I've tried to blot from my mind. Bootsie has noticed. She even told me that having you here was like a breath of fresh air."

"Wow. I don't think anyone has ever said that about me."

"That's not all she said," Uncle Forest continued. "But that's all I'll tell you right now." He leaned forward. "Next question?"

"Have you been talking to Mama?"

"Of course I have. Your mama—my sister—and I have talked once a week ever since I moved up here. Why?"

"Does she have anything to do with your change of heart?"

Uncle Forest quickly glanced away. "I didn't say that."

"Okay, so what's really going on?" Cissy should have known better than to think Uncle Forest suddenly took a liking to Tom Jenkins.

He massaged the bridge of his nose and expelled a whoosh of air. "I really didn't want to tell you this, but your old boyfriend...what's his name?"

"Spencer?" The sound still left a bitter taste on her tongue.

"Yeah, that's who I'm talking about. He might be getting out of jail soon, and she's worried he'll go looking for you."

Her knees went weak, and she fell back down into the chair. "Does he have any idea where I am?"

"He knows you're not in Hartselle, and since he's on probation, he can't come up here looking for you without getting into all kinds of trouble that might land him back behind bars." Uncle Forest paused. "We're hoping he'll be distracted before you even think about going back home. I've heard he's developed quite a following of young ladies who like the bad-boy image, so maybe he'll get over what happened soon."

Cissy blew out a sigh of relief. "We need to pray for those women. I'd hate for him to repeat what he tried to do to me."

"You need to let things happen as they will," Uncle Counts said. "Pray for everyone, including Spencer, but stay out of his way. Eventually something else will take over his thoughts, and then you can go wherever you feel led." He waved her off. "Now get back to work. I have things to do."

As Cissy left Uncle Forest's office, she thought about their conversation. Uncle Forest was right. Even if she wanted to return to Hartselle, she didn't think she'd be able to because of Spencer.

When Tom's phone rang, he saw that it was Forest Counts. As quick as this was, it probably meant bad news.

"Hey, Mr. Counts."

"Call me Forest. We'll be working together for a long time, and this Mr. Counts thing will get old real quick."

"So you've decided to accept my offer?"

"That's what I just said. I'll have my attorney call yours to draw up the papers."

"That was quick."

"I finally listened to my wife, and she told me to do this. We went over all the paperwork, and it looks like you have an excellent business plan."

Tom was surprised, and he couldn't help but grin. "Sounds good. If you have any more questions, feel free to call. I have nothing to hide."

"I do have one question."

Tom relaxed. "Shoot."

"How can someone so good in business be so dense with women?"

"Who are you talking about?"

"You. I know this merger has everything to do with the fact that you've fallen in love with my niece."

"Not everything. I've been working on a plan for quite a while."

"Then let's just say the *timing* is about her." Forest snickered. "You're too smart to be in this mess."

"Smart has nothing to do with it, I'm afraid."

"Let me give you some advice." Forest paused. "You don't mind taking advice from a geezer, do you?"

Tom laughed. "I would hardly call you a geezer."

"Okay, so let me rephrase that. Here's some advice from a wise, *mature* man who has messed up more times than he can count. Find a way to be with Cissy. Tell her to give you an hour to state your case. Let Cissy say everything she has to say to get it out of her system. When she's finished, apologize and promise you'll never hide anything from her again."

"But I didn't intentionally hide anything."

"Maybe not, but it's a nice touch. I'm sure she'll understand after the fact that she hid your relationship from me."

"Okay, then what?"

"Then keep your promise. Cissy might be a motor mouth, but she has a heart of gold. She would never intentionally do anything to hurt anyone, which is why she keeps getting herself into so many pickles."

"There is one problem," Tom said softly.

"Oh, yeah? Since when has a problem ever stopped you from doing what you need to do?"

Mr. Counts had a point. "Okay, so I'll do whatever I can to get Cissy to speak to me again. The rest is up to—"

"The Lord," Forest said.

"That's exactly what I was going to say."

"Then why are we still talking? You better get on the stick, Tom. My niece is a mighty pretty girl. If you wait too long, you'll miss out on the best thing that ever happened to you."

Tom hung up laughing. The Lord sure did work in the most unexpected of ways. If someone had told him a week ago that Forest Counts would be conspiring with him to get in Cissy's good graces, he would have wondered what planet they'd been living on.

Cissy propped her elbows on the tiny table in her apartment but lowered them when it shook. Charlene nibbled the edge of the cornbread as Cissy's phone started ringing again. "You can't keep ignoring the man forever. Why don't you put him and yourself out of misery and talk to the poor fella?"

"It's too awkward. I don't know what to say. I accused him of using me to advance his business."

Charlene put down the wedge of cornbread and leaned toward Cissy. "Okay, so you and I both know how much you love to talk. I'm sure he realizes you were just voicing your frustration."

Cissy squinted as she thought back to the times they'd been together. "Maybe."

"Okay, so you don't know where you stand with him. Why can't you at least sit down with him and clear the air? You don't have to marry him. Just communicate with him…and give him a chance to say something."

Charlene had a point, but Cissy's pride made her want to run and hide. "I don't know if I can do that without getting myself right back into a mess."

"I have an idea," Charlene said in a conspiratorial tone. "Set up a lunch meeting with him so you have a starting and an ending time. If it makes you too uncomfortable, at least you'll know you won't be there long. But on the other hand, if you need more time, you'll have an excuse to see him later."

"I s'pose I could do that." Cissy tilted her head. "Would you go with me?"

Charlene snorted. "Honey, that's the last thing you'd want. If I so much as heard a single solitary negative thing about you coming from his lips, I might just haul off and deck him."

"We certainly wouldn't want that, would we?" Cissy giggled.

"No sirree."

"Okay, next time he calls, I'll answer."

Charlene pointed to the phone as she stood. "Nope. I'm gonna go to my apartment, and as soon as I leave you're gonna call him right back."

"But I—"

"No *buts*. Call him now, and when you're done, come see me." Charlene went straight toward the door and turned around. "If you don't do this, I might have to resort to more drastic action, like dragging you over to his office or church myself." She planted her fists on her hips and bobbed her head. "And trust me, shoogie, that's not something you want."

After Charlene left, Cissy stared at her phone for a couple of minutes before picking it up. She scanned all her messages, trying to stall, but finally, she knew what she had to do. She pulled up his number and clicked call.

"Cissy, I am so glad you finally got back with me. Will you give me an hour to explain?"

"An hour is a long time. What do you want?" Cissy resisted the urge to ask him to come over. That would make things way too easy for him.

He sighed. "Okay, I suppose I don't deserve more than a few minutes." He cleared his throat and continued. "Look, I know why you're upset, and I'm really sorry. I've had the longest talks with your uncle, and I know I've made some mistakes."

"Yes, you have." She was a little taken aback by how quickly his apology came and the fact that he didn't make any excuses. "You should be ashamed of yourself."

"I know, and I am. Will you give me another chance?"

"How do I know you won't do it again?"

The sound of his breath brought back that familiar tingle in her stomach. "You don't. Only time and letting me prove myself will restore your confidence in me."

She'd almost forgotten how soothing the sound of his voice was and how he could make her feel from the top of her head to the tips of her toes. "I reckon we can give it a try."

"That's all I ask." An uncomfortable pause fell between them before he spoke up again. "Did your uncle tell you what we have planned?"

"What are you talking about?"

"We're merging our wholesale businesses, and I'm turning over all my accounts to him."

Good thing there was a chair behind Cissy, or she would have been on the floor. "You what?"

He explained the plans he had with her uncle. "I probably should have let him tell you," Tom said. "But I'm sure he'll understand, given what's been happening between us lately. Cissy, I didn't want to tell you this on the phone, but I can't get you out of my mind."

"Really?" In spite of her earlier anger, she smiled. "I have a confession to make. I can't stop thinking about you either."

"I've already told you that I think I've fallen in—"

She gasped. "No, don't say any more. We can talk later...in person."

He cleared his throat. "Yes, you're right."

After they hung up, she paced in front of her daybed and ranted about her uncle withholding information. "The least Uncle Forest could have done was told me he was gonna be Tom's partner."

"Did I hear you correctly?" Her door opened, and in walked Charlene. "It's been a while, and since you didn't come over, I thought I'd check in and see if you're okay. What's this about your uncle and Tom being partners?"

Cissy spent the next hour telling Charlene about her ten-minute conversation with Tom, leaving out what she thought he'd been about to say. It was hard, but she'd decided that if there was ever a time she needed a filter, this was it.

"That is just weird," Charlene said. "I wonder why they went and did that. It doesn't seem like a good business decision."

Cissy waved her hand. "It has something to do with wanting to create a niche market for designer notions with products made in the USA."

"Well, that makes sense."

"Maybe to you it does, but Uncle Forest sure does have a lot of explaining to do."

Chapter 28

THE NEXT MORNING Cissy arrived at the office early—at the same time as Dave but before Uncle Forest. "I never thought I'd see the day," Dave said. "So what got you out so early this morning?"

"I have to talk to my uncle." She plopped down in her chair and turned on her monitor, doing her best to avoid Dave's intense stare.

"Does this have anything to do with the merger?" Dave asked.

Cissy bolted out of her chair, spun around to face him, and planted her fists on her hips. "So you knew, and you didn't tell me?"

"Hold on there, Cissy." Dave made a lowering gesture with his hands. "You left in such a hurry yesterday. He called me into his office after hours."

"He could have at least called me."

"Oh, but I thought you wanted to be treated like a regular employee and not someone special just because you're the owner's niece."

"I do."

Dave folded his arms. "You can't have it both ways, Cissy."

That shot some of the wind out of her sail. "Yeah, I reckon you're right, but that doesn't mean I have to like it."

Dave laughed. "You do realize this will involve some restructuring, right?"

"Restructuring?"

He nodded. "Since he'll have more salesmen, he'll need

managers. Most of the senior salespeople don't want to give up their commissions and flexible schedules, so he's offered me another promotion." He puffed up his chest. "You're looking at your new sales and training manager."

Cissy smiled. "Congratulations! I know that's what you've been gunning for, so I'm super happy for you."

"He has a surprise for you too."

"I can't imagine anything that would surprise me at this point."

"Cissy!"

The sound of Uncle Forest's voice coming from the elevator caught her attention. "Oh, I didn't hear the elevator ding."

"That's because you were so busy chatting up the new sales manager. Are you gunning for a promotion for yourself?" Uncle Forest went straight to his office before turning around. "Because if you are, it's not going to work."

She followed him into his office, but she didn't sit down like she normally did. Instead, she leaned against the wall and watched her uncle as he sat down, still looking smug.

Cissy didn't even wait for her uncle to speak before launching into her spiel. "Now that this merger is happening, I'll certainly understand if you don't want me here anymore. It wouldn't be fair to let someone else go since they need the money." She swallowed hard and thought about going back to the town where Spencer still reigned and had more sympathy than she'd ever get. "I can't move back home for a while, so would you mind if I stay with you and Aunt Bootsie until I figure out what to do?"

Uncle Forest shook his head. "You need to quit jumping to conclusions and find out what's going on before you speak. Dave obviously didn't tell you that we're moving you to a new position."

"You're right. He didn't."

He stopped fidgeting with his desk supplies and looked directly at her. "You'll be my personal assistant."

"Why do you need a personal assistant?"

Uncle Forest gestured toward all the paperwork on his desk. "I'll be busy with the merger, so it would be nice to have someone running errands, making phone calls, and handling some of the details for me."

She glanced down as her mind drew a blank. This was all so unexpected she didn't have any idea how to respond.

"Understand, though, that it's just temporary, until Tom has the machines retooled. He wants you to be the person who tells him what kinds of decorative accessories he needs to make." He shrugged. "The man seems to think you might enjoy something more fun than selling sewing notions."

"What are you saying?"

"Apparently some of the accounts are asking for fancy buttons and beading, and Tom wants to make sure they can get what they want." He shrugged. "He and I both agreed that he's not the best person for that job, and it's too expensive to hire someone who already specializes in that sort of thing."

Cissy sat down in the chair across from Uncle Forest's desk before her knees buckled. "Okay, let me get this straight. You and Tom are merging companies, I'm changing jobs for a little while to be your personal assistant, and then I'll be designing buttons and stuff?"

"Yeah, well, basically you'll be taking the sketches from the designers and being the liaison between them and the company to make sure they get what they want."

"Liaison? So I'll be sort of like…the bridge between the new company and the accounts?" Even though she still wasn't totally sure of what the new job would involve, it sounded like a whole lot more fun than being a salesperson. And she wouldn't be stuck behind the desk all day staring at a computer screen.

He lifted his hands and let them fall back down on the desk. "That's pretty much it in a nutshell. It'll be a whole new thing for you...for all of us." Uncle Forest grinned. "How about it?" His attention was diverted to something behind Cissy. "Come on in, Tom. I was just telling Cissy about our plans."

Before Tom had a chance to open his mouth, Cissy bounded out of her chair and threw herself at Tom. "Uncle Forest told me about your plans, and I just—"

His rigid body relaxed, and he wrapped his arms around her. "This isn't the best place for affection," he whispered.

"Oh, yeah." Cissy pulled away from him and straightened her jacket as she cast a glance in Uncle Forest's direction. "Sorry about that."

Her uncle widened his eyes at Tom. "Do you think you'll be able to get any work done with her hanging around your office?"

Tom chuckled. "It might be difficult, but I think we can manage." He turned to Cissy. "So what do you think about our plan? Are you willing to give it a shot?"

"Are you kidding me? This is my dream job."

"You do realize it's not all fun, right?" Uncle Forest said.

"Of course, and I don't mind." She glanced up at Tom and felt the warmth of his smile before turning back to her uncle. "I love work. It's just that being a liaison seems more suited to my career goals." She saw that Uncle Forest was trying his best to suppress a laugh. "In spite of what you might think, I actually do have goals, ya know."

Uncle Forest held out his hand toward Tom. "There ya

go. I have a personal assistant to help with the transition for a few months, you'll have your accessories and embellishments go-to person, and Cissy will be in her dream job. It's win-win-win all the way around." He stood up and started to walk out but stopped at the door. "I was going to let y'all have my office, but I've changed my mind. Why don't the two of you go somewhere for coffee? I'll be here when you get back, Tom. We can do our planning then."

Tom gave him a clipped nod before looking down at Cissy again. "Let's go before he changes his mind."

"Take all the time you need, as long as it doesn't go over an hour or two." Uncle Forest waved.

As she passed Dave's desk, he looked back and forth between her and Tom and grinned. "Have fun, you two."

Once they got outside, Tom took Cissy by the hand. "We're going to brunch in a cozy little diner so we can talk."

Ten minutes later Cissy sat across a Formica table from Tom, and she couldn't get over how handsome he was. She'd always thought he was good looking, but now he had a spark she'd only seen when he was doing church work. "So what were you about to tell me on the phone?"

He grinned and took her hand across the table. "I think you know."

"I think I do too, but I want to hear you say it before I tell you something."

"Cissy Hillwood, I'm falling in love with you. There are no guarantees, and I don't even want to pretend I'll never make you mad again, but when I thought I might lose you, nothing else seemed important anymore."

Tears sprang to her eyes. "That is so sweet."

"So now what were you going to tell me?"

She tipped her head and gave him a coquettish grin. "That I'm not falling in love with you."

He suddenly stilled, and a look of pure shock took over the joyful look on his face. "I—"

She grinned through the tears. "I'm already there."

"Huh?"

"In case you haven't noticed, I don't waste much time. I've known since our second time together that I was in love with you."

The waitress had just arrived, but she slowly backed away. Tom got out of his seat and scooted around the table to sit next to Cissy. "This calls for a kiss."

As he put his arms around her and lowered his face to hers, she was certain she could hear music. The minute their lips touched, she sighed. She could so get used to this.

Coming in 2015 from Debby Mayne,
Book Two of the Uptown Belles series—
Trouble in Paradise

Chapter 1

CHARLENE STEPPED OUTSIDE her apartment building and glanced up at the blue sky peeking out from between the skyscrapers. Here it was a beautiful Friday morning in June, the day before her much-needed vacation, and Charlene still dreaded going to the office. She hadn't always felt that way. She had the job of her dreams, and she lived in the city that never sleeps. But hoo boy her new boss sure could be a bear.

And today would be extra rough since she had to tie up all the loose ends before her weeklong vacation, which she'd decided to take back home with her mama and daddy, who lived on fifteen acres smack dab in the middle of a sprawling Atlanta suburb. Grandpa had refused to sell his property to the developer, so now her parents lived on the old family homestead surrounded by modern mansions.

As Charlene hoofed it to her office in the heart of New York City's garment district, she took several deep breaths and then stopped to say a brief silent prayer before entering the building. *Lord, give me the strength to get through this day without any tears, or even a sniffle...* She opened her eyes for a second and then shut them again. *And help me keep my thoughts to myself, because You know how mouthy I can be!*

Once she entered her office building, she squared her shoulders and forged ahead, her shoes tap-tapping on the tan marble floor that sure could use a polishing. The white walls—with nothing but a metal directional sign and a list of businesses—seemed even colder this morning. She hopped on the elevator and rode up, hoping she wouldn't have to face Alan until the Friday morning meeting in a couple of hours.

Her heart sank the instant she stepped off the elevator. Standing there in front of her was the man of her nightmares. Alan glanced at the clock and then tipped his head toward her. "Ms. Pickford, nice to see that you made it on time."

"I'm always on time." She forced a smile to take the edge off the clipped tone that escaped her lips. *Lord, help me.*

He shrugged. "Maybe so, but I thought you might be in vacation mode. That's what generally happens the day before someone takes time off." His lips flat-lined, making him look like a marionette as he lifted an eyebrow, looked at her for several long seconds, and then turned around and strode back to his office without another word. She stood there staring after him as all kinds of comebacks flitted through her mind.

Ever since Alan Robards had arrived as the general manager of Paradise Promotional Products four months ago, she'd felt that she couldn't do anything right. She thought her hard work for the past three years had paid off when her boss and the general manager left and she got a promotion. Unfortunately that career boost came with a brand-new boss she would never have chosen to work for. Mama always said to be careful what you wish for. Now she understood that saying all too well.

Charlene skittered to her office and closed the door behind her. She'd do just about anything to avoid the usual interruptions. This was one day she wanted everything to finish on time so she could go home and pack for her early-morning flight.

As she pulled up different screens to print for the

meeting, her mind kept flitting back to Alan. If she'd met him anywhere else, she would have thought he was a looker—until he opened his mouth and showed what a sourpuss he was. His short, sandy blond hair gave him a boyish look, yet his deep blue eyes held something that she couldn't quite put her finger on. He was about average height, but when he entered a room, his presence loomed larger than life—and he didn't have to say a word.

Everyone else in the office chatted about everything under the sun, including where they were from and how they got here. But not Alan. She had no idea of anything about his past, and neither did anyone else. So they made stuff up. Melissa the receptionist came up with the best theory, saying he was in the witness protection program and the government had found him the job with his new identity.

Five minutes before the scheduled meeting Charlene got up from her desk and walked out to the printer to pick up the collated reports, stumbling for a split second as she strained her neck to make sure Alan wasn't close by. She caught herself, but Rodney's laughter behind her let her know her near disaster hadn't gone unnoticed.

She spun around and glared at him. "What?"

"Careful there." The finance manager lifted both hands to his sides. "Rough night?"

"Nah, it's just these heels." Shopping with Cissy was not only dangerous to her bank account, it also killed her feet.

He glanced down at her shoes and then smiled at her. "Is it worth it?"

"Prob'ly not." She smiled. "Now don't you have somethin' important to do, like crunch a few numbers before the meetin'?"

He held up a folder. "Done. See you in a few. I have to grab one more report before I go to the conference room."

She watched him head toward his office and sighed. She wished she had just a smidge of Rodney's ability to take things at face value when it came to their new boss. Nothing seemed to faze him, while as soon as she realized what a pill Alan could be, she started fretting and worrying about everything related to work.

Out of the corner of her eye she spotted Alan entering the conference room. She took her time stapling the pages because she didn't want to be stuck in a room alone with him. Once other people walked in, she followed and took her usual seat.

Alan had already taken his place at the head of the long table. His face remained expressionless as he scanned the room, clearly doing a silent head count. His right-hand man, George Foster, sat beside him, appearing to do the same thing.

Rodney gave his financial report first. Since it was all positive news, no one had any questions. Then Alan looked around the room before settling his gaze on her. "Ms. Pickford?"

Just then a loud crashing sound erupted from outside the conference room door. Charlene jumped, but not nearly as quickly as Alan, whose face turned a sickly shade of pale. A nervous giggle threatened to escape her throat, but she caught herself and cleared her throat. He glared at her.

When he didn't say anything, she stood. "Uh…this quarter's marketing program has barely gotten started, so I don't have any of the results in yet, but last quarter's number are—"

"Sit down, Ms. Pickford," Alan snapped. He lifted a shaky

hand but quickly dropped it to his side. "This meeting is now over. Please submit your reports to the management team via e-mail." He picked up a stack of papers on the table and walked out of the room, leaving everyone sitting there looking around, confused.

After an uncomfortable few minutes, Rodney grimaced. "I wish I knew what that was all about. That's the second time this week he's walked out on a meeting."

George lifted a hand to silence him. "This is not open for discussion. You heard what Alan said. Now go on back to your offices and send your reports in an e-mail to all the department managers. If we have any questions, we can handle them through e-mail or a one-on-one." His firm tone left no room for questions.

After the rest of the management team left mumbling, Rodney looked at George and then turned to Charlene, shrugged, and gave an I-don't-get-it-either smile. She nodded and went through the motions of gathering her things, hoping George would leave so she could talk to Rodney. When she realized that wouldn't happen, she got up and took off for her office, wondering why she even bothered coming in today. She could have e-mailed the reports at the end of the workday on Thursday and taken Friday off to finish getting ready for her trip. She certainly had accrued plenty of vacation time.

A knock at the door yanked her back to the moment. She glanced up as someone pushed her door open a few inches, and Melissa peeked in. "Mind if I come in for a minute? I asked one of the admins to fill in at the front desk for a few minutes."

"Sure, come on in." Charlene gestured toward the chair across the maple desk. "What's up?"

Melissa shook her head. "Sorry I messed up your

meeting when I dropped those boxes. You know how clumsy I am."

"Don't worry about it," Charlene said. "It was just an accident."

Instead of accepting that and leaving, Melissa remained seated with her head down, shifting in her chair, obviously itching to say something else. Charlene watched the fresh-out-of-college office receptionist squirm for a moment before speaking up herself.

"Is something else bothering you?" Charlene asked.

Melissa sniffled and slowly raised her head, and that was when Charlene noticed her eyes were rimmed in red. "George gave me a warning."

"A warning?" Charlene repeated. "What kind of warning?"

"Apparently my little accident can cost me my job." Her chin quivered and she swallowed hard. "I really want this job to work."

"That's ridiculous." Charlene frowned as she remembered herself when she was Melissa's age and willing to take any job just to get her foot in the door. "Want me to talk to George?"

A look of panic shot across Melissa's face. "No. I mean, I don't think that would be good. They'll think I'm blabbing, and it'll make things worse."

"I understand, but if you ever feel that your job is in jeopardy, let me know, and I'll see what I can do to help. You are probably one of the most valuable people in this office. I don't know what we'd do without you."

Melissa forced a quivering smile as she stood. "Thank you, Charlene. I better get back to the desk before someone comes looking for me...if you know what I mean."

After Melissa left her office, Charlene leaned back in

her chair and thought about the past four months. The former marketing manager and general manager of the office had left, leading to her promotion, and leaving her and Rodney with an office full of new people, including Alan and George, who arrived as a boxed set. It quickly became obvious that these two men had a history together when they finished each other's sentences during meetings. It was odd, though, because George was clearly old enough to be Alan's father and seemed to have more business experience than Alan, but he always deferred to Alan. This only added to the intrigue in the office.

She worked at her desk all morning, but her mind kept wandering to the trip ahead. In spite of the fact that she knew Mama loved her with all her heart, tension hovered between them, creating tiny skirmishes that, once one of them realized what was happening, they ended. Abruptly. So abruptly that they'd sometimes spend hours in silence to prevent it from happening again, and that only made their time together uncomfortable.

Charlene sighed. In spite of knowing what she had to look forward to, she was still eager to get back home and sleep in the bedroom Mama hadn't changed since she'd moved out almost ten years ago. "Just in case," Mama had said. Just in case what, Charlene wasn't sure, but she still appreciated the fact that she had a place to stay when she visited her parents.

Lunchtime arrived, but Charlene waited until she saw Alan leave to grab her bag and head for the place where she met her best friend Cissy most Fridays. And today she was happy to see Cissy sitting on the bench in the middle of a small patch of grass waiting for her.

"You look like you've been wrestlin' a bear," Cissy said.

"What on earth happened to get your face all puckered up like that?"

Charlene shook her head as she opened her bag and pulled out a peanut butter sandwich. "Alan."

"Say no more. I don't get how he's even in that job, bein' he's such a…" Cissy shrugged and made a face. "Sorry. I shouldn't feed your frettin'."

"The tone of that office sure has changed since he's been there, but I'm gonna try not to worry about it." Charlene took a bite of her sandwich as she stretched her legs out in front of her as much as she could with her five-foot-two frame. She chewed in silence as Cissy gave her a moment to gather her thoughts.

"Let's change the subject, okay?" Cissy grinned as she pulled a magazine from her tote. "I've been lookin' at bridesmaid dresses, and I found one I think would be super cute for you."

"Let me see." Charlene welcomed the diversion as she pored over the dresses. Could Cissy have found anything tackier? "Have you nailed down a color yet?"

Cissy shrugged. "You said you liked purple or cranberry, so I'll probably pick one of those. It really doesn't matter to me since I'll be wearin' all white."

"But it's your weddin', hon." Charlene glanced back at the dress Cissy had put "#1" beside and wondered why she didn't think the embellished jewel neckline and draped lace overlay combination was anything but tacky.

"Yeah, I know, but I have a feelin' I won't know up from down that day, and colors won't matter a single solitary bit." Cissy giggled. "Tom told me he'd just as soon wear jeans and skip all the fancy stuff." She wiggled her eyebrows. "But he looks so good in a suit, I can't let him get away with that. I want some great pictures to show the grandkids."

Charlene grinned. "You'll be a wonderful grandma, Cissy, but don't you think it's a little early to be talkin' about grandkids?"

"At least I'm thinkin' ahead. It took me a while, but between Uncle Forest and Aunt Bootsie workin' on me I think I'm in the groove."

Charlene flipped the page to Cissy's second favorite dress, chewed her bottom lip for a moment, and looked back at her friend. "Maybe you should consider skipping all the fancy stuff." At least that would save her from throwing money away on either of the hideous dresses Cissy had picked out.

Cissy crinkled her nose. "I don't think so. Mama expects me to have the princess weddin' of her dreams."

Charlene glanced at her watch and groaned. "I sure wish I had longer, but I gotta get back." She stood up, tossed her trash in the receptacle by the bench, and gave Cissy a hug.

Cissy patted her on the back. "Have a great time and try to forget about that mean ol' boss of yours."

"I'll do my best."

The remainder of the afternoon Charlene managed to get everything done and in order for her weeklong absence. She was about to leave when Alan appeared at her door. "Got a moment?" he asked.

"Um...sure." What else could she say?

He walked in, pulled the door halfway to, and walked over to the chair where Melissa had sat earlier. "Mind if I sit?"

"Of course not." She cleared her throat as she realized she sounded rather terse. "I mean, you are the boss and all."

He flashed one of his rare smiles. "I bet you think I'm an ogre."

She blinked. "An ogre?" She'd been thinking much worse things than ogre.

Alan shifted in the chair before settling back and holding her gaze for an uncomfortably long several seconds. "I haven't exactly been Mr. Congeniality since I've been the manager here."

You can say that again. She tightened her jaw to keep from making a snide remark and forced a closed-mouth smile.

"Before you leave for your vacation, I wanted to clear the air between us."

"Okay. So what did we need to discuss that would...clear the...you know."

He laughed. "I'm sorry I ended the meeting before you had a chance to give your report. That had nothing to do with you."

She glanced down at her desk. "That's good to know."

"It's an issue I need to deal with."

Ya think? He narrowed his focus on her as though he could read her mind, so she fidgeted with papers on her desk.

He stood. She watched him, hoping he'd give her more of an explanation, but he didn't. Instead, he edged closer to the door before stopping and turning back to her. "Have a nice vacation."

After he left, she let out a breath of...she wasn't sure if it was relief or frustration. Surely Alan had come to her office to clear things up, but he'd left her with more questions than answers. What was he trying to hide?

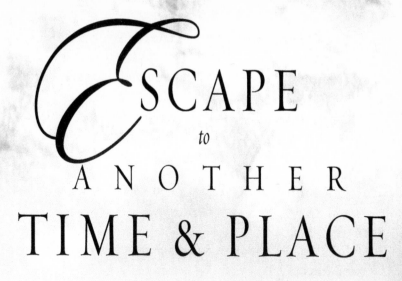